From Pillar to Post

From Pillar to Post

Fiona Bullen

Riverside Books
Fairview Farm
Littley Green
Essex CM3 1BU

ISBN 1 904571 14 X

Printed and bound in the United Kingdom

To my wonderful Kit
who delayed this book by two years,
and to 2RGJ
none of whom are in this book, so relax!

Chapter One

She glanced over at her husband's sleeping form, the covers bunched up over his freckled shoulders and tucked in tightly around his back where he had just wrenched them. Her side of the covers. She lay uncovered and cold, wondering. Why, she thought, why in God's name had she ever married him? The clock glowed three-fifteen. Dimly, she considered murder.

The tale of the wife who dashed her husband's brains out with a frozen leg of lamb, and then calmly cooked the roast for the police investigating the murder, had always amused and intrigued Laura. What delicious irony, the detectives eating the murder weapon and destroying any incriminating evidence! And besides, Hugh really deserved it, she thought, calmly lying there and considering the matter more fully.

Poor little Private Dutton ... He had only meant to compliment ... it was only a hand that had strayed around her waist as he guided her down the hallway. Nothing really ... and yet Hugh had 'accidentally' struck Dutton with his cane when he next saw him, across the knuckles of that offending hand. No one had any doubts. It had happened too often. Laura sighed sharply. Hugh had had no business doing such a thing. Not an officer to a soldier who couldn't even fight back and wouldn't dare report it. No, Hugh deserved a good hefty thwack across the head, she decided grimly. Oh, why ever had she married him!

Of course, that was nearly four years ago and she could barely remember the sense of frustration and claustrophobia that living on her parent's farm in the Nandi Hills of Kenya had produced in her at the time. And Hugh had seemed so strong, so knowledgeable, so . . . what? Confident? Powerful? Or had it all been bluster? God knew the other officers pulled faces behind his back, grew rigid with annoyance when he did something that wasn't quite right. Nothing you could put your finger on. Just something about the way he handled the men, or asked for a drink in the mess, or even wore his beret. Subtleties that Hugh would never grasp, never even notice.

And now all she could think of was the golden light she had left behind, stretching out across the dry landscape, the feel of warmth right through her bones, the sense of possibilities all there for the taking. And she had taken Hugh. She sighed again to herself.

Her father had thought him wonderful, of course. Strong enough to control his flighty daughter, someone determined in his career, commanding, and yet charming when he put his mind to it. Oh yes, Hugh had won Dad over with no trouble at all, Laura thought bitterly. Dad was a snob and thought she was marrying an officer and a gentleman. Her mother had been more reserved, more wary. She didn't like small men with ginger hair, she said vaguely, in that rather unfocused way of hers. They were bullies. But Laura hadn't listened to her mother then, any more than she had ever listened to her mother. A timid, conservative woman thoroughly under her husband's domination, Laura had dismissed her at an early age. But Mother had been right, she sighed to herself. Hugh was a bully. She fingered the soft bruised flesh on the upper part of her arm.

And the only way she could get back at Hugh was to embarrass him. The corners of her mouth turned up slightly, thinking matters through, planning her next campaign. Divorce wasn't an option, Hugh had told her firmly on the one occasion Laura had been foolish enough to mention it. Officers didn't divorce, he had told her in a grimly pompous voice. Which was nonsense, of course. Everyone divorced these days – even officers, even the Prince of Wales, apparently . . . But not Hugh.

And, Laura had to admit, she didn't much care to work for a living or have to survive on the pittance Hugh would provide. No, no, much better to look for a replacement while still comfortably taken care of. And then she could act. She glanced coldly across at her husband's head and imagined a meaty crunch.

Emma sat heavily and massaged her stomach. It still ached. She forced her mind away from the familiar circling pattern of why, why, why. Why me? Why my baby? Would it have happened anyway if she hadn't fallen, if Hugh hadn't shoved past her like that at the top of the stairs, gone on oblivious to the fact that she had overbalanced . . . There was no point.

The doctors had no answers and even if they had, they couldn't have done anything, couldn't have made the baby viable when it simply wasn't. It was very unlikely the fall had caused the miscarriage, they said. Nearly a week had elapsed between the events. Just one of those things, they said . . . And there was no reason to think it would happen again. Everyone seemed to have at least one miscarriage these days. Everyone.

She sighed and Fergus, bending down to kiss the nape of her neck, was wrenched with such sorrow that he had to move away, stare out at the tree line where some young louts were churning up the sports field with their crossbikes. He focused his anger on them, willing them to crash, to roll, to break a few bones, trying not to think about Hugh.

'Bill dropped by earlier, did I tell you?' he spoke casually, as though his mind were on other things, not on his pretty, dark-haired wife sitting so quietly on the garden bench, trying to come to terms with the loss that had devastated her so. Devastated both of them.

'Really? What did he want?' Emma forced a smile, trying to be sensible and down-to-earth about the whole matter. A coper, a manager. That's what she was expected to be. She tried to smile a little wider but it wobbled at the corner of her mouth and she gave up the attempt.

'Oh, nothing, really. Just wanted to see you, tell you – how sorry he is.' He broke off, rubbing his long nose furiously. 'He was on his way up to London so he couldn't wait. I told him you were having a nap, so he just sent you his love and said he'll see us both at the wedding.'

Emma turned her head, intrigued. 'The wedding? Alex and Kate's? But that's not for several weeks yet. Where's Bill going?' She was surprised. Bill Ovington had been back with the 1st battalion only a couple of months after a stint abroad with the 2nd. Gorgeous, lazy-eyed Bill with a heart of gold and wandering feet, she smiled to herself. Where on earth was he off to now?

'Where do you think?' Fergus grinned ruefully, raising one eyebrow. There was a twinge of envy there, Emma thought. Grown men playing at soldiers . . . except, of course, they weren't really playing.

'Oh, I see . . . is he with the Intelligence bunch now? Close Observation Patrol or something?' She wrinkled her brow. 'Belfast, by any chance? Or further south?'

'Mostly the Belfast area, I imagine. But no, he's only going for a look-see. He's nothing to do with Intelligence really. But when he takes over as Operations Officer, he'll need to know the area at first hand.' Fergus paused, musing, 'It'll seem strange with no patrols out on the streets. Much harder to pick up what's going on. Odd for us altogether. Makes me feel quite uneasy, being in a sort of no-man's land, not deployed and not stood down either . . .'

'Is anything?' Emma frowned, her dark hair whipping in the strengthening breeze off the Downs behind the house. She shivered at the thought of the approaching winter. 'Going on, I mean? I thought it was all over, bar the shouting and squabbling over arms . . .' She looked up, a trace of anxiety smoothed out quickly from her calm face. No point in fussing, no point in letting it show.

'Well, not just yet. Let's face it, everything's still going on much as it always has except they're not actually pulling the trigger or detonating the bomb. It's a bit early to say it's all over. It's a pretty shaky "Peace" what with all this decommissioning mess.' Fergus grimaced again at the high-pitched whining of the crossbikes. 'So . . . we'll have to wait and see.'

'And if I had still been pregnant? Would you have been

happy for me to have the baby out there?' Emma glanced at her husband, wishing he would come over and put his arms around her instead of standing there, arms crossed in annoyance as he glared his defiance at the local lads. He caught her eyes and smiled.

'Not "out" there, Emma. You say "over" there or all the locals get terribly offended and think they're being referred to as the colonies.' He grinned. 'Listen, we'll be there two years, sweetheart, and you'll have a baby by then. There are several very good hospitals and the Troubles won't bother you in there, or anywhere else, you'll see. So you better start thinking of Irish names. I've always liked Patrick. It goes well with Kennedy, don't you think?'

Emma made room for him on the bench and snuggled in against his woolly jumper, looking up at her husband's comfortably irregular features that made him look much like an attractive bear. 'And what makes you think she'll want a name like Patrick?'

Mrs Dalton, rich, erratic and prone to minding everyone else's business but her own, raised her eyeglasses and peered at Kate.

'I hear you're marrying a soldier?' It wasn't so much the question, rather the tone that gave away her opinion. Kate smiled tightly. Mrs Dalton was American with an American's opinion of the army.

'That's right. In December.' Kate continued to leaf through the Colefax swatches, searching for the exact shade she had in mind, ignoring the obvious irritation swirling in Mrs Dalton's mood. Finally, unable to raise Kate's attention, Mrs Dalton sniffed.

'Rather late in the year for a wedding, isn't it? In fact,

you've only been engaged a few weeks, I understand. Why the rush?' For a few seconds Kate continued to look down at the fabric in her hands, counting silently to herself, the flush rising inexorably up her pale cheeks. God, how she hated this bloody woman! Then she turned her head and fixed her client with a cool stare, choosing her clipped words with care.

'There is no rush to speak of, Mrs Dalton. We prefer to get married as soon as possible, that's all. People in love often do, you know.' And she was so very much in love with Alex, she thought with a thrill that was half fear. It was dangerous to love this much; it made one vulnerable. Something the Mrs Daltons of this world would never comprehend. She wouldn't have married for love, merely for security, to be comfortably well off, rich. Kate sniffed in return.

Besides, the battalion was off to Northern Ireland soon, very soon. And if they didn't marry now, then when? When would ever be a good time for the army? She turned away the thought, rejecting it, sure in her choice . . . well, almost.

'How will you manage – with the business, I mean? It'll be rather difficult if you're only here certain days of the week. I like to be able to just drop in and discuss things with you,' Mrs Dalton complained and Kate thought ah, yes, as you've been doing for the last five years of my life, plaguing me with your silly little whims and flights of fancy, changing your room décor like you would change your hat and then complaining that nothing ever looked really *settled*, really *established*. Mrs Dalton longed to belong to the old guard of London society but couldn't comprehend the undercurrents. Kate smiled, almost with relief, that she would be leaving Mrs Dalton behind.

'I shan't – manage, I mean. I'm selling my half of the business to a friend of Milly's who wants to come in with her. I'm going to be an army wife, Mrs Dalton, going wherever Alex is sent. I can hardly run the business from some garrison town in the north, now can I?' Or from Belfast, despite the 'Peace', she added to herself. Or could she? No, no, that was ridiculous. She had seen Belfast on the news enough times. That was hardly the place to set up a business in interior design! She tried to sound firm and positive, not to let the niggling worms of doubt in her mind destroy her calm.

She loved Alex, she wanted to marry Alex, and he had no choice where he went in his career. It was obvious that he was a flyer – so many people had given him the nod – in a very good infantry regiment. Sound career prospects, despite all the army cuts, she'd been told. Would go all the way, if he wanted. So she would have to be the one to compromise. There was no choice. But still, she doubted and worried and regretted – just a little, not enough to want to change her mind in any way, no, not at all. It was just such a wrench to give up a successful interior design partnership in Pimlico to become Mrs Alex Aldridge, army adjunct, rootless. She stifled another sigh.

Mrs Dalton, watching her, was far from surprised by the sigh. There was something about Kate Gordon that fascinated her. Always had really, from the first moment she had walked in the newly painted cream and pale green door with the name Gordon & Tait Design discreetly in gold above it and had seen the slender, fair-haired girl leaning forward from her desk, a look of anticipation on her face. Barely into her twenties at the time, although she had had four years' experience with onc of thc morc established design firms, Kate Gordon looked every inch the part. Immaculately dressed, her ash blonde hair caught up in a tortoiseshell barrette, her surprisingly dark eyebrows over green eyes lifted in expectation, she had entranced and obsessed Mrs Dalton from that moment on. Besides, her father was a lord and that meant her taste had to be just right, Mrs Dalton was sure.

And of course, she *was* so very good at what she did. Wonderful eye, so subtle and yet not boring at all, the way she knew exactly which material would go with what you already had, it was quite extraordinary. And Milly was the other side of the partnership, a design degree making her the less exciting colleague, to Mrs Dalton's mind, but still so useful when one needed an extra foot or two for an alcove here or new cupboards there to make the kitchen that bit more like a friend's she admired. Such a good pair!

How on earth could this young woman be contemplating giving it all up? She had scores of young men dangling after her, her business was successful and becoming more so every year, her flat was *sooo* beautiful, Mrs Dalton thought covetously, having been invited in once when Kate had left a swatch at home. Who on earth was this man that he could expect such sacrifices from the dear girl? And why?

'Where will you get married?' Mrs Dalton tried her best to sound interested but it came out, even to her ears, rather petulant. Well, she couldn't help it if she were peeved. Kate was her discovery. She had introduced all her friends to Kate as clients and now the wretched girl was snapping her fingers at her. Of course she was cross.

'At home.' The word sent reverberations crashing through them both, Mrs Dalton wishing she could so casually refer to a family home that had been there for generations, Kate wondering if she would ever be able to refer to a succession of army quarters as home. Would her children feel they belonged somewhere, have strong roots and ties to a house, a village, a community, the way she had? Or would they be yet more army brats dragged around the countryside and abroad, not knowing where home really was?

The doorbell chimed and she glanced at Mrs Dalton and then beyond her right shoulder. Suddenly, she smiled, all her doubts resolved. A light-hearted bubbling frisson of delight burst through her. 'You haven't met Alex yet, have you, Mrs Dalton? Let me introduce you now.

'Hallo darling! I had no idea you were coming up today.' Kate came around from her desk to grasp the hand of the man who had strolled casually into the shop. He was tall, dark and undeniably handsome, although it was a face that held a certain graveness, a certain detached seriousness when he wasn't smiling. A deep, thin scar cut across one cheekbone where he had been cut once by flying shrapnel and it gave the regular features a quirk that spared them from being too good-looking. The dark blue eyes held thoughts that were not always revealed immediately and the straight, carved lips could be both sensual and stubborn at will. But he was light-hearted today.

'Couldn't keep away.' He kissed her disarmingly. 'Besides, there's a regimental dinner tonight at the club. Thought I might cadge a bed for the night and shoot back in the morning, if that's all right?'

'Wonderful! I've been missing you all week. Alex, I'd like you to meet a – very valued client of mine, Mrs Dalton.' Kate pressed herself briefly against him, before turning to include her visitor.

Mrs Dalton swivelled her corseted bulk, glancing backwards as she prepared to smile briefly and insincerely. And then she surprised herself by feeling a jolt that she hadn't felt in years. Ah, she thought to herself, smiling slyly. Now I understand. Sex appeal. The wretched man had it in spade loads. Not to mention being damned good-looking, all dark and lean with those piercing eyes. She hadn't seen a man so all-out gorgeous in a long time, nor so obviously unaware of it. And she sighed, a shade annoyed with herself, at feeling that momentary pang of envy.

Sex appeal faded, she told herself firmly, and then money had a way of being a major comfort. So, Mr Dalton might not be a god to look at, but his bank balance made up for it. Kate would find out, she told herself. And then she'd be back. Mrs Dalton could wait.

Chapter Two

'No sign of a bump, is there?' Joanna, more than a little discontented by Alex's whirlwind romance, engagement and now wedding, observed nastily. 'But then, she's so skinny. Nothing would be showing yet, would it?' She peered around her largely unkissable-under hat at the pair slowly making their rounds in the garden. A glorious day, high-washed sky and thin winter sunshine gilding the winter jasmine until it shone like gold, still caused her to shiver in her woollen suit.

'What makes you so sure there's anything to show, Jo? I would think the reason he snapped Kate up so quickly is entirely obvious. She's quite stunning,' an effete voice lisped in her ear. He smiled at Joanna's thinned lips.

'Anyone is on their wedding day, Tim, even your precious cousin. Three inches of makeup and a white party dress does not make her Claudia Schiffer—'

'Now, now, let's remain civilised, shall we . . .' Tim tugged at his shirt-cuffs, wondering idly if the bow-tie was perhaps too much with a morning coat. 'No, no, that glow's quite natural. Look at them both,' he sighed. 'They're besotted.'

'Darling! What you don't notice—' began Joanna.

'Why can't they just be in love?' Tim argued stubbornly. 'After all, Alex isn't rich—'

'Besides, who'd want to marry army – even for gorgeous Alex's sake, isn't that what you're really saying?' A third voice, that of Tim's twin sister, intervened, laughter hovering in the words. Nicky would mock, Joanna thought viciously, ignoring them both as she stared out through eyes half-shut against the spiralling smoke from her cigarette. The wind whipped at Kate's veil, sending it soaring out behind her from the small diamond coronet encircling her hair. Joanna closed her eyes even more tightly.

'Jo would,' Tim interposed, a sly grin on his too-pretty face. 'And quite a few besides. Don't kid yourself, Nicky. It's a closed, privileged world still, no matter what outsiders might like to think. Soldiers saluting and "ma'aming" you, the chance to become General Sir Someone-Terribly-Important and Lady Thing. Protected from the grim reality of the world outside and just think of all that pomp and circumstance . . .'

'Oh, what crap!' Nicky started to laugh for real. 'Fifty years ago, yes, or even twenty but not any more. What the hell has it to offer these days? Dreadful postings, minimal leave, and never knowing where you're going next . . . Father says it isn't at all as it was—'

'"In his day", but wasn't he just lapping up having Alex around to reminisce with? Once army, always army, according to Father, and those were "the best days of his life",' her brother corrected her with a satiric grin. Too close to love each other, and yet unable to be apart, the twins made everyone around them uncomfortable with their sniping. Joanna, her patience strained beyond bearing, turned away abruptly. If only she hadn't walked away, if only she hadn't demanded Alex give up his career and take up something more suitable in the City . . . The thought caused a sharp pain to lodge in her chest.

'Oh, shut up, the pair of you! Like old women constantly bickering!'

'Better than bitchy women . . .'

'Oh, you'd qualify for that too, Timmy darling,' Joanna snapped. 'Nicky, do take him away, will you? He's setting my teeth on edge. I can't think how you put up with him.'

'Come on, Tim. You're not needed or wanted. Jo wants to spit her venom into appreciative ears and we don't qualify. Family, you know. Can't say what she wants without remembering Kate's our first cousin. Besides, we introduced them, so we're deeply in the poo . . .' Nicky rolled her eyes drolly.

They drifted away. 'You'd think she'd realise she's not the only disappointed party today,' Tim remarked disconsolately, earning a sharp look from Nicky. 'But that's Jo all over. Me, me, me. I can quite see why Alex ran for the hills, can't you?'

'Aren't you over him yet, my pet? I thought it was just a school crush, years ago? Good heavens, does Simon know?' Nicky shot a curious glance over to where silly Simon, as she liked to call him, was busy chatting to some dowager. Tim's face darkened.

'Don't be absurd. There was never anything there. Alex isn't at all that way inclined. No, I meant on the other side. All those male eyes watching dear Kate, wishing they'd moved a bit faster, wondering whether she'll be content

. . . if they can catch her on the rebound. It's a difficult life for a young woman with career prospects these days, they'll be thinking, hoping . . .'

'Good lord! Jo's quite right! You *do* sound like an old woman. Go and rescue Simon, why don't you? He's run out of safe gossip and about to embark on the more titillating. And I've just realised that's Kate's other grandmother, for God's sake, the dowager Lady Greaves. Frightfully uptight and so old she looks quite mummified. Mustn't shock her or she might just keel over.' Nicky grinned mischievously, kissing her brother's cheek and shooing him towards the far corner of the lawn.

'She looks quite unshockable but – all right, I'm off. Behave yourself and don't get yourself engaged again.' Tim smiled sweetly. 'It becomes quite ridiculous after a while.'

'Oh, sod off, Tim!' Nicky turned abruptly and sought out a waitress circling with a tray of champagne.

'Have you noticed?' Kate murmured in Alex's ear, as they smiled and sauntered on to greet more friends. 'Your lot's on one side of the garden, all in a huddle, talking shop, and my lot's on the other, all in a huddle, talking gossip. And every now and then someone realises they know someone who knows someone and the two sides briefly meet. I feel like I'm straddling a stream, with people yanking me both ways.'

'Just as long as I yank harder than anyone. And you have to realise that our shop-talk is gossip. Nothing different, I promise you,' Alex murmured, kissing the nape of her neck where the fair hair was drawn up off it and wishing to God they hadn't decided to stay on until late. It had seemed like a good idea at the time, to enjoy the party with everyone else, to dance and have a long chat with people they hadn't seen for ages but now, smelling his young wife's lightly perfumed skin, all he wanted to do was whisk her off to the hotel and ravish her in her ivory silk dress with all those petticoats. But there were hours still to go . . .

'God, we were lucky with the weather, weren't we? It's more like spring today than late December. Do you think it's a good omen?' Kate interrupted his thoughts and he smiled tenderly down at her.

'For what? Our marriage?' The serious look in his eyes was belied by his twitching mouth.

'Yes, why not? Think how dreary it would be if it had just rained all day long . . .'

'Or thunderstormed . . .'

'That would have been your wedding day with Joanna,' Kate quipped and then relented. 'Sorry. I just feel as though her eyes are boring into my back like lasers. Why ever did she come?'

'She has a strong masochistic streak in her,' Alex replied drily. 'Try and ignore her, if you can.'

'Um, fat chance. Oh, look, who's that?' Kate paused, squinting in a slightly short-sighted manner. 'The gingerish man over there by the fountain, scowling. The mini Mussolini. What's he looking so ferocious about?'

'Where?' Alex followed her line of sight. 'Oh, lord . . . that's Hugh Mallory, OC "S" company – one of the company commanders,' he clarified, as Kate's eyebrows rose enquiringly. 'And I imagine – yes, there she is, in amongst that gaggle of male admirers, as usual.'

'Who?' Kate craned around to watch a particularly vivacious flame-haired woman, her arms interlinked with two men's, laughing uproariously at something someone had said. There was a similarity to Joanna there, she thought, that wasn't just the colour of the hair. The flamboyance, perhaps? The edge that was just a little too forced, too manic?

'Laura, Hugh's wife. Difficult pair. There's going to be a scene if she keeps that up—'

'Not here, surely? Goodness, their colouring must clash terribly – ginger with red. What a horrible combination!' Kate's colour sense was offended.

'Believe me, they are. They bring out the very worst in each other. And where Hugh's concerned, that's not all that difficult.'

'Well, I do hope they behave themselves here. My mother would be devastated if we had a scene—' She was interrupted before she could demand that something be done, as Alex murmured in her ear.

'Ah, here's Colonel Joss. His wife's name is Suzy. You met them at the Beating of Retreat, remember?'

'Yes, yes, of course I remember. Such a dear.' She glanced back at Hugh. It really could be awful if left to run its own course, she thought worriedly as she watched Hugh's puce face bunching in rage. Reluctantly, she turned instead to greet her husband's commanding officer.

'Alex! Kate! Finally, I've fought my way through the throng. Come and give me a kiss, my dear, and then Suzy can't accuse me of molesting you. Wonderful church ceremony, wasn't it? Got all choked up over "My Country" as usual. Fabulous voices, that choir.' A trim voice, sharp and precise, preceded a tall, slightly stooped man with fair, thinning hair neatly brushed back from a high forehead. A distinct type, Kate thought, that couldn't be other than English, well bred and deeply conservative with a small c.

'They thought they'd have to contribute most of the sound, Colonel. Haven't come across a military crowd before, used to belting out the hymns. I think they were a bit taken aback, actually.'

'No, it was your Great-Aunt Maud's ear-splitting screech they were dumbfounded by,' Kate laughed at Alex, 'and everyone around her is still partially deaf. Ringing in the ears – what do they call that? Tin-something. Hallo Joss, how are you?' She kissed the colonel's cheek fondly, thinking what a Nice man he was, with a large N. Small c, large N, oh dear, she smiled to herself, she'd been in London too long. Just as well she was getting away.

'Lucky them. Then they won't have to hear my speech,' Alex remarked feelingly and Joss laughed.

'Ah, stretching the nerves a bit, is it? You can stand up in front of six hundred cynical, hard-bitten men without batting an eyelid, but God help you at a family gathering. Terrifies us all. My advice is to keep it short and sincere, thank the parents, bridesmaids and pages, and have done. By the way, have you seen Hugh?' He nodded significantly towards the fountain. Alex grunted.

'You'd think they could lay off today, of all days. People are meant to fall in love at weddings, not stage family dramas.'

'Oh, you know Hugh – and Laura provokes him so. She enjoys making him squirm, belittling him. It's her revenge, I imagine.' Colonel Joss turned to Kate, who was eyeing the pair warily. 'You'll find out all about the battalion's little foibles soon enough, my dear. Ignore them for today. I'll keep them in check, I promise. And if I can't, I'll pick up the pieces!' And then Kate was swept away by Milly to greet other friends, throwing a rueful smile at Alex over her shoulder.

'Gorgeous in uniform, isn't he? I've never seen him in it

before. Those long, long legs and that straight back, yumm!' Milly was remarking and Kate focused back on her with a secretive look.

'Even more gorgeous out of it!'

'Don't! My heart can't take it!'

Kate laughed. 'Mind you, I had to convince Alex to wear uniform today. He wanted to wear a boring old morning coat, like everyone else.'

'Mad. Uniforms are so utterly hunky!' Milly, square-built and sturdy with beautiful skin and eyes beneath a mop of unruly dark hair, shook her head enviously. 'And you've got two long weeks to enjoy it all. Lucky cow! Any ideas yet where you're off to?'

'Don't tell me you don't know?' Kate raised her eyebrows. 'And I thought Alex had you in a huddle sorting out details . . .'

'Ah, but that would be telling . . .'

'Wretch,' Kate remarked fondly. 'You're supposed to be loyal to me.'

'Look who's talking!' Milly retorted, with a little more feeling than she had intended. 'Abandoning the business and me to go gallivanting off in Alex's baggage train. Sorry,' she amended as she saw Kate's eyes widen in dismay. 'Didn't mean it. I'll just miss you, that's all.'

'Oh, Milly! It isn't as though we won't see each other all the time still. But what was I supposed to do? There's no way we could work it both ways, is there?'

'No, no, I guess not. And I don't blame you in the least. If Alex had so much as blinked in my direction—'

'You are madly in love with Robby, so don't give me that.' Kate laughed off Milly's comments, knowing it was all bluff. There was never a pair better matched. 'He just happens to have a more sensible career in the City that makes life easier for you both.'

'Heavens, cous,' Nicky, appearing from behind Kate, interrupted, 'does this sound like regrets? Don't say it around Jo. She's frothing as it is about losing Alex.'

'Regrets? Hardly! Poor Jo . . .' Kate tried hard to sound sympathetic. 'It must be terribly difficult to come today and smile at everyone, pretend she's happy. Not that I actually expected her to turn up . . . it was really just a politeness to invite her . . .' Kate glanced coolly over at Joanna in a group by the border, gesturing largely with those strong pale hands of hers. Sculptress hands. She could have had her cake and eaten it too, married to Alex.

'Don't be so mealy-mouthed, Kate. You know you loathe her and she certainly hasn't a printable word to say about you. Wants to know if you're preggers – you're not, are you?'

Nicky laughed at Kate's expression, covering her mouth briefly with scarlet-tipped fingers as it lengthened into a yawn. 'Lord, I'm tired and cold. All this standing about, being polite. Can't think why we all turn up again and again at these dos, can you?'

'Waiting for our own turn?' Milly suggested, good-naturedly baiting Nicky who had a habit of getting engaged at weddings and ending it the following week. 'But there are fewer and fewer eligible men left.'

'You'd better get a move on with Robby, then, hadn't you? You want him to look half-decent on your wedding day, not balding and fat,' Nicky retorted rudely. As he was veering towards, even in his early thirties, all three girls knew. Milly gave Nicky a strained smile, her mouth parting to give battle.

'Oh lord, look,' Kate broke in hastily, half to deflect each girl's irritation with the other, half in fascinated dismay. 'There's going to be a scene after all. That wretched Hugh Mallory's just taken a swing at Joanna's arty friend. You know, the painter creature with the pony-tail.'

'What! No! Where?' Both girls craned forward to see over the gathering crowd. 'Why?'

'Being too familiar with his wife, I imagine. Hugh was scowling like thunder before and she was lapping up the attention.' They pushed forward slightly to see the men being separated by friends, Colonel Joss muttering sharply to Hugh; Suzy, the colonel's wife, drawing Laura away inside the house where she could try to sober her up a little, wild red hair floating across both their faces in the strengthening breeze. The painter was still sitting aggrievedly on the lawn, feeling his jaw while Joanna talked to him quietly and flashed venomous glances around at any army people in sight. Kate suppressed a smile.

How one knew they were army, exactly, she wasn't quite sure. They wore morning dress just like everyone else. But it was still instantly apparent. Possibly it was their bearing, or their slightly shorter hair, but she didn't really think so. The fresh, clean, scrubbed look? The air of command? What was it? Because she could tell them at a glance and so could Jo.

'If looks could kill, that Mallory fellow would be writhing on the ground right now,' Nicky observed with amusement. 'Jo isn't having a good day, is she? Do you think it was the red hair that set him off? Jo's man, I mean? Not the short one.'

'Probably. And I'm quite frankly surprised someone hasn't shot him years ago. The short one, Hugh, I mean.' Alex caught Nicky's startled glance, having come up quietly behind her. 'Negligent discharge or the like. If he keeps it up, he'll be lucky to come back in one piece from Ireland. Laura likes to bat her eyelids at the men too and Hugh lets them have it on the q.t.'

Nicky shot her eyebrows heaven-ward. 'How thoroughly disgusting – the whole set-up, I mean. You are an incestuous lot, aren't you? Must go and take another peek!' And she nipped off smartly to the house to see if there was anything more to be witnessed. Failing that, she could at least find another bottle of the Tattainger to sock away for later, she thought brightly, eyeing a rather good-looking man whom she knew had formed part of the honour guard. He eyed her back warily.

Alex came to collect Kate and start leading people into the tent for tea. A bit early, perhaps, but anything to break up the awkward atmosphere, he remarked shortly, his firm lips pressed together unsmilingly. Kate glanced at him. His eyes were dark with anger, the single lock of hair that tended to fall forward over his brow pushed back with a gesture of irritation.

'It's embarrassing, Alex, but . . . people forget. Don't make a big thing of it, don't let it spoil our day,' she murmured hesitantly. Beside her, she felt him shift abruptly.

'Oh, Kate, I wouldn't mind if it were the first time. But they make a habit of it. And quite frankly, Hugh's the sort who might just collect a quick bullet in the back, and think what a stink there'd be then. The tabloids would have a field day. And God knows the battalion doesn't need any more bad publicity,' he added feelingly, a spate of violence within the regiment lately having made his life as Adjutant all the more difficult.

His voice, though still quiet, had become hard and clipped, a tone there that Kate had never heard before. Suddenly she understood how he could command men in the field, make them obey orders. There was an inner strength or, perhaps, just confidence in himself that registered respect. Not fear exactly, but definitely the knowledge that one should tread warily. But Alex was continuing on, oblivious to her surprised thoughts.

'Swaggering, pompous, petty and vicious – he's a thoroughly dreadful man. He doesn't look after his men or earn their trust in any way – just assumes because he's an officer that he can do what he likes. God knows what he's doing in the regiment.'

'Not the right sort?' Kate mocked lightly, hoping to jolly him out of his mood.

'Not ours, anyway,' Alex replied, frowning. Kate pulled a face.

'Now who's being pompous?' For a moment he froze, his dark eyes stilled as they looked at her. Then he turned away and pulled her gently towards the marquee. She could see he was trying to retain his dignity but a reluctant smile kept tugging at the corner of his mouth as he led her towards the tent. She saw him shake his head.

So, that was all right, she sighed contentedly to herself. Alex could, at least, laugh at himself.

Emma patted Laura's hand and wondered if another cup of black coffee would be a good idea. Hugh had left, screeching out of the driveway, scattering gravel, dogs, and wedding guests, and he would certainly not be returning. Joss had told him off rather sharply and he had been humiliated by his wife yet again in front of people who very much mattered to him. So, no, he would not be back, Emma thought. Laura laughed.

'Don't look so tragic, Em. I really couldn't give a stuff. Besides – you'll take me home, won't you?' Her words were barely slurred.

'Can't this time I'm afraid, Laura. We're heading on up to Scotland for the week. But we'll find someone going back, don't worry. Maybe Bill?'

'Ah, yes! Definitely Bill! I've always liked Bill.' Laura punctuated each statement with a kitten-like lick of her tongue against her bottom lip. Definitely more coffee, Emma thought. Poor Laura. What a completely miserable existence, living simply to make another person unhappy. She tried to feel sorry for Hugh too but even her placid, sweet nature found that too difficult.

'Kate looked stunning, didn't she? That dress! Quite the loveliest I've seen,' Emma remarked, leaning forward to pour out two more cups of rich, very black coffee. 'It'll be great having her on the patch – she's terribly nice, don't you think?'

'Don't know her,' Laura shrugged, indifferent. 'I expect she must be quite something for Alex to marry her. Yet another gorgeous man out of bounds.' She sighed sharply. Laura had her own peculiar brand of ethics. She might be married but that in no way curtailed her own amusements, but other marriages, ah, that was different, they were not to be invaded. No, only bachelors for her. And then she thought of Bill, lovely, light-hearted Bill, and brightened immeasurably. She liked Bill.

'So,' she said suddenly, focusing on the room around her and taking in the quietly grand air of old family and old money. 'Alex has done rather well for himself, hasn't he?

Hope she's not terribly snooty. I really could do without any more frilled and bowed disapproval.'

Emma smiled. 'Like Amanda and her cronies? Kate's lovely, don't worry. I'm sure we'll all be good muckers.'

Laura laughed. 'Oh, Em, you're so completely sweet through and through, I'd be nauseated if you weren't actually my only friend.'

'I am not sweet!' Emma retorted, a sudden flush rising on her cheeks. 'I just happen to prefer to like people rather than bitch about them – at least, until they prove themselves thoroughly unlikeable.'

'Like Hugh,' Laura flashed quickly and Emma sighed.

'Oh, well, yes, I suppose. Like Hugh.' She glanced around as Fergus peered in the doorway, and smiled at his raised eyebrows. 'Are we wanted?'

'Scoff's on. You've missed the speeches. Bill did very well, made 'em all laugh no end. Alex sensibly brief and to the point. Kate's pa made a bit of a muff of it – forgot Alex's name. Called him Adam. But since he's titled and loaded no one's said very much. Kate's mortified of course. Thought you might come and cheer her up?'

'Yes, of course we will. And poor Alex too. Besides, I'm starving.' Emma started to rise, smoothing down the emerald green silk jacket and skirt that she had found in a designer second-hand shop for a song. Laura bobbed up quickly, indifferent to the fact that her wickedly expensive suit was stained with wine. She would just buy another and charge it to Hugh. Serve him right.

'I'll come and cheer Bill up,' she announced brightly. 'Will that do?'

Chapter Three

It was the bomb-shaker that did it. She had managed everything else so well, Kate thought, but how was anyone expected to react when jolting over a brick maze designed to loosen bombs from the underside of your car? And to add to it, Alex took it so calmly, so matter-of-factly, joking about the eggs on the back seat, his laughing profile turned slightly towards her as they lurched sickeningly over the obstacle.

Kate felt like screaming. But what would she have screamed, exactly? '*I'm* not in the army, so why should anyone put a bomb under *my* car?' That was hardly relevant, was it? She was married to someone in the army. As of three weeks ago she had become – dare she say it? – an army wife. And people like that had to worry about bombs, under cars or otherwise. Even with all this peace talk going on. The thought dimmed the beauty of the morning for her, a vague fear surging forward that she had always pushed to the back of her mind, avoided, caught up instead in the glamour of Alex and her love for him.

Sabre-teeth, watch-towers or 'sangers' as they seemed to be called, bomb-shakers and now a toll-gate forced them to a halt, the guard coming out at a leisurely pace, clipboard at the ready, while he jotted down their licence plate number and belatedly sauntered over to the driver's window. Birds sang, the sun shone, a light breeze ruffled the hedge beside them. All so normal, Kate thought, except that her new home had a bomb-shaker.

'Morning, sir.' The guard saluted smartly as he suddenly recognised Alex. 'Morning, ma'am. Have you just arrived, sir?' The soldier smiled in at Kate, his young, snub-nosed face seemingly absurdly out of place beneath an army helmet, his merry eyes taking in all the details of the captain's new wife. The word would be out all over camp in barely an hour that the boss had married a corker, Alex thought wryly.

He fished in his pocket and produced his identification.

'Good morning, Private Edloe. Yes, we're straight off the ferry. Things quiet?' The boy nodded back benignly.

'They are now, sir. Had a bit of a barny with the last lot when we took over. Took a few casualties but we gave even more. You'll hear all about it, I expect.' He grinned as he returned the identification and saluted again. 'Captain Lambourne's expecting you, sir, at some point, to brief you and Mrs Aldridge about security and then I expect the Families Officer will show you your quarter. You know the way, do you, sir?'

'Yes, yes. I was marched in a week ago, so we won't need to be shown where to go. Thank you,' Alex was saying and Kate again had to adjust herself to this new phrase. Marched in. It sounded so absurd. How could you be marched in to your own home? Did you do a goose-step or simply strut, she giggled to herself. But apparently people took it terribly seriously, the checking of the oven, the mattresses and so on, before agreeing to sign for it all in triplicate. When you signed, you took on all problems and agreed they were yours, Alex had told her.

The really excruciating part was the march out, however, as Emma, relating the saga to Kate over a stiff glass of wine in London, had found to her cost. A posse of men from the various housing departments turned up and went over the quarter in detail, running fingers along the tops of doorways and inside cupboards, going over the carpet with such care that Emma had thought one of them was going to walk around the house on his hands and knees! And, then, of course, the oven . . .

Emma, whom Kate had thought the most scrupulous of people, had had her oven rejected three times. It didn't seem possible or even sane, but the army actually expected the oven to be returned in the same pristine condition in which it had been bought. Nothing, not the merest speck of baked-on cement in the farthest cranny of the oven was allowed to remain. As Emma had drily told Kate, the man had brought a torch . . .

After having threatened to leave Fergus or insist he leave the army, if she had to deal with such humiliating inspections ever again, Fergus had decided, wisely, to employ professional contract cleaners in future who signed for the quarter and were then responsible for bringing it up to the martinet standard the army required. No toothpaste plugging of holes, no talcum powdering of mattresses. The place would be industrially cleaned. And no doubt fail at least once . . . Emma advised Kate strongly to do the same.

But Alex had done it all, seen to everything while she, Kate, had packed up her little London flat and said goodbye to her friends, her workmates, yet again, and then they had driven ten hours north to Stranraer in Scotland, taken a ferry across to Larne, and driven down to Belfast. And now it was time to take on this strange army life.

Kate sighed imperceptibly as Private Edloe asked Alex if he was satisfied with the security of his vehicle and then they were waved through, the toll-gate coming down behind them. They were inside and the world was locked out and for just a moment Kate breathed deeply with relief and thought that it wasn't such a bad idea at all to have high, barbed-wire fences around your house. Not if you needed bomb-shakers to keep you safe.

'What happens if a bomb actually drops off?' she asked suddenly, struck by this new fear. Alex slowed to ease over speed bumps in the road and glanced at his wife, thinking how fetching she looked in her casual London clothes and with her fair hair caught back behind her ears. But it was the look of concern puckering between her dark eyebrows that made his heart unexpectedly lurch for a moment at how lucky he was.

'I expect it'll either go off and then you won't know much about it, or it'll be a dud in the first place which is why you're still alive and driving. But it's not a real worry, my love. There are too many other targets that are far more enticing than a boring officer's wife. Bad PR anyway. Don't forget they're trying to talk peace these days.' He tried to make light of it, knowing Kate would adjust, forget about it all within a week or two. All the wives did. Besides, what choice was there?

'Oh, how reassuring! I'll try and remember that next time I'm crawling around on my knees peering under the bloody car,' Kate commented waspishly. 'And what's all this about "red areas" that we're not allowed into?'

Alex shrugged awkwardly. 'They don't really concern you. I'm not allowed into those areas on pain of courtmartial. You are simply advised not to go unless you have a good reason.'

Kate stared at him, horrified. 'Why? What are these areas?'

'Trouble spots,' Alex replied calmly. 'Loyalist and Republican flashpoint areas that could be dangerous. Then there are orange areas that aren't quite as bad, and so on. We have large maps up around camp to remind everyone where they can and can't go in Belfast.'

'How would I know where I was going, if I were lost . . .'

'I'll drive you around and you'll quickly get the hang of it all. Mainly it's just West Belfast with a couple of other little patches . . . it's not so bad, you'll see.'

'Good heavens, I had no idea it would all be so difficult. Bomb-shakers and barbed wire and red areas . . .' Kate was aghast. Alex, watching her with a sympathetic grin, was nevertheless pragmatic.

'You knew the pitfalls . . .'

'Yes, yes,' she sighed and looked around her instead, trying not to let him see just how bizarre she was finding it all. The steady drone of a tractor mower circling the far perimeter fences, making sure the grass didn't obscure a possible terrorist, and the bickering of a couple of magpies over a nesting site was all the disturbance she could find in the stillness of the morning.

It was a large camp and no doubt the work went on in another sector. But just here, as they passed landscaped gardens sweeping down towards what looked like stables in the distance, and turn-of-the-century red brick buildings standing curiously quiet in the sunshine, it was quite still. Idyllic really. No soldiers marching back and forth, no movement almost at all.

'Empty, this bit.' Alex read her thoughts. 'The camp used to house several battalions at once. Now there's just us and a handful of the Royal Irish. Part of the Treasury cuts.' His voice was unemotional. He had come to terms with the first round of cuts and the diminishment of his regiment by one battalion. The men found it harder, he said, than the officers. Their pride suffered more.

'Who's Captain Lambourne? And why do we have to see him?' Kate asked idly as she looked around. The car rose and fell over another speed bump and Alex laughed.

'Nick. You've met him several times. He's the Intelligence Officer. Every new arrival has to get briefed on security and they show a couple of video nasties to remind everyone to keep on their toes . . .'

'Video nasties? Like bombed cars and so on . . . ?' Kate turned pale at the thought. Alex nodded, hoping it was nothing more than that. In the past they had shown bombed people as well, just to drive home the point about security. He hoped Kate didn't have to see that.

'Oh,' she replied in a subdued voice. 'But . . . it is peace at the moment, isn't it?'

'Yes . . . yes, it is, but it could all fall apart at any minute and we don't expect to get a lot of warning. Word is, it'll fail before Easter. So don't go getting complacent.' Alex hated to tell her such dismal news but he desperately wanted her to understand and to be careful. Sometimes telling the news as it really was, was the only way to make sure it was taken in.

'What happens then?' Kate's eyes were large and fearful. Alex shook his head.

'We don't really know. Most people here want peace. They're desperate for it. So . . . if trouble starts up again, there'll be an outcry. Who knows? Maybe it'll be listened to. If not, well, we'll be back out there on the streets and spend some time in West Belfast on a rotational basis. You'll be safe here.' From the tone of his voice, Alex didn't want to discuss the matter further. Kate subsided quietly against the car seats, trying to memorise her way around the camp instead.

Further down the hill, sweeping around in a cul-de-sac hidden behind ancient trees, Alex pointed out their new home and Kate laughed unexpectedly, the sound forced out of her more by surprise than amusement.

'Brookside? Or am I imagining things?'

'Well, the local council estate's fairly outraged at having us as such a blot upon their landscape,' Alex remarked wryly. 'But wait until you get closer. You'll like it even more.' He swung past several identical houses, the lawns neatly mown and flowerbeds turned and tended, even in winter.

'I think I'm close enough, actually. Do you think it's too late to get my flat back?'

'It's a bit of a commute. Anyway, I thought you enjoyed a challenge. What's the point in me marrying an interior decorator if you can't improve upon an army quarter?'

'Designer, please!' Kate sniffed. 'And besides, there are limits . . .'

'I shall hold that against you, you know.' He leaned over

to stroke her cheek with the back of his hand. 'You told me there were no limits and I believed you. I'd never have married you otherwise. Well, maybe just for the sex . . .'

'You always were gullible with women, Alex,' Kate retorted, smiling in spite of herself as she caressed her husband's hand, giving it a quick kiss. 'But . . . oh, Lord,' her voice became wistful, 'is this really it?'

'You can refurnish it from scratch, you know. Get rid of all the G-plan, put in our own stuff . . . And it's not a bad view across the lough, if you ignore the gas works in the way.' The concern on Alex's face, the slightly crestfallen look of someone who had tried so hard to please, speared Kate with guilt and remorse.

'Oh, darling, it'll be fine. I'm sorry, it's just all so strange and quite frankly the *Sunday Times* talked about quarters being palaces and I've never seen a married patch before . . . What's G-plan? Surely not that 1960s stuff . . . ?' Her tone of contrition suddenly turned sharply to suspicion. Alex brought the car to a halt in their new driveway and opened his door, gesturing for her to follow. He grinned wickedly.

'Come and see . . .'

Laura Mallory kicked her legs idly, admiring the way the water slid enticingly over her long, shapely limbs. That was what had first caught Hugh's attention, she realised ruefully. Her body. Tall, slender, very curvaceous, she was the Barbie-doll embodiment of most men's fantasies. And she had accepted within a few weeks of arriving in England that huskies, pedal pushers and alice bands were simply not her style. Thank God.

Whereas, sexy black one-piece bathing suits really were

her style. Or, at least, the men covertly glancing her way clearly thought so. She tossed her flame-coloured hair and fluttered her grape-green eyes slowly and languorously at the young sergeant in charge of the gym. So nice to be appreciated by such a good-looking young man, she thought, with a laugh that caught in the back of her throat and emerged as a sexy chuckle. The young sergeant blushed and walked away quickly.

'Laura, do stop it. You're embarrassing the men, and in those hideous little trunks there's not much they can do to hide it.' Emma laughed in spite of herself, in spite of the reproving words. She liked Laura but, oh dear, what a potential disaster the girl was for Hugh. It then occurred to Emma, not for the first time, that that was exactly why Laura did it. She sighed.

'No, I'm not. They like it.' Laura glanced at Emma, her neat, slender, boyish figure more appropriately clad in a navy and white spotted swimsuit that hinted at rather than revealed her possible charms. 'They like you too but you never catch their eyes,' Laura added pointedly, 'you just smile and talk to them as though you were still wearing your twinset and pearls. You've got a great figure, so why not show it off? What's wrong with a little flirting?' She glanced around at the other wives, also sensibly clad, holding small children splashing and shrieking in the shallow end of the pool and felt absurdly, angrily out of place.

'Nothing. There's nothing wrong with flirting, so long as that's all you do. But . . . it's not fair to do it with the men,' Emma protested, flushing slightly. 'You know they get ideas and then Hugh comes on all heavy-handed . . . and it just isn't fair,' she repeated stubbornly. 'If you want to flirt, do it with the other officers or people outside the battalion where it won't cause such a stink.'

'You sound as though you're accusing me of doing more than flirting.' Laura raised an eyebrow quizzically.

'No,' Emma flushed again, thinking perhaps she was. 'No, I'm not,' she lied. 'I know you think I'm being stick-in-the-muddish, but you don't seem to realise what havoc it can cause when personal problems arise between men who may have to fight together, or rely on each other for their lives.'

'Oh, here it comes,' Laura yawned, 'the Colonel's daughter's advice to the "gels" of the regiment. "Chin up, gels, support your men, do your bit!"' Laura squeezed Emma's arm to take the sting of her words away. 'I know you're a good girl, Em, and I know you care about the battalion and the regiment and the happiness of all, but,' Laura sighed sharply and turned away, 'I don't. I'm married to a – well, to Hugh, not your lovely Fergus or Alex or Bill, damn it all, and I have to have some fun in life.' She grinned. 'So be a sweetheart, will you, and button it? I'm going for a swim. Coming in?' She stood, all five foot eleven inches of pale beautiful curves and winked at Emma as several of the men sucked in their breath sharply. Emma laughed reluctantly.

'Oh, all right, and I'm sorry about the lecture. I'll mind my own business in future.' She stood up beside Laura, sharply aware of how meagre her own charms seemed in comparison. Barely five foot seven and too skinny these days, what with the miscarriage and all, she had no figure to speak of. She couldn't blame Laura. With Hugh for a husband, no one could blame Laura.

'Race you to the far end and back,' Laura challenged and Emma gauged the distance.

'You're on,' she agreed. Maybe all those luscious curves would slow Laura down in the water? After all, she privately sighed to herself, not much else would.

Theirs had been a whirlwind romance, Kate conceded as she sat nursing a much needed cup of tea on her lap and staring around her at the bleak, magnolia-painted interior. The stiff chair beneath her yielded only slightly as she squirmed into a more comfortable position, its faded floral pattern at odds with its square geometry. Thin, mismatched curtains blew lightly in the chill breeze where she had opened a window to air the house, and the ox-blood red fireplace gaped like a large mouth that happened to be plugged with the metal braces of a particularly unattractive gas fire. So, this was army life . . .

She had met Alex at a drinks party barely eight months ago, hardly seen him in uniform until after they were engaged. And then the glamour of a Sounding of the Retreat, a dinner in the officer's mess, all the silver gleaming and men strutting around in mess kit, it had all been too exciting, too awe-inspiring to raise any doubts. Why should she have doubts when everyone was so envious of her? Alex was wonderful, gorgeous, loving and generous. Their lifestyle would be one long party, her mother assured her. And she had believed it.

All young unmarried officers drove around in sports cars, as far as she could see, and they all knew everyone in London, dashed back and forth from Germany or whatever camp in England, had huge overdrafts but somehow always had money to spend. And Alex had been the most dashing, the most dazzling of them all. He still was, she mused as she drank the warm, sweet tea from thick green army china, but somehow, overnight, their life had changed dramatically. She looked around again, her dark eyebrows drawn slightly together.

In the hallway Alex could be heard muttering on the telephone to the estate warden about the possibility of wharfing the furniture, the dreaded mock teak G-plan that was more hideous than anything she could have imagined, and Kate felt a sudden surge of love for him. He was trying so hard, she thought, and all she had done was complain. What sort of wife was that? She wasn't a pathetic child to be humoured and besides, he had to get back to work, not ring around everyone sorting out matters that she could easily handle herself.

All right, so she didn't know the terminology yet, had no idea exactly what 'wharfing' was, or the PSA or ASA or any of the other acronyms the army was so fond of, but she could find out. And most people understood plain English, didn't they?

I'll be a good wife, she vowed silently to herself. I'll make this hideous box look like a home and I won't fuss over bombs or Red Areas or terrorists or the long separations, or the constant moves – I'll try to make him happy. Because I do love him, she thought fiercely, catching sight of Alex's dark hair curling in an unruly cowlick over one blue, blue eye as he peered around the doorway. I do!

The estate warden was still talking and Alex was trying to pay attention, but distracted entirely by the way his wife's sarong skirt had parted to reveal long, smoothly brown legs that stretched out forever. Two weeks in St Kitts had turned her fair skin a golden tint that he longed to caress and that looked strangely out of place in winter Belfast. He shook his head and turned back into the hallway, disappearing from

Kate's sight. Reluctantly, he focused upon the intricacies of who exactly was responsible for what.

When he finally emerged again, triumphant at having arranged that legendary impossibility, a partial wharf, some of the spare bedroom furniture staying, most of the rest going, he found Kate sitting on the floor surrounded by unwrapped newspapers as she piled the framed wedding photographs around her. She looked like a child, thoroughly absorbed in some exciting game, he thought. Except that the new game was marriage and army life and he was terrified, deep down, that she would rebel against its dangers and constrictions and leave him. She looked up abruptly and smiled at him, so that his heart suddenly swelled with love and relief.

'Leave it. We'll sort it out later,' he said abruptly, coming forward to take her outstretched hand and pull her to her feet, holding her slender body tightly against him. His mouth sought hers and again he felt that surge of warm relief when she responded eagerly. 'Come to bed,' he coaxed, leading her towards the stairs. Kate looked around her at the complete disarray, then back at Alex. Unhesitatingly, she let him draw her up to the bedroom.

Supper that night was taken care of, Kate remembered with sudden relief, as she lay propped up against Alex's chest, listening to his quiet breathing. Fergus and Emma Kennedy had invited them around for a bite and a quick break from their unpacking. A nice, light-hearted couple, thoroughly in love and happy with life, they were an inspiration, Kate thought. She had met them several times before, of course, at parties or in London and liked them more and more each time.

Fergus, big, bear-like and gruffly charming, was one of

Alex's best friends, as well as a brother officer. Emma was pretty, bright and level-headed, a former solicitor who had given up her practice to marry Fergus. Kate thought her a saint to have given up so much without even a murmur. Particularly when her new life involved march-outs and ovens that were impossible to clean. Ah, the love of a good man, she murmured to Alex's chest and he stirred slightly, swatting her hair away blindly in sleep.

When the telephone rang, she jerked slightly in surprise. Who had her number already? Alex was reaching for it, his eyes still shut, his hand groping across the side table and knocking the lamp so that it teetered before settling back into place. He placed the receiver against his mouth and ear.

'Hello?' The conversation was one-sided, Alex mostly groaning and sitting up with irritation, his long fingers scrubbing at his mop of dark hair, his eyes slowly opening to peer around at Kate and smile with blue intensity at her.

'All right, Colour. Tell the Jocks we'll take him but if there's any trouble, we won't promise to keep him safe. I'm not endangering any of my boys over a child-molester. Where's his wife? Well out of the way, I hope? Fine, well, lock him up in the Guardroom overnight and I'll interview him in the morning,' Alex was saying and Kate slid from beneath the sheets to walk, naked, across the room to her robe. Except that it wasn't there, behind the door as it was supposed to be. It was still packed. She sighed, shrugged and with a glinting smile at the way Alex was watching her so intently, sauntered out towards the cold linoleum of the bathroom.

Thank heavens her own bed was arriving shortly. She

couldn't deal with that squeaking monster with its latched-on side tables for more than a few nights at the most. In fact, thank heavens all her own things were coming. But, at least the moving-in pack had provided them with sheets and towels, without which they would be in a bit of a pickle, she thought and then, abruptly, wondered who the child-molester was. What a charming bunch Alex must deal with as adjutant, she smiled uncomfortably to herself in the mirror. An uneasy face smiled back at her.

Chapter Four

'Are they having an affair?' Kate didn't say it, merely thought it, her fractionally raised eyebrows and enquiring eyes flickering at Emma who glanced awkwardly back. Maybe, Emma's dark eyes signalled. Quite likely, in fact. Both sets of eyes turned back to Laura and Bill. Laura was perched on the arm of Bill's chair, her body turned in towards him, her riotous tumble of hair half-obscuring her face as she laughed at something he had said. Her entire being was intent upon him, flattering him, puffing him up with a sense of his own importance. And then Bill glanced across at the other two girls with a look of mock alarm that had them relaxing, laughing, turning back towards each other.

Captain William Ovington was the third member of the fraternal club comprising of Alex, Fergus and Bill. All much of an age and background, all handsome and charming, they had caused havoc in their younger days when they hunted as a pack. Now two were happily married and only Bill, the youngest, the most flighty, was left to bachelor on alone. Except that Laura had seemingly decided she wanted Bill. And with her husband Hugh away, Bill was powerless to deny her. Kate looked at Laura coolly, disturbed by how much she resembled Joanna.

'I found Jo quite . . . difficult, to be honest,' Kate was replying to a careful scouting question of Emma's. She cast a wary look over at Alex. But he was safely absorbed in conversation with Fergus.

'You and me both, I'm afraid. I always felt so uncomfortable with her. It was really rather a relief when she walked out on Alex, thinking that would bring him to heel with ring in hand. I think, well, she's basically quite arrogant, you know. Unable to see what other people are thinking . . . or perhaps, simply unconcerned.' The candle-light glowed warmly on Emma's skin, lighting her clear, forthright features.

'Dear Jo . . . the bane of my life,' Kate sighed. 'Yes, I know what you mean,' she admitted with feeling. 'Terribly demanding and theatrical all the time. Everything had to be larger than life. The most dramatic break-up, the most romantic reconciliation . . . ttch!' She sat back, nursing her coffee, glancing around the room.

Emma had transformed the drab interior of the quarter with her own furniture, paintings, flowers. Kate took it all in with a professional eye and silently applauded. Time she got to grips with her own. Then, as Laura threw back her head and laughed, the image of Jo doing the same thing flashed across Kate's mind. The surge of indignation it provoked made her indiscreet. 'I had the hardest time with her when Alex and I first started going out, you know. Practically accosted me in the street over it. I mean, it wasn't my fault they had split up—'

'Of course not! Jo was never going to make Alex happy,' Emma soothed. 'She's far too self-absorbed. But she had her talons in deep . . .' She drifted off again with a relieved sigh. 'I was terribly worried for a while that she would prevail, despite everything. She would have been such an awkward person to have around permanently.'

'She's very strong. In all senses. And they'd been going out together, on and off, for nearly five years. You know what she said when we became engaged?' exclaimed Kate, irritated all over again at the memory.

'Of course!' Emma's eyes glinted with amusement. 'We all heard. "But darling,"' Emma mimicked Jo's deep, throaty tone, '"does that mean we won't be able to go to Mauritius after all? We always planned to, you know, and you promised me . . ."'

Kate joined in Emma's laughter. 'The bloody cheek of it!' Miss Number One all the time. Ah well, it's all past history now. I can't think why she even came up in conversation—'

'Because I was saying how unsuitable she would have been as an army wife. Truly bolshie, knocking everyone and everything and let's face it, there's enough that's fair game in the army as it is. The last thing Alex needed was a difficult wife.'

'And am I suitable?' Kate asked with irony, feeling faintly uncomfortable at the thought. She glanced down questioningly at her severe black jeans and cream knit top.

'I don't mean you have to wear frilly blouses and pearls, or line up panting for coffee mornings to kowtow to the senior wives and promote your husband's career,' Emma retorted with a laugh. 'Those are just clichés that people like to make up about us – or perhaps they were true once. I don't know. I just mean you aren't likely to purposely embarrass Alex to score off him. That doesn't go down well within the battalion. Too small, too intimate for things like that to go unnoticed.' As she said it, she flickered her eyes uncomfortably over to where Laura was dangling her glass precariously above Bill's lap.

'I can imagine,' Kate said with emphasis. 'But tell me,' she hesitated, trying to phrase the matter lightly, yet delicately, 'just how important is a wife to a man's career in the army? How much does her behaviour influence his advancement . . . ?'

'Or otherwise? Is that what you mean?' Emma raised her eyebrows mischievously. 'Well, judging from past performances, the answer is not much. Not anymore, anyway. Maybe at Brigadier or General level, where wives have quite a serious role to play in entertaining on a political level. But not down at scrubby Captain and Major level. These days, thank God, we're free to do what we want, as such. It's just so uncomfortable within such a tight community when people don't try to fit or be . . .'

'Convenable?' Kate smiled ruefully. 'Like going to a large family gathering and having one of the cousins behave appallingly over the inheritance or go off with someone else's wife?'

'Exactly!' Emma agreed with satisfaction. 'Everyone shudders and leaves with a bad taste in their mouths.'

'Ah, I see.' Kate smiled down at her hands, absorbing the information with mixed feelings. 'Just general good manners, then? Normal behaviour? No lengthy duties or forelock tugging to senior wives?' She sipped at her coffee, admiring the Limoges service, noting briefly but carefully the silver framed photographs, the general air of sophisticated living that the house proclaimed. Appearances clearly did matter. Despite claims to the contrary.

'Good lord, no! That went out with the Dark Ages!' Emma protested so loudly that Laura finally glanced away from her seduction of Bill to laugh mockingly.

'Whatever Emma's telling you, don't you believe her, Kate. Wives are still expected to toe the duty line. You won't really notice it at first, it's such a subtle thing. You'll just be invited to meet the other wives, help out with cake bakes and SSAFA lunches, the occasional flower arranging for dinner nights – and then, slowly but surely, you'll start to feel little tugs on the leash for you to come to heel.' Her mouth, generous and red-painted, opened in a wide grin, pale pink tongue lapping her teeth. Her eyes glinted with disdain as Emma pooh-poohed the notion.

'That really is ridiculous, Laura.' Emma's tone was cool. 'Who, after all, tugs you into line, might I ask? Apart from Hugh, of course.'

A slantwise look, another mysterious mocking smile irritated Emma further. Slim shoulders raised themselves nonchalantly. 'Oh, I think we both know what I'm talking about, don't we, Em? You don't mind because you're a conservative creature at the best of times. And Kate will learn, all too soon,' she sighed plaintively, raising her glass to drain off the last of the wine and dangling it out above Bill's head. 'Any more of this? It's rather good, isn't it?'

'Are you sure, Laura? I don't want you blaming us tomorrow for getting you thoroughly soused. Or Hugh blaming us either!' Fergus laughed good-naturedly as he went to replenish glasses.

'Hugh won't be back until next week, as you know very well, Fergie darling, so I really don't give a damn what he thinks. Besides, none of you are going to tell him, now are you? About anything?' Laura added, smiling around at everyone pointedly as they quickly shook their heads. 'Good!' Bill laughed as she deliberately slid from the arm of the chair onto his lap. She had a bottom like a ripe melon, lush and curved and taut. Bill clasped her comfortably around the waist and whispered that fact to her, his lazy, half-closed eyes running over her appreciatively.

'Then I'd better be careful where I squirm, hadn't I?' Laura teased in a half-whisper. 'I don't want to go bruising the goods, do I?' The others shifted and glanced quickly away.

'Have you thought what to do with your quarter yet?' Emma hastily enquired of Kate. 'Everyone's waiting for you to do something miraculous, so we can all copy it. But quite frankly, if you can do anything to make that box even half-way presentable, we'll all start tugging our forelocks to you.' Her own quarter was larger, Fergus having been promoted to major earlier in the year. The captain's quarters really were nothing more than tiny, ugly bungalows with patches of scrubby lawn that passed as gardens.

Kate shrugged. 'I gather there are rules. No wallpapering or you have to strip it all off and repaint the walls magnolia again before you leave. That sort of thing.'

'Well, apart from which, it would cost you a fortune each time you got posted. And that could be as soon as six months' time. I tend to paint a couple of rooms the colours I want and hang my own curtains and that's it. It's not worth doing more, really.'

'Besides, we have a cottage in Dorset that we hare off to whenever we get a chance and that's soaking up all our non-existent money in renovations. We're trying to get it ready as a permanent base before we embark on children,' Fergus added, giving his wife a gentle kiss on the cheek.

'Aren't we, darling?' Emma flushed, biting her lip, the words causing unexpected and unintended pain. Glancing over at Laura, Fergus wondered if she knew what Hugh had done. The surge of anger momentarily baffled him and he had to shake his head to clear it.

'Oh, but this is lovely here!' Kate protested. 'I've been admiring it all evening, wondering why I'm supposed to be the decorating expert when you've clearly done such a wonderful job—'

'Well, I've always enjoyed making things look nice,' Emma glowed suddenly with the compliment, 'and I'm quite handy with the sewing machine, but we just don't have the budget to do anything spectacular. Army pay doesn't leave a lot over, you'll find. I just wish I could find someone really good who would do all my decorating on a shoestring budget for me and save me the hassle!'

'Maybe that's what I'll do then, darling,' Kate teased Alex. 'Start up a budget decorating operation locally. What do you think?' She was surprised when Alex paused and then nodded.

'Maybe you should at that,' he grinned, 'and then you can support me in the style to which I would like to become accustomed! I've always fancied a private income to splash around like old Bill here . . .' But Bill merely grinned good-naturedly and gestured for Alex to do something that Alex and Fergus laughed at and the girls looked puzzled.

'Really?' Kate wasn't sure whether to be delighted or not. 'Well,' she temporised, 'I'll experiment a bit at first. I'm not used to having to watch the prices.'

'That,' Alex slid an arm around his wife and drew her close to kiss, 'my darling, comes as no surprise. No surprise at all.'

Chapter Five

Five days passed before Kate emerged triumphant from beneath the MFO boxes and her own more delicately crated belongings to declare that that was as good as it was going to get. The tiny sitting-room walls were now sponged a delicate shade of biscuit yellow against which her many paintings and prints looked cosily established.

The dramatically fringed pale silk curtains from the flat in London had been adapted to the boxier windows of the quarter by looping and puffing them, and the green checked wing-chairs and yellow two-seater sofa arranged to enhance the limited space. She had had the gas fire removed and painted the oxblood red fireplace a soft cream. A cheap pine mantelpiece, carefully stained a pickled antiqued shade, had been added to frame the fireplace and could be moved on with her to the next quarter. Her travelling mantelpiece and her travelling curtains, she thought with a sense of parsimonious satisfaction. What an old army hand she was becoming!

An antique writing desk, damask and rose needlepoint cushions, silver and leather framed photographs, and spring flower arrangements made the place both elegant and relaxed at the same time. She felt as though it were finally her own.

In the dining room, the walls were now a soft shade of coral, the curtains a warmer coral and green flowered chintz, and a mahogany drop-leafed dining table, a present from Kate's maternal grandmother, gleamed beneath Herend china candlesticks. The hideous G-plan sideboard and writing desk were gone and in their place was a simple painted chest of drawers on which a flower arrangement and large porcelain lamp lightened and brightened the room. The gilt mirror that hung above it reflected the colours back at her.

Curtains from her own bedroom in London hung in the master bedroom and her own double bed had replaced the sagging monster that the army provided. The fresh china blue and white colour scheme of the curtains and bed linen blended surprisingly well with the existing magnolia on the walls and Kate had decided, wisely, to follow Emma's advice and keep the rest of the decorating to a minimum. These were the main rooms they would live in and the rest would just have to wait.

The other wives had lost no time in bringing around welcoming gifts of flowers, home-made biscuits and cakes in the hope that they would be invited in the inspect her efforts. First among them was Suzy Mailer-Howatt, the colonel's wife, small and rounded, her dark, robin-like eyes darting around brightly, taking everything in at once.

'My dear! It's quite enchanting! And those pots of topiary

and daffodils by the front door. I thought I'd strayed into Chelsea by mistake. How very established you are for newly-weds!' She deposited her cake on the hall table, kissed Kate airily and set off to explore. Kate stood holding the front door with a bemused expression on her face.

Belatedly she caught up with Suzy in the sitting room, examining the wedding photographs. 'Don't you photograph well! So much nicer in black and white, I always think. Good heavens, how have you managed all of this in five days? It takes me that long to draw breath and get the screws out of the MFO boxes!'

'Ah! Electric screwdriver,' Kate confided. 'Bill gave us one as a wedding present and I was totally taken aback by it at first, thinking what an odd present. But now I bless his name every time I unpack another box. He clearly knew what he was about.'

'Bill? That does come as a surprise! Charming, gorgeous, funny – but practical? That's not the Bill I know!' Suzy grinned good-naturedly. 'What about all the rest of it?' She swept her hand around at the furniture.

'It all came from my London flat. We've rented it out unfurnished for the time being, so I grabbed everything including the curtains since the new couple moving in have everything of their own. The movers even packed all my pots for me!' Kate laughed at the memory of the burly men lumbering out of her flat, delicate ferns and begonias in their meaty hands.

'How wonderful for you. I remember sitting in a damp heap in my first quarter, crying my eyes out to my mother down the telephone that I couldn't cope. I couldn't even boil an egg. Joss had to teach me. But then, I was ridiculously young. So much more sensible these days the way girls establish their own careers first, do a bit of living.' She beamed at Kate and Kate wondered what other career she could have visualised Suzy in, other than as a wife and mother . . . Nothing came to mind.

'Umm,' she agreed, non-committally. 'Like some tea?'

And after that, there were Amanda and Penny and Victoria and a rush of others, their names a blur to Kate at first as were their husbands'. Emma and Laura both dropped in, approved, made helpful suggestions and explained the mysteries of the boiler, the thermostat and the plumbing. At least, Emma did while Laura perched herself on the kitchen table and swung her long legs to and fro, admiring her reflection in the kitchen window and rubbing red lipstick off her teeth which she bared in a ferocious grimace at herself.

And the estate warden, Mr Elliot, surprisingly spry and enthusiastic, despite what Kate had heard to the contrary from the other wives, had the lawn mowed for her and the flower beds rotavated. She might even get a small terrace, she was promised, if there was any money left at the end of the fiscal year. And after a day of planting bulbs and a few roses, Kate felt there was little left to do. She wondered, uneasily, what wives did do all day long?

'Moan about the quarter, the estate warden and all workmen. You don't realise, Kate,' Laura drawled, 'that now that you've done your garden, you're bound to have them in to dig up the paths and cement over your new plants some time in the next week. It happens every time. It's quite infallible.'

'But Mr Elliot was charming—'

'Oh yes, all new wives say that, thinking they have

some special power over the ASA. Then, when the roses are cemented into place, the back door is replaced by a plastic replica and your doorbell no longer works, and the bathroom is tiled in white as you specified but they add a particularly lovely pink floral pattern smack in the middle of it all, you begin to realise what everyone else is on about. Particularly as it generally takes several months to get any of these little matters put straight, if ever . . .'

'Don't!' Kate laughed in mock horror. 'Besides, it isn't my place so I don't really care.' She glanced at Emma and said, 'No, really, what do you all do?'

'Have babies, of course,' Emma smiled wryly. 'Haven't you noticed what an incredible amount of time babies take up? Besides, you're running at London speed at the moment. Give yourself a month or so and you'll wind down considerably.' She examined her nails. 'I find it can take me hours to do a weekly shop now, whereas before, when I was working, I did it on my way home.'

'Is that meant to be reassuring?' Kate grinned, liking Emma's dry humour more and more.

'You needn't worry.' Emma waved her arms around airily. 'Your brain will atrophy at the same rate so you won't even notice.'

'Alex would!'

'Nonsense. They like us pudding-brained and domesticated,' Laura interrupted. 'Makes life easier for them.'

'The sexy bimbo in an apron?' They all giggled at the thought. 'As though Fergus would have married anyone who couldn't think for herself, Mrs ex-solicitor!' Kate chided Emma who had plucked an apple out of the bowl on the kitchen sideboard and was delicately peeling it with a knife. 'Or you, Laura!'

'Oh, Hugh would've! In fact, that's what he hoped—' Laura began but Emma was taking the question seriously.

'Umm . . . Fergus does like coming home to a cooked meal and the house all clean, I have to admit. You mustn't forget they're used to mess staff to run around after them. It took me quite a while to train him to drop his clothes in the laundry basket and I promise you, a separate dressing room for them and all their kit is essential. Then you can just shut the door on it.' She popped a quarter of apple into her mouth.

'If, after all that and the babies business you've got time to solicitor a little or decorate and bring in some extra income towards future school bills, well, fine and dandy. If not, well . . . priorities are priorities!'

Laura rolled her eyes and Kate burst out laughing. Neither Fergus nor Alex was like that, she thought, although Hugh might just qualify . . . And besides, she was enjoying being little Mrs Homemaker just for the moment. Emma was just joking, after all. Wasn't she?

Laura grinned at her doubtful face. 'You know what? We're the only three wives without babies at the moment,' she saw Emma's eyes darken and plunged on hastily, 'so we really ought to think of something to do together. Pool our resources. What do you think?' The other two glanced at her thoughtfully.

'Like what, exactly?'

'I don't know! What are we all good at? Take you, for instance, Em – you've got a great legal brain and you're a pretty handy seamstress on top of it all. Kate's a decorator. And I'm . . .' she paused, thinking.

'A decoration?' Emma teased.

'Exactly!' Laura shrugged her shoulders. 'And I have

the gift of the gab. You know how persuasive I can be if I put my mind to it. I could tout for clients. You could do the decorating, Kate, and Emma – you can do everything else.'

'Oh well, thanks very much!'

'No,' Kate paused and looked at Emma with rising excitement, 'Laura's right. We could take the next month to get ourselves set up and find our way around Northern Ireland, the auction rooms, the fabric warehouses and so on, and then we'll launch ourselves into business. We could call it "Decorating on a Shoestring", and just think of all the wonderful antiques and linens over here . . .' She turned bright eyes on Laura. 'Northern Ireland's opening up to all sorts of businesses, according to the newspapers, and they'll need their offices and homes done for them. Well, what do you think?'

'I'm game,' Laura replied promptly.

Emma snorted. 'So, what's new?' She wondered, privately, if either Kate or Laura realised quite how shaky the Peace was. But then, life had to go on and she, for one, could do with the extra money. She smiled at the others. 'Oh, well, why not?'

'Great! We'll sort all of that out later, then.' Kate, pleased with herself at moving ahead so quickly, looked at the list of things to do in her hand. 'In the mean time, do either of you know the way to the big shopping mall everyone keeps talking about? The one down Bangor way?'

'*Bang-gor*,' Emma corrected, with a giggle. 'Sounds rather rude otherwise. And yes, I'll draw you a map. But you can just shop in Stewarts in Holywood, you know. You don't have to go all that way.'

'Oh, and have them load all my shopping from one trolley

into another, and then I have to repack it a third time over at the bags counter . . . ! Have you ever come across such a chaotic system?'

'Not to mention the prices over here. Quite frankly,' Laura yawned disinterestedly, 'I've found it just as easy and cheap to shop entirely at M&S. Saves a whole pile of hassle.'

'You don't care if it costs twice as much, Laura, just as long as you're sticking Hugh with the bill,' Emma retorted with a laugh.

Laura nodded. 'True. But that way I don't have to cook a great deal either. Suits me just fine. Life should be as easy as one can make it, I feel.'

'Speaking of which,' Kate looked at them both, faintly embarrassed, 'do you really check under your cars? Nick briefed us and told me I really should. Do you?' The other two women looked at her with half-smiles.

'Yes.'

'No.'

The two answers came simultaneously. They all laughed. Emma shrugged. 'It's really up to you, Kate. The chances are very slim that anyone's watching your particular movements or your car, but . . .'

'But, it can't hurt to be on the safe side?' Kate clarified.

'Well, it looks pretty odd if you're on your hands and knees peering under the thing,' Laura disagreed. 'I mean, you might as well shout out loud, "Look at me, everyone, I'm very clearly something to do with the security forces over here."' She grinned. 'I mean . . . it does become pretty bloody obvious, doesn't it?'

'Check out the underneath here, in the privacy of the patch, and get to know what it looks like so you'll notice anything unusual pretty quickly,' Emma advised casually. 'Then, if you're out and you're feeling uneasy about where you parked it, just "drop" your keys or something under the car and then pretend to hunt for them.'

'Oh, lord! I really can't believe this!' Kate shook her head and the other two gave awkward shrugs. This was reality, their smiles said. This was army life.

The car wasn't ready. Alex's car, that was. He'd put it in to be serviced the night before and caught a lift in with Fergus in the morning. And now it was evening and it still wasn't ready. Kate groaned when Alex rang to tell her he was stranded and could she come and pick him up please?

'I'm right in the middle of trying out a new recipe, darling,' she pleaded, glancing around at the clutter of the kitchen, 'and the wretched thing will go flat on me if I turn the oven off—'

'It'll take you five minutes, round trip, I promise you. I wouldn't ask but it's pouring cats and dogs outside. Leave the oven on and just run out the door right now.' Alex grinned to himself at the thought of Kate being so domesticated. It wouldn't last, but he would enjoy it while it did.

But when Kate turned in to the main camp, pulling up before the closed gates, the sentry didn't hurry forward as he had always done when Alex accompanied her. Instead he signalled for her to turn her engine off while he noted down her licence plate. And then he pointed to where the Guard was standing to attention, the flag being lowered and the bugle playing raucously. Guard Mount. Oh shit, Kate thought to herself furiously. There goes my soufflé. She stared broodingly at the sign proclaiming that the state of threat was currently 'Amber'.

It was nearly a quarter of an hour later, the Guard Mount completed, Kate's identification checked and car pass issued, before she angrily strode into battalion headquarters in search of her husband. And walked straight in on Hugh Mallory shouting incoherently at Alex, his face a deep puce, his bantam strut rigidly uncompromising as he crossed the room back and forth in front of Alex's desk, his silver-topped cane swatting at imaginary heads. Alex rose from his chair politely as he saw Kate hovering in the doorway.

'You remember my wife, Kate, don't you, Hugh?' Alex's voice, so cool and disinterested cut through Hugh's tirade, causing the man to falter and lose his train of thought. He swung around in irritation.

'Yes, of course.' Hugh forced his features into an unconvincing smile and went forward to greet Kate, kissing her on both cheeks and ushering her into the room. 'Are you here to drag your new husband home early?' he asked roguishly and Kate raised her eyebrows even further.

'Early, Hugh? It's after six. Though I admit that probably is early for Alex. Are you waiting for Laura to pick you up?'

Hugh's face lost some of its determined cheer. 'Laura?' He laughed heartily. 'Good lord, no! We have two cars, you know. Two proper cars, I might add,' he laughed abrasively, 'not silly sports cars that never work.' The patronising smile to Alex set Kate's teeth on edge. 'No, no, I don't expect Laura to have to wait on my whims.'

'How fortunate for you,' Kate smiled politely and Hugh's eyes searched hers, wondering if she were hinting more than she was saying. But Kate was unaware. 'Darling,' she turned back to Alex, 'I hate to hurry you but I did leave the oven on and Guard Mount's delayed me badly already. We really must go.'

'Of course you must, Alex,' Hugh agreed blandly. 'Can't go keeping the little wife waiting. Nice to see you thoroughly under her thumb already.' He laughed with pleasure at seeing Alex's colour rise. 'You'll sort out that problem, will you? I can't have you just demanding whoever you like for Bosnia. I know you think you're God in HQ but it is my company, after all. Just sort it out. See you tomorrow, Kate.' And with that dismissive nod, he smiled again at Kate and strode towards the door, only to nearly collide with Bill walking in. Both men stepped back sharply.

'Hugh,' Bill nodded, looking past him at Alex who beckoned him in.

'Ovington,' Hugh replied sharply and Bill glanced up, a laugh in his eyes. He hadn't been called 'Ovington' since he left Sandhurst. 'What keeps you here?' Hugh remarked witheringly, as he strode off. 'Hardly work, I imagine.'

'No, no,' Bill leaned against the door jamb and called after the square back retreating down the hall, 'friends.' For a moment Hugh missed a stride and then he turned the corner and disappeared. Bill laughed ruefully and rubbed a finger along the side of his sharply elegant nose in a gesture of resignation.

'Shouldn't have, I suppose,' he drawled feelingly.

'No,' Alex agreed with a wry smile. 'You'll pay for it. He's been letting me have it for the last half-hour until Kate interrupted, thank God. You and your soufflé!' His firm lips compressed into a straight line, then he took a deep breath and slowly released it as though allowing his rage to evaporate. Bill grinned lazily.

'Oh, dear.' Kate's face fell. 'Have I messed things up for you?'

'No, of course not. Nothing I can't handle. Just Hugh

being his normal, delightful self.' Alex's dark blue eyes showed a glint of humour. 'Tell me, darling, how do you feel about going out tonight?'

'And sod the soufflé?' Brightening, Kate perched herself on the corner of her husband's desk.

'Sod Hugh – I have news . . .' Alex looked both pleased and excited at the same time. Kate was bewildered but Bill raised his eyebrows. 'Ah, and does that explain Hugh's little temper fit just then?'

'Probably, if the rumour mill's been as efficient as usual,' Alex agreed with quiet satisfaction.

'It has. I came to congratulate you,' Bill bowed, 'oh, old and smelly OC-to-be.' He grinned at Alex's face. 'It comes to us all – well, to most of us. I still seem to be waiting.'

'You're a year younger. Be patient, my boy,' Alex advised mockingly.

'For what? What are you talking about?' Kate demanded.

'Promotion, of course.' Bill put an arm around her. 'The subject that obsesses us all. But you'll note Alex has acquired just the right tone of patronising wisdom suitable for a lordly major in the span of an afternoon. He should do well.'

Alex switched off his computer, rose and picked up his own silver-topped cane. 'Eff off, Bill,' he smiled. 'Let's get out of here before the phone rings again. Come on, Kate,' he kissed her forehead, 'I'll explain as we go.'

'Company commander! But I thought you were going to stay as Adjutant for another six months to a year and then go straight to Camberley?' Kate fought to keep the dismay from her voice.

'Yes, I was, but they're going to be short a company commander now that Charlie's been offered a place back at Hereford, and Joss says they can get someone to fill in for six months as Adjutant before Nick takes over.'

'Hereford? You mean . . . ?'

'Yes, he's going back as a company commander, lucky bugger.'

'Oh,' Kate said wonderingly. She'd never thought she'd actually know someone in the SAS. She blinked. 'But – you haven't been to staff college yet, have you?' Kate puckered her brow, not sure if she had it quite right. Surely you did staff college before you went on to being a major and a company commander, didn't you?

'No, but they're changing things so that this job will count as one of the three required reports you need as a major, even before staff college – well, as long as I do it for at least a year as a substantive major and I should be picked up for promotion on the beige list next time round . . . Besides, they're closing down staff college for a year while they amalgamate all three services together, so I'd miss my slot anyway. So . . . what do you think of that? Your husband will be Major Aldridge within the month.' Alex was so obviously delighted that Kate had no difficulty in smiling even if she didn't fully grasp the intricacies. Substantive, beige list, heavens; why couldn't they speak in plain English!

And what did she think? She thought Alex was going to be in Ireland for only a year or so, before staff college, that's what she thought. And now it was going to be a minimum of two years. Her smile became stretched.

'Wonderful, darling. I'm very proud of you.'

'Suddenly I'm really looking forward to our time here. The chance to have my own company and be out with the men rather than stuck endlessly in an office—'

'Don't you enjoy being Adjutant? I thought it was meant to really be a finger-on-the-pulse sort of job?'

'Oh, it is. And I've loved it so far, but I really prefer working with the men. I've just had enough of being a paper-shuffler for the time being . . .'

'And what about when you get promoted straight into an office permanently? What'll you do then?' Kate sipped her drink slowly. The buzz of voices from the wine bar receded as she listened intently to his answer.

'. . . I'm not sure. It'll be a question of seeing what happens to the army altogether by then. But all that's a good ten years off, always supposing my career goes well . . .'

'Mmm,' Kate nodded, 'always supposing.'

'You don't sound thrilled . . . ?'

'Well, I am and I'm not. I'm very pleased for you, of course, but I hadn't expected to be in Belfast quite that long, you see . . .'

'You'll love it here, Kate, I promise. Everyone says what a good time they have in Ireland, how friendly the locals are—'

'Oh, right!'

'No, really. The vast majority of people over here are perfectly charming and very kind. You just need to get out there and meet them. Stop skulking at home. The red areas don't apply to you and there are very few areas you really shouldn't go into. After all, it's only the tiniest minority—'

'That's all it needs.'

Alex was quiet for a long moment. 'It's good for my career, Kate. And it's what I want to do. But if you really hate it over here, you can always go back and live in London until Camberley comes up.'

Kate's eyes grew wide. 'You're not serious?'

Alex shrugged. 'A lot of wives choose to do that. You can too if you really want to.'

'What on earth was the point of us getting married if we do that?' Kate asked indignantly and Alex slowly smiled.

'Then you'll stay?'

Kate sighed. 'What choice do I really have? Well, I suppose it'll at least give me the chance to try and make a success of our business.'

'Business?' Alex raised an eyebrow. 'Is there something going on on your career front that I don't know?'

Kate explained what she and the other girls had decided upon and Alex was warily enthusiastic.

'Great. But you'll have to be careful, you know. For a start you're not allowed to run a business from a quarter and there's the security on the patch, so you won't be able to bring clients in without having them vetted and then the fact that you shouldn't run a business will come to light. No, you'll have to have a shop or something in a nearby town and then you'll have to take great care that no one knows who you're married to . . . But,' he sighed suddenly, unable or simply unwilling to explain all the difficulties, 'I can get you briefed on all that by the Nick.'

'Honestly, Alex! One minute you're telling me it's as safe as houses, the next, that I'll have to be terribly terribly careful. Which is it?'

'Both. Now let's change the subject. What're you wearing tomorrow night?' Alex drained his glass abruptly and gathered his jacket from the back of the chair.

'Tomorrow night?' Kate cast around in her memory but nothing came to mind.

'Yes, you know,' Alex urged, a shade impatiently, 'the

Ladies Dinner Night in the mess.' Kate looked blank. 'I'm sure I told you about it. Look in your diary.' But there was no entry. He grimaced ruefully. 'Oops.'

'What time – and what exactly should I wear?' Kate asked drily.

'It's generally 7.30 for 8.00. And something reasonably smartish. One step up from a drinks party, one down from a ball. Ask the other girls. They'll tell you.' He was standing now and waiting for her, his hand poised to help her rise.

'Are you cross about something, Alex? Have I said something to annoy you?' Kate stood slowly, knowing that the stiff impatience was not like him. He shrugged, silent for a long moment until they were outside the wine bar, the evening air fresh and earthy around them from the newly dug flowerbeds.

'I thought,' he hesitated, 'I suppose I thought you'd be proud of me, being promoted so early.' His voice became tighter, 'and stupidly, perhaps, I thought you'd be eager to support me.'

'I am proud of you and of course I intend to support you. Why? Does my wanting to set up another business interfere with that process in some way?' Kate enquired with concern. 'After all, you were the one who said army life wouldn't put a crimp in my style, weren't you? You were the one who said you wanted me to continue working, wanted me to have my own career? How does that change now that you're suddenly promoted to a major? Or are you now "old and smelly" – as Bill put it – and prefer to have a wife at your beck and call?'

'Don't be ridiculous,' Alex sighed. 'I just wanted a little more recognition, that's all. Forget it, it doesn't matter.' He was silent for a moment and Kate refused to help him out. She stood equally silently by the car, waiting for him to unlock the door. 'Just don't forget about tomorrow night, will you?' was all he said, finally. Kate shook her head.

'I'll make it a priority to find out what to wear, since it's clearly so important to *your* career,' she remarked and Alex winced at the irony in her voice.

But it seemed no one ever knew quite what to wear to this particular sort of function, Kate discovered to her cost. Emma said she was wearing a little black dress, Laura, a slinky evening dress, Suzy, a long skirt and silk blouse. Kate spent hours going through her wardrobe, trying on one thing after the other and conferring with both Laura and Emma who were sprawled on the bed watching with interest and some envy the selection of evening clothes on offer.

'What about this?' Kate wrapped a midnight blue dress with tiny white daisies across her, the sleeves nothing more than cuffs off the shoulder, the skirt very short, full and flirty.

'Divine,' Laura pronounced enthusiastically. Emma eyed it carefully.

'How short is that on you?' she asked non-committally.

'Short.' Kate laughed.

'And when you sit down?'

'Very very short,' Kate admitted, suddenly eyeing the dress herself with misgivings. It seemed wonderful in London, but perhaps, after all—

'So what, Em? For heaven's sake, lighten up a little. Kate's got the legs for it and the men'll love it!' Emma shrugged and Kate put the dress down and stared thoughtfully back into her wardrobe. 'This?'

'A long skirt? You must be joking. You might as well wear

a frilly shirt and pearls with it,' Laura complained instantly. Emma paused.

'I think it's lovely but probably Alex would prefer something a little sexier.'

'This?' The clothes session went on for some time, different shirts being tried with different skirts, long dresses versus short, evening trousers, sarongs . . . Finally Kate stood back with her hands on her hips and eyed the devastation around the room. It had never taken her so long to decide on anything in her entire life and she still didn't know for sure quite what was expected of her. She blinked, shut her eyes, twirled around with her finger pointing out and came to a giddy halt. 'I'll wear this,' she announced, her eyes still shut.

'This' was a white, stiffly embroidered jacket and a black velvet skirt slightly above the knee. Emma smiled. 'Perfect,' she said. Laura sighed slightly but admitted it was very elegant. Kate nodded her head with satisfaction. She'd wear the all-in-one black basque and black stockings underneath, she thought. That should be sexy enough for Alex . . . and perhaps would smooth over the awkwardness still between them. She smiled at the others, not allowing the worry gnawing at her inside to show.

Chapter Six

'Strap me into this, Kate, will you?' Alex begged, sucking in his breath as he wrenched on his mess kit trousers and craned around his back for the brace that kept eluding him. Kate watched him with laughter dancing in her eyes.

'Bit tight, is it?' she enquired.

'It was cut skin-tight for me when I was straight out of Sandhurst and just a skinny lad. And considering the cost of these bloody monkey outfits, I'll be damned if I'll order another just yet.' Alex huffed and puffed, limbering his long legs in the tight woollen trousers and raising his foot for Kate to strap them under his polished boots.

'Looks a bit like a bellhop's uniform to me,' she remarked, eyeing the tiny frogged jacket and the bow tie. 'But you still manage to look gorgeous in it, despite being a few pounds too heavy.' She mockingly patted his washboard stomach. He was now a full-grown man as opposed to a slim adolescent. It was hardly surprising the mess kit was too tight. 'Tell me, is everyone going to be as uncomfortable as you tonight?'

Alex grinned. 'A damned sight more uncomfortable, actually. These contraptions are a subtle form of torture, designed to see if you're tough enough to carry a social smile and witty remark at the same time as being disembowelled by your trousers. You girls have it easy.'

'Oh, of course we do,' she agreed. 'We simply wear boned underwear to make our lives cosier,' and she casually unwrapped her robe and tossed it aside on the chair before sauntering over to where her own outfit was still hanging on the wardrobe door. Alex drew his breath in sharply.

'You know,' he began in a conversational voice that didn't fool Kate for a moment, 'I don't think you've strapped me into this quite right, Katie, my love. Why don't you come and undo it and try again?' He grinned appreciatively at his wife's slender body pouting fully at the breasts and whipped into a wasp's waist. Her stockinged legs seemed to go on forever.

'Really?' Kate smiled slowly and hesitated, provokingly out of reach. 'Have we time?'

They arrived slightly late, drinks nearly over and the first guests beginning to drift into the long dining room. Joss raised his eyebrows at Alex, glancing over at the couple of dignitaries whom Alex was supposed to have helped entertain with the colonel. Alex grinned sheepishly and glanced at Kate once, so that Joss nodded faintly and turned away with a tight smile. Newly-weds were allowed a certain latitude, after all.

'Kate, my dear, how lovely you look,' Joss murmured, as he kissed her cheek, 'I thought perhaps we'd have a quick drink to officially celebrate your arrival. Sergeant Hoskins?' The colonel nodded at the mess sergeant hovering behind him, who immediately produced a silver tray with champagne flutes and a bottle of Veuve Cliquot. Flushing slightly with pleasure, Kate accepted a glass and the warm smiles and congratulations of several couples grouped around them. Alex slipped an arm around her waist and she leaned in against him as she tilted back the glass and drank deeply.

Through the straw-coloured liquid, the room glimmered around her, with candles in vast silver candlesticks, heavily scented flowers in even larger oriental porcelain urns, darkly bloody battle scenes on canvas, the gilt frames glinting in the flickering flames. A gaudy swirl of silk-clad women rustled by; the men, stiffly elegant in their mess kit, held silver goblets casually as they leaned against pillars or mantelpieces. For a moment time seemed to spin out beneath her, a long silent moment of history where she could have been participating in an event a hundred years earlier. Or more.

The officer's mess, it was said, was originally intended for India in the days of the Raj but had, for one reason or another, ended up in Northern Ireland. With its cavernous ceilinged rooms and huge windows, Kate could well imagine it surrounded by jungle behind and a polo padang in front, punka wallahs idly twitched on fans overhead as officers and their ladies gently sipped on iced limes.

And then, out of the corner of her eye, she caught a glimpse of the mess furniture pushed up against the walls. G-plan with linen slip-covers that struggled to hide the rigid lines of the chairs and failed completely. She laughed delightedly.

They had been seated together when they were unmarried, Kate noted, but now they were separated. She was on the opposite side of the huge, many leaved, mahogany table and several places down from Alex, so that she could do nothing more than catch his eye occasionally. Instead she had Fergus on her right and, by sheer misfortune, Hugh on her left. She raised her eyes to gain sympathy from Emma and was startled to see her watching Hugh with a look of quiet hatred. Kate glanced away, unnerved and baffled.

Laura was next to Bill and further down the table toward the ends where a great many of the younger officers and their girlfriends were placed; far enough away not to disturb the dignitaries in the centre of the table, but close enough for the colonel still to keep an eye on their behaviour. Kate wondered briefly if Laura had swapped the name cards around. The flame-coloured hair flung itself back as Laura laughed and Kate saw Hugh fold his lips in tightly. Was that simply disapproval, or was there some pain involved as well? She really couldn't tell.

'Must be exciting being married, eh, Kate? Or are you used to it all already?' Hugh was trying to sound worldly and amused. It came across as patronising.

'I'm enjoying it thoroughly, Hugh. And Alex does try to make it as easy a transition as possible.' Kate smiled warily.

'Ah well, Alex does try hard in all ways, doesn't he? A real tryer . . .' Hugh's words trailed off, his voice stiff with annoyance. 'Of course, he's quite ambitious, isn't he? Determined to get ahead. Perhaps you'll be Lady Aldridge some day?' He smiled blandly, as though letting her know that he had seen through her secret desires and they were all too familiarly common.

'What a thrill that would be,' Kate remarked curtly before

turning across to Fergus. But he was intent on conversation with the plump woman on his left and Kate had no choice but to turn back to Hugh.

'Your father's titled, isn't he?' Hugh continued on his theme, oblivious to Kate's thinned lips.

'Yes,' she replied shortly.

'What is he? An earl? A duke?' Hugh badgered, the amusement in his voice turning faintly sour. Kate wondered how long he had been drinking. Since well before he arrived, she suspected.

'Merely a baron. Surely you were at the wedding? But no, of course, you left early, didn't you?' Kate retreated in some confusion. 'And you? Where are you from?' She hadn't meant it to sound cutting but Hugh bristled.

'From Hampshire, near Winchester. My family's lived there for generations. A large estate,' he added with what Kate was beginning to recognise as his bluffer's tone.

'How nice for you and how nice for your children to come,' Kate remarked as kindly as she could manage. 'Continuity is good for children, don't you think?' She knew from Laura that the 'estate' comprised of an ugly house and a few acres of land but did not want to antagonise Hugh further. Why he thought it necessary, she couldn't imagine. Most of the other officers seemed to spend their time bemoaning their status as the *nouveau pauvre*, though, of course, there still were some with private incomes, like Bill. Now, wouldn't that be nice . . .

'Laura doesn't want children.' Hugh interrupted her musings with the bald statement, as though it had been wrenched out of him.

'Oh?' For a moment Kate was nonplussed. 'Well, I expect she will when she's a little older,' she soothed.

'She's bloody twenty-eight. If she waits much longer, she'll be past it.'

'Oh, nonsense, Hugh. Twenty-eight's nothing. More and more people are waiting until they're in their thirties—'

'Laura's waiting all right. But not for the right time. More for the right man. And it seems I'm not it.' The bitterness in his voice was corrosive. Kate could think of nothing to say. Her cheeks flushed, she looked for help around her but could see none.

'I, uh, I'm sure you're wrong . . . um,' she murmured deprecatingly, 'I don't suppose you could reach the water for me, could you? I expect it's all the candles in here that make it seem so hot.'

'More like the company. Lots of hot air trapped in here tonight,' Hugh laughed and lurched forward in his chair to reach for the water bottle. He poured it deftly enough into Kate's glass and then replaced it with a hard thud on the polished taple-top. Kate noticed Joss's eyelid twitch briefly over Hugh's perspiring face before he returned his attention to the wife of the Lord Lieutenant on his right.

'Thank you,' she murmured.

'Mind you, Kate, I wouldn't drink too much of that or you'll be in agony by the time the port's gone round twice.'

'In agony? I'm sorry – I don't quite . . . ?' Kate's lips hesitated over the glass, while she wondered if the water was perhaps contaminated in some way.

'Frowned upon, you know,' he smiled tightly and even more obscurely. 'Must wait until after the port. Of course, some will always go, but . . . well, not really done, you know . . . I'm sure Alex wouldn't like it.'

Kate blinked. 'What's not done, exactly, Hugh?' she asked gently.

'To leave the table . . . you know, answer the call of nature, wash your hands,' Hugh's voice dropped lower. 'I'd have thought Alex would have explained . . .'

'Oh. I see. I didn't realise.' Kate put down her glass with a feeling of impending doom. Surely Hugh couldn't be serious?

'Didn't you see all the gels flocking off to the loo before we sat down? Don't want to get up in the middle of the meal and disgrace your husband, do you? Disastrous thing to do in the cavalry, I understand. Young subbies think it a great joke to whisk away your chair and make you kneel at the table for the rest of the meal.' He laughed approvingly and Kate stared at him aghast.

Kate remembered the mass exodus now only too well. But she had been finishing her champagne and talking to Joss and hadn't wanted to seem rude. Besides, she had thought she only had to wait until after the main course . . . Oh lord, she thought, now I'm really in for it.

'Yes, of course. Well,' she smiled brightly at Hugh, 'I hope there aren't too many speeches or I shall be thoroughly uncomfortable.'

'No speeches, don't worry. Frowned upon.' Hugh seemed to think a great many things were frowned upon, Kate decided, merely wetting her lips on the first of the wines. But thank heavens he had warned her. How embarrassing otherwise!

By the time the fifth course had been removed and the fifth wine glass replaced with a port glass, Kate was sitting tightly, discomfort having turned to actual pain. Her conversation had become stilted and preoccupied but since most people around her had enjoyed all of the wines thoroughly, they didn't seem to notice.

A silver-topped cut-crystal decanter was passed to her and she picked it up to pass it on to Hugh. 'Have some, Kate, you'll enjoy it,' Fergus insisted. He was the wines member, in charge of ordering wines for the mess and had repeatedly asked for her opinion throughout the meal. Reluctantly, she shook her head.

'No thanks, Fergus.' Her smile was tight. 'I've had quite enough already, I think.' For another half-hour she sat, feeling light-headed and giddy as the port circled the table. Then, as she saw Suzy smile and leave the table, Kate bounded up and out the door, leaving Fergus in mid-speech. When she returned, she coloured up brightly at Fergus's ironic, 'Feeling better?'

'Um, yes, thanks. Rather a long dinner wasn't it, nearly four hours?' She wondered how on earth everyone else managed. Not that people hadn't left the table, but . . . she hadn't wanted to disgrace Alex.

Fergus lifted an eyebrow. 'You haven't been waiting all that time, have you?'

'I understood from Hugh that it was frowned upon . . .'

'Good God, that old chestnut!' He gave a snort that was half-laugh, half-annoyance as he peered past Kate to Hugh. But Hugh had his back to them and was loudly pontificating on some point that was leaving his audience cold. 'You mustn't believe a word Hugh says, Kate. He's fossilised into a time he would have liked to live in, rather than present reality. You do whatever you'd do at any dinner in London and just ignore all these silly conventions. Now,' Fergus smiled gently at her, 'some port?'

'Um,' Kate sighed, relaxing back against her chair in relief, 'love some.' She glanced at Hugh, wondering if she could club him with the heavy port decanter without anyone noticing. But it seemed a shame to damage crystal on such dross. She'd just poison him next time he came to dinner instead. She sat back and, with pleasure, imagined him writhing in agony.

When the doors at the end of the dining room folded back and the bandmaster led his men through the first of the night's programme, Kate's eyes grew wide with a mixture of amusement and wonder. But as the music went on, through the regimental, battalion, and company calls, each of the men at the table nodding their heads or beating lightly with their hands on the table, Kate began to see how important the music was to them. And then the finale of 'Soldiers', 'High on a Hill', and 'Sunset' left her moved beyond all her expectations, her vision misting as the bugle notes soared through her, poignant and desperately sad.

She glanced quickly around her, at the way people were caught up in their own thoughts, their laughter stilled as they allowed the music to flow through them. She knew many of them were thinking of their jobs there in Belfast. Would the Peace hold? Or would some of them not be coming back? She glanced across at Alex only to find him watching her, a faint curve to his lips, an enquiring look in his eyes. She smiled at him and he raised his glass to her and sipped it quietly.

Oh God, she thought, the uneasiness of the past few months suddenly swelling out into her chest, bludgeoning her with emotions that she had tried so hard to dismiss. How could she ever bear it if something happened to Alex? How did the other wives bear this fear? Furtively, she stole a glance at Emma who smiled and laughed and chatted to the man beside her, seemingly unmoved. But then a twitch of her eye in Fergus's direction revealed it all in devastating clarity. You didn't get used to it, didn't learn to ignore it. You just controlled it. Kate swallowed hard.

Emma, wandering around the gallery at Farrer's, paused to admire a charcoal sketch of a donkey. She peered at the number and consulted the list in her hand. No guide price. How annoying, she sighed, and peered over at where Kate was laughing at a rather appalling watercolour by a different artist.

'Come and look at this, Kate,' she called lightly, turning back to the donkey. The setting reminded her of Dorset, the beast both ugly and appealing, the chalk strokes clear and bold. 'Do you like it?'

'Oh, yes! That's wonderful!' Kate's eyes sparkled. 'How much, do you think?'

'Not the foggiest. There don't seem to be any guide prices at all. I'll just go and nab the director, I think. Are there any prices you want?'

'Not really. I'm thinking of going through into the furniture auction side. Why don't you join me in there?' Kate didn't really need any more pictures at the moment and certainly had no intention of buying a local artist just for the sake of it, as many of the other wives seemed intent upon doing. But Emma was right about the donkey. That really had charm.

'All right, I'll see you in there.' Emma moved off, catching the director's eye and smiling at him as he approached. He was tall and distinguished with an appreciative twinkle in his eye and Emma warmed to him immediately.

'I don't suppose you could advise me on one of the sketches, could you?' she began tentatively, and was rewarded immediately with a charming smile.

'Of course. Let me see which one . . .'

Kate watched them wander over in the direction of the donkey, their heads close together as they peered at the list in Emma's grasp. How different life would be for Emma, she mused, if she were married to someone like that instead. But Emma loved Fergus and was bravely realistic about army life. No different, she said, from many large companies. Just a tad more dangerous, that was all. But, for Kate herself? She shook her head. The difference was enormous.

London seemed miles and years away. No casual popping out for a drink locally of an evening. Alex preferred not to drink anywhere where the men might, since it undermined his authority as adjutant. And besides, all the local pubs were working men's bars, not somewhere where a wife might feel comfortable. And just at the moment, Kate added mentally, they were out of bounds to all soldiers anyway.

Restaurants were all right as long as you didn't go to the same one too often. And as long as you booked out with the Guard Room and remembered to book back in again when you came home. Kate sighed again, looking around at the crowd of people examining the antiques. Who knew who was charming and friendly and pleased the army were there to protect the Peace. And who was not?

She had been asked by several people if she were newly arrived, and where she had moved to. Blithely, she had answered them before realising that everyone in the Belfast area was aware of a new battalion arriving and had mentally pegged her even before she had opened her mouth and revealed her accent. Should one pretend one wasn't army, Kate wondered, colouring up at the thought of lying. Oh yes, my husband's a schoolteacher. Or a ship builder. Or a civil servant? Or did you just brazen it out. Yes, we're with the new battalion . . . and hope for the best?

She was interrupted in her musings by Emma's return, eyes sparkling with excitement. 'Guess what?'

Kate raised her eyebrows. 'What?'

'The sketch is going for about £50 and I've gone ahead and placed a bid. Ian Hayle thinks it's a bargain and that the artist is going to be very big in the next few years. I hope Fergus doesn't mind!'

'And who exactly is Ian Hayle?' Kate grinned, seeing Emma was clearly taken with the director. Emma gave a flustered laugh.

'You know only too well! Such a nice man! He was so discreet and merely asked if we were with "The Big Firm" that had recently arrived.'

'And what did you say?' Kate laughed as Emma rolled her eyes.

'What could I say? It's obvious to everyone, isn't it?'

'I hope not absolutely everyone.'

'Them too,' Emma added thoughtfully. 'Or perhaps, them most of all. Come on, let's go and see what Laura's about to put a bid on. Probably a ruby ring, knowing her! Hugh'll strangle her if she spends any more money.' It was said lightly, laughingly. Not for an instant did either of them ever imagine such a thing happening.

As they approached, Laura turned around and dangled a heavy antique gold chain out for them to inspect. They both groaned.

It was nearly a week later, as Kate sat around the large kitchen table in Suzy's house, all the other officers' wives absorbed in conversation with each other, that she first noticed the mark on Laura's neck. A darkly discoloured sphere, much like a thumb-print, just behind and below her ear. The high-necked cotton polo that Laura wore would have normally hidden it, even if her hair weren't down, but Laura was unconsciously stroking it as though it pained her and Kate, sitting beside her, could hardly miss it. Was it? Kate smiled to herself at the thought. A love bite? From Hugh? The thought seemed absurdly adolescent.

'Nice one, Laura,' she murmured teasingly as she looked down at her plate. 'Can't say I've seen one quite so impressive in a long time. Glad to see you and Hugh are on better terms . . .' She swivelled her eyes laughingly in Laura's direction only to see Laura flush an ugly red before the blood drained to leave her face paler than ever.

'Shut up, Kate! It isn't what you think,' Laura hissed between her teeth. Startled, Kate pulled a quick grimace.

'Sorry. Didn't mean to—' she began, but Laura cut across her.

'Oh, it's Hugh's mark all right,' she remarked jerkily, her voice barely raised enough for Kate to grasp what she was saying. 'But it's matched by one on the other side of my throat too.' She turned her eyes, pale limpid green and frightened, on Kate. 'He nearly choked me to death.'

Kate went cold. Her mouth opened and shut without a sound. A burst of laughter around the table, as Suzy told an amusing tale, seemed to come from far away. Finally Kate managed to ask, 'When?'

'Sunday. We were at lunch with friends. He'd had too much to drink. I suppose I had too.'

'Was Bill there as well?'

'Yes.' She fingered the bruise again and sighed. 'That's what triggered it all off. Bill was a bit obvious.'

'How close was it?

'You mean, how close did Hugh come to strangling me?' Laura snorted. 'Close enough for my vision to blur. When he finally let go, I couldn't stand up.'

'Very close, then.' Kate thought for a moment. 'Didn't anyone else see it? Bill?'

'No, of course not. Hugh's not stupid. He waited until we got home.'

'Did you report it? Go to the doctor?'

'Are you joking? Hugh'd kill me for real. Besides . . . one doesn't, not something like that! No, I've got to get away, get out of Hugh's clutches . . .' Laura broke off as though she realised she was talking wildly. She shrugged. 'I just spent a day in bed and the rest of the time avoiding him. It'll fade.'

'If you're frightened of him, why do you provoke him so?' Kate asked, curious and shocked at the same time. Wife-battering didn't happen to people she knew, she had thought. How thoroughly naive and stupid of her. Laura shrugged again.

'Because I hate him.' She raised her eyes to Kate's and smiled sadly. 'And what else is there to do?'

'Kate.' A hand on her arm caused Kate to turn, wrenching her mind back to the casual conversation around her. 'Kate, you'll do one, won't you?' It was Amanda, thin-nosed and high-foreheaded, smiling brightly at her. Amanda's straight, chin-length fair hair was pulled back by a velvet alice band and she wore a navy guernsey over a pleated skirt. Everyone else, including Suzy, wore jeans. Kate sighed to herself, even before Amanda continued.

'One . . . ? Sorry, I wasn't—'

'Cake. For the Open Day. We gels are running a bake

stall. You'll take a slot, won't you? Everyone else has. Say, from ten until eleven, perhaps?' Amanda half-turned away, announcing sharply, 'Good, that's settled then,' to herself as she wrote on the small pad beside her before Kate could think of a reply. She had meant to agree but suddenly she understood how Laura could feel rebellious at being taken for granted, at being bossed into things without consultation. She closed her teeth together with a firm bite and smiled at Amanda. What else could she do?

'Of course, I'd be happy to,' she murmured with a wry emphasis on the word 'happy'. Amanda was oblivious. Emma swallowed her wine with an amused choke and even Suzy grinned apologetically at Kate.

'Amanda's a great one for organising people,' she said lightly. 'And I'm afraid I'm rather busy at the moment with the Wives' Committee, getting everyone settled and making sure they're happy. Amanda kindly offered to take over.'

'Well,' Amanda replied firmly, 'someone has to help you out, and Philip is, after all, the 2IC. It's only natural I should be the one.'

'Yes . . .' Suzy smiled around at the other wives, just the faintest twitch to her eye. 'Now, tell me, does anyone know where I could find capers? The local shops just don't seem to know what I'm even talking about . . .'

The dogs leapt and scurried, chasing back and forth across the hard ridges of earth thrown up by the tractor, before scenting something that enticed them out in a circling arc across the field. 'They're working dogs,' Emma explained, the wind gusting at her hair and whipping it free of the barrette that attempted to hold it back. 'Not much sense, just yet, but they're very young still. Fergus is training them up.'

Kate laughed as one of the spaniels gave an excited yelp and started digging furiously, her little stump of a tail wiggling with delight. 'Don't they normally go in with Fergus?'

'To work? Yes, most of the time. But he's away at a conference at the moment so the girls stay home with me.' Emma smiled. 'They're good company and very easy to look after. Just give them a walk twice a day and a hug or two and they're anyone's. Why? Is Alex talking about getting a dog?'

'Yup!' Kate rolled her eyes. 'It's not that I mind. I like dogs. But I don't really feel like dealing with a puppy just yet. But you can't tell Alex anything. He says he'll do it all, but you know perfectly who's going to be left holding the baby . . .'

'What does he want? A black lab?' Emma asked drily.

Kate laughed. 'Like every other officer? God forbid! No, he'd really like a Jack Russell but I've objected strongly to that one—'

'Snappy with children.'

'Exactly! So now he's talking about a Border . . .'

'Ugh, smelly little beggars!' Emma wrinkled up her nose in disgust. 'Why a terrier at all? Why not a spaniel, or a retriever, if he doesn't want to be stereotyped with a lab? Or a lurcher?'

'Why not a cat, I say?' Kate demanded and Emma burst into laughter.

'Not the right image for a soldier, I'm afraid.'

'Not rufty-tufty enough, I suppose?'

'Nope. He might as well have a gerbil or a hamster. Can't you just see a gerbil sitting on his shoulder during lunch in the mess? Or being stroked politely by a visiting general?' Emma was still laughing and Kate reluctantly joined in.

'Umm, I see your point.'

As they cleared the last of the fields and headed for home, Emma whistling for the dogs, Kate looked up and glimpsed Laura slipping over the stile that led into the woods near the sports field. The sound of a rugby game being played echoed dimly back to them through the trees. Wednesday afternoon – sports afternoon for the men. She wondered if Laura was going to watch. Hugh wouldn't like that at all.

Calling out, Kate waved her arms but Laura disappeared from view between the trees without turning around.

'Oh, lord, she's asking for trouble if Hugh catches her,' Emma remarked worriedly, having rounded up the dogs and clipped them onto their leads. 'He's getting more and more paranoid every day. Have you seen the way he watched her? The look in his eyes? Pure murder.'

Kate glanced at her. 'You've seen the marks, then?' Emma nodded. 'Well, d'you think we should catch up with her and persuade her to come home with us?'

'You can try. Run after her before she's seen. I'll follow on with the dogs.' She pulled both dogs sharply in to heel, snapping 'Daisy! Daisy!' as one tried to escape after Kate and pull her over. Tilly sat obediently, as always. Kate had already taken off, vaulting the stile in a manner that left Emma raising her eyebrows in surprise. Who would have thought the impeccable Kate was so sporty? But then, she looked like a greyhound, Emma mused. Perhaps that was what they should have?

Kate ran lightly along the woodland path, hoping Laura would not be irritated at her interference. But the thought of the bruise marks on Laura's throat was spur enough. The first snow drops were out, flooding the dappled sunlight through the trees with a frosty haze and Kate longed to linger and enjoy the scene. But just ahead she could glimpse Laura's red hair slipping through the foliage. She opened her mouth to call out again but suddenly Laura was not alone. A flash of yellow appeared from the opposite direction.

Kate came to an abrupt halt, almost teetering as she tried to freeze into immobility. A sudden sense of voyeurism overwhelmed her as she realised it was Bill and that the meeting was not by chance. Guiltily, she stepped behind a tree, breathing hard. She watched with dismay as Bill, tow-headed and ruddy cheeked, his light blue eyes flashing with laughter and his rugby shirt half unbuttoned, was pulling Laura into his arms, bending his head to hers. Kate closed her eyes. Oh, lord, now this was really trouble!

She opened them to see Bill stroking Laura's unruly mop of hair back behind her ears and gently examining the bruises on her throat. His actions, even from a distance, were so indescribably tender that Kate felt the hard knot in her stomach begin to dissolve slightly. Surely Bill would do nothing to hurt or endanger Laura? This wasn't a light-hearted flirtation. They both clearly cared too much for that. Kate quietly slipped away.

Emma was still holding the dogs near the stile when Kate reappeared alone. 'Too late?' she called in surprise.

Kate nodded and shrugged. 'I'm afraid so.' She pressed her lips together. 'How about coffee back at my place? I think we need to talk.'

Laura leaned against Bill's hard, warm chest and sighed heavily, the shudders leaving her weak and sleepy. His hand brushed her tears gently from her lashes, caressed her hair, soft and serpentine as it coiled around his fingers. Moving his mouth along the skin of her throat and up to her full, quivering lips, he kissed her again deeply.

If anyone had come across them at that moment, they would have had no difficulty in reading the situation and coming to the conclusion that Captain Ovington was committing adultery with Major Mallory's wife. Practically a courtmartial offence and certainly one that would have Bill banished from the battalion. But, strangely enough, it wasn't true. Nothing had happened bar a long, lingering kiss or two and a great deal of soul-searching. But it couldn't continue as it was. Either they stopped seeing each other or they had a full-blown affair. Bill sighed.

'You're going to have to ask him for a divorce, you know. You can't go on like this, hating him, baiting him – and getting half throttled for your pains,' he added and Laura sighed too, half angrily.

'That's all very well, Bill, but he's likely to throw me off a cliff just for mentioning the word.' Her leaf-green eyes shimmered. 'And besides, what am I supposed to do with myself, always supposing he agrees? Where do I go?'

'What about your parents? Wouldn't they put you up for a while, just until you decide what to do?' Bill was oblivious to the heavy-lidded look Laura gave him. It truly hadn't occurred to him that Laura might be planning her future around him. All he knew was that he had never been so excited, so unsettled, so desperate for a woman in all his life.

'I'm twenty-eight, Bill. I can't go running home to my parents and besides, I really don't want to.' She glanced at him thoughtfully, her face guileless in repose. 'I just know I don't want to lose you,' she whispered.

'You won't,' he said without hesitation, feeling suddenly protective and strong and willing to do battle with anyone for her. His fresh, boyish features hardened into those of a man who contemplated actions distasteful to him but necessary. 'We'll sort it out, Laura. I promise you.' I'll sort that bastard out for you, he murmured beneath his breath, by God I will! He kissed her again, breathing in her scent deeply. Reluctantly he pulled himself away. 'I better go. We're at half time and I'll be missed if I'm gone much longer.'

'Is Hugh playing?' She swallowed. 'Or is he working out?'

'Neither. Said he was going running. Don't know where, though. So, we'd better be careful, right?'

Laura nodded, glanced around uneasily, and shivered again.

Chapter Seven

'Mother, no, Mother, really, I promise you, Alex hasn't got a batman.' Kate rolled her eyes at Alex, while cradling the phone to her ear and preparing sandwiches for lunch at the same time. Alex was sitting at the kitchen table, working. He grinned in amusement at the thought.

'Well, of course he manages . . . no, he cleans his own boots. Yes.' Kate listened some more and then burst out laughing. 'No, I'm afraid I don't have any house staff either.'

'Those were the days . . .' Alex murmured, getting up to find a sharp kitchen knife to plane his pencil with. Kate frowned at him but he ignored her. 'Well, I don't really know, Mother. Hold on, I'll ask.' She held the receiver in her palm and grinned. 'Mother wants to know if the cavalry still have batmen and if so, why aren't you in the cavalry?'

Alex twirled the knife in his hand and gave Kate a jaded look. 'Tell her because the cavalry are irrelevant, despite what she might hear from all her cronies. Now,' he glanced at his watch, 'you've been on that phone for nearly twenty minutes and your mother still hasn't come to the point.' He knew his mother-in-law only too well. Elegant, inconsequential chatter was her hallmark followed by the *coup de grâce* when she calmly told you that unfortunately Cousin Becky or Aunt Florence or Great Uncle George were coming to dinner, to visit, to stay and did you mind? Actually, he thought, this time, he did.

'Oh, nonsense!' Kate had pulled a face at him and turned her back, but now she stiffened slightly as she listened to her mother's bright chat. 'Tim and Nicky? Really? On their way to Dublin? Want to stay overnight and leave their car here for a couple of weeks while they tour around by train?' She grimaced at Alex, who sighed heavily. 'Well, yes, that'd be fine . . . No, no trouble at all. Alex'd love to see them both . . . What? Oh? Four of them?' Kate swallowed and deliberately didn't look at Alex. 'Fine,' she said bravely, 'fine.'

But it wasn't fine, she could tell instantly, when she eventually put the phone down and turned to glance at Alex. There was a tight set to his chin that she knew, from past experience, meant he was truly irritated. She couldn't entirely blame him.

'You know . . . I really don't like either Nicky or Tim or their weird friends,' he announced conversationally before she could say anything.

'Well, hold on a minute, Alex. They *did* introduce us, after all and you've known them almost as long as I have—'

'But I don't make a point of keeping in touch. Tim's a bender and has always fancied me, which makes me feel bloody uncomfortable, even if he is bringing simpering Simon with him—'

'For heaven's sake, he can't help being gay! I think he's charming with it and besides, he's never made a pass at you. It's just you being paranoid like all military men—'

'And let's face it, Nicky's a complete tart—'

'She is not!' Kate felt a surge of defensiveness that made her thoroughly cross. Nicky wasn't her favourite cousin but she was family. 'She just gets engaged a lot. And they are my first cousins, I'll have you remember, and I truly don't need to hear this sort of thing about my own family—'

'You do if you want them to come and stay and don't consult me on the issue,' Alex retorted baldly. He whittled furiously at his pencil.

'Don't do that with my best kitchen knife. Anyway, what was I supposed to say?'

'"No." Just a short two-letter word and quite easy once you get the hang of it. It's time you did, Kate.' Alex looked up sharply. 'You can't say "no" to anyone.'

'Oh, fine. Then you ring my mother back and say it. Let's hear just how easy it is.'

'Why should I have to speak to your mother at all? After all, she's your mother!' Alex knew he was being childish and bad-tempered but he didn't care. There were times, like right now, when he wished Kate had been an orphan.

Kate took a deep breath. 'And your mother-in-law, you might remember. Besides, I put up with a great deal because of you and your career. I think you could just about manage one evening with my cousins. And if you don't, then I may just feel it necessary to rethink a few things,' she added darkly.

'And just what's that supposed to mean?' He looked up, wary and annoyed, both at the same time. 'Rethink what, exactly?'

'I think you know exactly what I mean.' Kate plucked the small paring knife from his fingers and dumped it in the sink before drying her hands and walking out of the room. She threw herself into an armchair in the sitting room and picked up a magazine, tapping it crossly with her finger and waiting.

Alex finally emerged, some long minutes later, a cup of coffee in his hand. 'Want some?'

'No.' She smiled sweetly. 'There, that good enough for you?'

Alex sighed heavily. 'I don't want to argue . . .'

'Then why did you? It's just one little night out of all the nights that we spend here in this delightful quarter with all your army buddy friends dropping by. Not so totally terrible, I'd have thought.'

'They're your friends too . . .'

Kate gave him a tired look and flicked her magazine again. Alex tried once more.

'All right, fine. It's done now, anyway and they're clearly coming no matter what I say. But, in future, I'd like you to ask me. I do live here as well, you know.' He sipped at the coffee, watching her and gauging her temper.

'You'll be telling me next that you pay the rent. Yes, fine, I'll ask you in future. But if that's the case, then I expect you to do the same, not just walk in the door with Freddie or Johnnie or Nick and ask if we've got enough extra for supper and then spend the entire evening talking army which no sensible outsider can understand or wants to understand.'

'Lord, what's ruffled your feathers? Where's all this suddenly coming from?' Alex sat down abruptly, looking alarmed. 'Are you trying to tell me you're unhappy with me being in the army?'

'No, no, I'm thrilled with it, darling. I always wanted to live in a box, be dragged from pillar to post every two years, have a husband who gets paid a pittance compared to my London friends', and be told I can't see whoever I want because it involves you exerting some charm instead of just issuing dogmatic orders. Not to mention giving up my own career, of course.' Kate smiled tightly. 'But that's a whole issue on its own, isn't it?'

Alex was silent for so long that Kate thought he wasn't going to reply at all. He didn't like emotional confrontation, she had begun to realise. A straightforward disagreement with another person over work was one thing, but an argument with her where the parameters of their own behaviour in marriage was the issue didn't appeal at all. He pursed his lips and looked deeply depressed. Kate felt a pang of sympathy for him. She hadn't meant to say all she had, hadn't even really meant it. Just sometimes . . .

'Is this going to be thrown in my face every time we have a disagreement?' he asked finally. Kate shrugged. 'Because I can't change things, you know. This is my career and you knew that when you married me and you knew what the life was like—'

'No, that's not true. I had no idea what army life was like and you knew it. But I'm willing to change and adapt—'

'It doesn't much sound like it. I'm sorry I don't get paid more and can't give you a stable home like all your friends, but what do you really expect me to do? Give up the army? Give up my career—'

'That's what I did for you,' Kate snapped.

Alex paused and put his coffee cup down carefully. 'I thought you were happy here,' he said.

Kate shrugged. 'Most of the time I'm fine. Not as happy

perhaps as I would be still living in London surrounded by my friends and having a really good career of my own, but I'm willing to deal with that, for your sake. What I won't put up with is you dictating to me, on top of it all.'

'I wasn't aware that I was,' Alex replied stiffly.

'Well, you are. So think it over.' And Kate stepped past him and returned to the kitchen to finish the sandwiches. Eventually, she heard Alex close the front door behind him as he went out without a word to her. She slammed the piece of bread she was buttering down on the chopping board and mashed it with the palm of her hand. Damn you, Alex, she swore to herself, damn, damn, damn!

'So,' Fergus called loudly, 'what did the doctor have to say?' He had just finished turning the compost, the evening breeze growing chill and the steam rising from the flaky soil as the fork lifted yet another load. Emma appeared, waved casually to him through the window and disappeared from sight again. She reappeared, leaning out the window to hold out a can of beer. Fergus grinned and took it, wiping his brow on the back of his hand.

'Wants me to see a specialist.' Emma disappeared again and Fergus's grin disappeared with her. He marched around to the back door and cornered her in the kitchen, unpacking a week's shopping.

'Why? I thought we could just start trying again? Isn't that what he said last time?' He swallowed some of the cold beer with relief. God it was hot work forking through a pile of dung!

Emma continued to unpack, her back to Fergus as she efficiently stacked the vegetables in the refrigerator and the tinned food in the larder. 'He says I'm underweight and he's fairly sure I'm not ovulating. They're going to do some tests and maybe a scan. I'm booked in for a month from now, which was the earliest appointment they could get me.' Her tone was matter-of-fact but Fergus knew her. He came up behind her and wrapped his arms around her, one hand massaging her flat stomach.

'Then we'll go privately and get this sorted out fast, all right?'

Emma paused, putting down the bag in her hand and leaning back against her husband. 'Oh, Fergus! What if I can't conceive again, what if some real damage was done?' She closed her eyes. 'I so want . . . but she broke off, knowing Fergus knew what she wanted and not being able to say it aloud without her voice breaking.

'Sh, sweetheart, sh. You had no trouble conceiving the first time, now, did you? So, that's not going to be much of a problem again. All we need is to get you to put on some weight and take life a little easier. It'll be all right. I'll have a chat with the doctor myself and just see if we can't bring the appointment forward a little by going privately. Okay?' He kissed her temple and glanced up to see Alex hovering in the doorway, the dogs twining around his legs begging for affection.

'Alex! Come on in. Want a beer?'

'Sorry, I've come at a bad time. I'll catch you later—'

'No, no, Alex, come in,' Emma sniffed and smiled, going over to kiss his cheek. 'Come and distract us.'

'I was hoping you were going to do that for me,' Alex admitted, giving Emma a hug and bending down to look at her face. 'What's up? Or am I butting in?'

'Doctors,' she replied cuttingly. 'That's what's up. Trying

to get appointments, trying to get answers or at least reassurance.' Alex continued to look blank and Emma grimaced. 'They say I'm not ovulating.'

'Oh,' Alex patted her shoulder awkwardly, 'I see. I didn't realise you were trying again. I'm sorry . . .' He took the beer that Fergus handed him, stretching down to ruffle Tilly's ears absent-mindedly while thinking how bloody unfair life was. People like Fergus and Emma, good, gentle, loving people couldn't seem to have the baby they so desperately wanted, and then depraved bastards like that Jock child molester had three or more.

'We weren't.' Fergus shrugged. 'But clearly it doesn't much matter one way or the other at the moment. We'll just have to get some tests done and get Emma to relax and put on some weight.' He smiled at her encouragingly and Emma gave him a twisted smile back. If only she hadn't lost the first one, Fergus thought, if only she hadn't taken that fall . . . if only Hugh . . . But he had to switch off his thoughts abruptly there, before the anger took hold of him again.

'So, what's wrong with you?' Fergus grinned at Alex, noting the carefree good looks were dimmed, his eyes worried. Kate, he thought. Has to be.

'It's Kate,' Alex echoed Fergus's guess. 'I didn't realise, or maybe,' he scrubbed at his face, 'maybe I am being dogmatic, or . . .' He raised worried eyes to Emma. 'Is she so unhappy? Does she hate the army?'

'Oh lord, that one, is it?' Emma laughed knowingly in a tone that said, been there, done that. He relaxed a little as she went on. 'No, I really wouldn't have thought so, Alex. It just takes a bit of getting used to. Particularly in the first year. And particularly when you're used to having a career yourself. It's a lot to give up, a lot of spare time to fill.' She gave him an understanding smile and gestured to the table. 'Let's sit. My back's killing me.'

They pulled up stools and grouped themselves around the small kitchen table, Alex swallowing down the beer with sudden relief. So, it was all right after all. Just something he hadn't understood, something time would smooth over, something minor . . .

'Should I not invite people home without asking Kate first? Would that help?' he asked, thinking back over what Kate had said and deciding that must be it. Emma raised her eyebrows.

'Oh, Alex.' She gave a half laugh. 'I really don't think it's quite that simple. Let's start at the beginning, shall we?'

By the time Alex finally reappeared, Kate had begun to work herself up into a mixture of terror that he had taken everything she had said too seriously and was going to ask for a divorce, and anger that she couldn't say it without him overreacting. Imagine if she had expected him to give up his career and sit in London with all her friends' husbands, trying to decide how to fill his day and then she came home and told him he couldn't have some old army muckers to stay the night because she didn't like them much.

Put that way, Alex's behaviour was outrageous, she told herself furiously. But then again, she had agreed that he had no choice in his career and this wasn't making it any easier. Oh . . . ! She turned abruptly from where she'd been painting a small pine wall shelf, as the back door squeaked open and Alex walked in.

He stood there, with that look on his face that Kate knew meant he was sorry and depressed and worried but couldn't bring himself to say any of it. She held out her arms and he pulled her in tightly and hugged her so hard she thought he might have crushed her ribs. A rather nasty bouquet of multi-coloured dahlias from the local garage was thrust into her face. She hastily put down her paint-brush, hoping she hadn't painted his back when they embraced.

'I don't want you to hate our life, Kate,' he began miserably but Kate held up her fingers to his lips.

'I don't, Alex, I don't. Not really.' She sighed. 'I'm sorry, I'm just going through an adjustment period, all right? Things get pent up inside me because I'm trying so hard to be the wife you want and need, and then whoosh, it all goes up in flames suddenly when I feel you're not trying as hard as I am in return. You do need to learn to compromise too, you know.' She caressed the sharp planes of his face, wishing she knew what the answer was. Loving someone desperately clearly wasn't quite enough for things to run smoothly. Perhaps all marriages were just that – a question of compromise?

She sighed again as Alex murmured. 'I know, I know. I didn't realise just how awkward I was being. I'm sorry too, you know. I didn't mean to upset you.'

'Then let's just forget it, all right.' She kissed him slowly and deeply, breathing in the scent and warmth of his skin, wanting to regain their old intimacy. It was a wrench to finally stand back.

'Now,' she said shakily, looking at the garish display of flowers and smiling, 'I'd better sort this lot out and perhaps you could go to sort out the spare bedroom for our guests – since it's all your clothes on the floor!' Alex's dressing room was a euphemistic term for Alex's dumping room. He leaned over and kissed her again.

'When are they turning up?'

'Tomorrow after tea, I think.'

'Then, how about we sort out our room, instead? They can wait. Besides, I don't really want to think about their sleeping arrangements.' He ran his hands down her waist and Kate shivered.

'What's wrong with our room?'

'Not used enough. Let me show you.'

Tim eyed the PVC window frames and rolled his eyes at Simon. Simon sipped his wine and winked back. Kate saw both gestures but chose to ignore them.

'I can't think where Alex has got to,' she said instead, glancing out the windows again. It was nearly eight in the evening. 'He's normally home by now.'

'But it's Friday, Kate,' Nicky protested. 'Surely he doesn't work late on Fridays?'

'Oh yes, quite often. And there was a disturbance down town last night, so he had things to sort out anyway. I just thought he'd have been home long ago.' She glanced out again. 'I hope nothing's gone wrong.'

'What sort of disturbance?' Their fourth visitor, a languid, rather beautiful Eurasian girl called Serena looked interested. Kate wondered what she did.

'Some sort of punch-up at one of the nastier pubs in town. The local lads versus ours, I gather.'

'Really? Anyone badly hurt?'

'Well, yes, unfortunately. Someone got run over – a couple of times – if that gives you any idea.'

'Heavens, how sordid!' Nicky, as usual, looked delighted at the thought. Simon, who rarely ever said anything, sat smirking in his chair, giving off offensively amused vibes that made Kate want to tip him backwards through the PVC window into the rose-beds. He was sporting a tiny goatee beard, recently grown and rather sparse still. Kate found it quite repulsive.

'Ghastly people to deal with, I imagine. However does poor Alex cope?' Tim murmured in his soft voice and Kate breathed in more deeply.

'Don't be so precious, Tim,' she snapped. 'This is the army, not your local needlepoint class. Of course they get drunk and have violent punch-ups occasionally. They're trained to be physical. It's the whole point of what they do. But Alex actually likes and enjoys the job, believe it or not.'

'Care to enlarge upon that?' Serena asked and Kate blinked slowly and gave a half laugh.

'Not really. Tell me, Serena, what is it you do?'

Serena shrugged. 'Oh, this and that. A little freelance work from time to time, some modelling . . .'

'Really? Freelance . . . ?'

Serena smiled and didn't reply. Nicky gave her a fleeting smirk that left Kate wondering just why she had bothered to have an argument with Alex over people like this. And why did she feel there was some undercurrent going on, that everyone else knew about except her. She eyed them levelly, took a deep breath and tried again.

'So, tell me, you've just come from Edinburgh and you've a couple of weeks over here. Is that right? And where are you all going? Mother said the south of Ireland, near Waterford, I think?'

By the time Alex returned, supper was nearly over and dark had fallen long ago. Kate didn't bother to ask how things had gone. The mere fact that he was still in combats meant he'd had to deal with official matters. And that meant trouble.

'Alex! There you are at last,' Nicky cried, leaping up from the table to throw her arms around him. 'Goodness, don't you look warry in those things.' She snuggled closer for a moment. 'Whatever have you been doing?' she demanded as she kissed him overeffusively. Kate smiled as Alex caught her eyes.

'Nicky, lovely to see you. All of you.' He gave a fair imitation of being pleased to see them, shaking hands with Tim and Simon, nodding politely at Serena while introductions were made. He kissed Kate with a long sigh that made her want to wrap her arms around him and tell the others to just get lost. Instead, she sat Alex down and dished him up some supper.

'You haven't answered my question,' Nicky began roguishly. 'Whatever have you been doing all this time? Anything exciting?'

'No, just fairly boring and thankless tasks, I'm afraid. I'm sorry I'm so late. Bit of trouble up at the camp.'

'But we want to hear all about it, don't we Tim?' Nicky insisted and again Kate noticed, uneasily, how interested Serena seemed. Alex drank his wine back and looked amused.

'No, you don't, Nicky, I promise you. And I'd much rather hear the gossip from London . . .'

'No, no, you don't get off that lightly. Tell us all. How's the thug who got run over? Dead?' Nicky was all brightness and determination. Alex shot a quick glance at Kate who grimaced in apology.

'No, he'll live,' he replied lightly. 'It was nothing. Just a punch-up.'

'Nothing?' Serena smiled, her eyebrows arching enticingly, her long dark hair seeming to slither over her bare shoulders with a life of its own. 'Attempted murder is nothing?'

'Who said it was attempted murder?' Alex smiled politely and warily. 'Just a mistake. Someone trying to get away from the punch-up, someone else trying to stop him. He went under the wheels. A dreadful accident but luckily with no fatal consequences.'

'Kate said he was run over twice,' Simon remarked slowly and Kate closed her eyes.

'By accident.' Alex stirred the food around his plate and pushed it to one side.

'Oh, come now, we're all aware these things don't really happen by accident—' Simon began.

'What about that poor woman? The live-export protester? She was driven over by accident in a similar sort of rowdy, noisy brawl. These things really do happen, I'm afraid, Simon, though perhaps not in your circles.' Alex shrugged. 'You mustn't get so worked up about it.' Kate looked down at her plate in amusement. Alex loathed Simon.

'Well! I hardly think—'

'What was it all about, the punch-up, I mean?' Serena rode rough-shod over Simon's huffy response, quelling him with ease. Alex leaned back in his chair and swallowed some wine.

'Just the usual – who's tougher than whom? Tell me, Serena,' he smiled, 'just what is your interest in all this? You all seem uncommonly fascinated by a very boring little fracas. Any particular reason?' There was a note in Alex's voice that had Nicky glancing nervously at Tim. Simon continued to smirk, enjoying the confrontation.

'Whatever made you ask that, Alex?' Serena countered. 'There's no law against being curious, is there? You don't have something to hide, do you?' She laughed, a throaty, sexy chuckle that made Kate, listening to it, feel naive and immature. This girl knew her way around.

'Hardly.' Alex sounded bored. He watched Serena fishing around in her pocket for a roll-up instead. She held it out. 'You don't mind, do you? You've all finished dinner?'

Alex hadn't eaten his but clearly he had no appetite. Kate stood and collected his plate. 'Let's go through into the sitting room, shall we?' she suggested, hoping the move would diffuse the tension in the air. 'I'll bring coffee in there.'

'Wonderful,' Nicky stretched and leaned back in her chair, not offering to help in any way. 'I could do with some coffee. Got one for me, Serena?' She reached for the roll-up that Serena held out and Alex watched her with eyes half-closed. Abruptly, he stood and held Nicky's chair back for her.

'I thought you preferred Silk Cuts?' he remarked casually. 'Or are you out?'

'Oh, Alex! Lord, aren't you becoming a fuddy-duddy these days? Surely you can recognise a joint when you see one?' Nicky laughed dismissively as both she and Serena lit up. They inhaled deeply, holding it between thumb and index finger. 'After all,' Nicky blew out the sweetly scented smoke in Alex's face, 'you did once yourself, didn't you?'

Alex laughed ruefully. 'Yes, a long time ago, Nicky, at university.' His gaze became mocking. 'But I'm afraid that these days I really would prefer you not to. Not here.' He smiled evenly. 'Hope you don't mind?'

'Oh, don't be so wet, Alex,' Simon interjected quickly, enjoying putting down someone he saw as a rival for Tim's affections. 'Heavens, half the judiciary are trying to legalise it, it's so harmless.'

'But it is still illegal,' Alex sighed, as he pointed out the obvious. 'And I spent quite a lot of time today having to bring charges against some of my men for just this offence. The army's very clear on the issue and we're regularly drugs-tested for just that reason. After all, you don't want someone stoned in charge of a semi-automatic, do you?

'So, right at the moment, you are causing me to become a passive smoker and it could show up in my blood.' He paused, eyeing them all steadily.

'And even more importantly, I am the adjutant in the battalion. In charge of disciplining the men. How do you expect me to be so hypocritical as to ruin one man's career over drugs during the day and then return home and allow them to be used in my own home?' He looked at all four of them with some irritation. 'I'm sorry, but that's the way it is. So, please, don't.'

'Good lord, Kate,' Nicky complained, as Kate walked in with a tray of steaming mugs, 'Alex has become the most righteous prig these days. However do you stand him?' She ground her roll-up out in one of Kate's porcelain knick-knacks. Kate put the tray down carefully and looked up at Alex.

'I'm so sorry, darling,' she replied deliberately. 'I can't imagine what you must be thinking. Nicky?' She turned to hand her cousin a mug. 'Please try and remember that you are a guest here. Mother would be so mortified if she were to hear of your behaviour.'

Nicky stiffened angrily and Tim, who had decided he really didn't like his sister enormously, laughed. 'That's right, Kate. Pull the big guns on her. Nicky'd never dare offend Aunt Harriet in case she became a social outcast. And then what would become of the poor girl? She might actually have to marry one of the poor sods she keeps getting engaged to.' He grinned maliciously.

'And you, of course, don't care,' Nicky snapped, 'since you've already burnt your bridges being a complete bender.'

Simon tittered, putting a hand on Tim's arm. 'Hardly! It's very socially and politically correct to be gay, these days,' he disagreed sweetly.

Serena had silently curled herself up on the sofa, having nipped the glowing ember out of her joint and slipped it away again in her pocket with further protest. Alex had the distinct impression she had done it to test him.

'Oh, do stop it!' Kate sighed, passing the rest of the mugs around. 'Tell us about London instead. How's Milly? Do you see her? Is the business going well?'

'Surely you're in contact, Kate?' Tim gave a quizzical frown. 'You must talk to her all the time on the telephone, even if you don't dash over to London yourself. This isn't Outer Mongolia, after all.'

'Well, sometimes it feels like it!' Kate joked. 'And I've tried not to interfere. I thought I'd let her get on with it herself for a while, without feeling I'm butting in or making suggestions—'

'Well, she's doing terribly well,' Nicky interrupted, 'so clearly she doesn't need your help after all. Or perhaps she never did.' She saw Kate's face lose brightness and added with satisfaction, 'And speaking of people doing awfully well, Joanna's become a real celebrity with her latest showing. Sold half of them on the preview night, I gather, and not for a song either. She's becoming such a name that everyone wants to have one of her pieces. Nice to have an income in five figures, wouldn't you say, Alex? That'd help get the children through school.'

'Yes. Well, good for old Jo,' he took an even breath, looking at Kate and commenting coolly, 'I don't think any of us were even in doubt that Jo'd be successful. She has a fairly one-track mind.' If one likes the ruthless type, he added to himself.

Kate slowly replaced her mug on the tray, smiling with determinedly good cheer.

'Well, and what time is your train in the morning?'

'Crack of dawn,' Serena yawned and stretched. 'So I, for one, think I'll call it a night.' She stood up and the others, taking their cue, also declared that an early night would do them good. 'Don't get up for us in the morning. We've ordered a taxi to meet us outside the gate. So, we'll just slip out and be on our way,' they insisted, finally finding their manners, Alex thought wryly. Within a few minutes they had all disappeared upstairs, leaving Kate and Alex to clear up alone and in peace.

They leaned against each other, laughing weakly. 'Don't ever, ever let me agree to their visiting again,' Kate pleaded. Alex folded her in tightly against him and kissed her.

'That, my darling, is one promise I'll have no trouble in keeping. The only problem is they'll have to come back and collect their bloody car. Oh well, maybe just once more, then . . .' He felt Kate move against him, so that she could look up into his face.

'Do you mind?' she asked softly.

'About . . . Jo?' He knew her well enough, he thought, to understand how much the news had hurt. He laughed. 'Not in the slightest. In fact, thank heavens she's becoming successful. She'll get on with her own life, then, and leave us alone.' He pulled her chin up and kissed her softly. 'You are the one I want. You are the one I married. And Jo means less than nothing to me. All right?'

Kate sighed happily. 'All right.'

Chapter Eight

Saturday morning was quiet and drowsy, the droning hum of a model airplane drifting in through the window, along with the cheerful bickering of several sparrows over the bread Kate had left out the night before to help them through the last frosty days. Occasionally, the sound of gunfire from the 30-metre range startled Kate but Alex didn't react at all. By now Tim and Nicky and the others would be in Dublin, she thought with relief, and well and truly out of their hair. She snuggled in against Alex. Just a lovely, lazy Saturday with nothing to do except enjoy themselves.

She glanced at the clock. Nearly ten o'clock. Bliss. And then something tugged at her mind. Dimly, she groped for the memory. And sat bolt upright in bed with an aghast, 'Oh, my God!'

Alex stirred. 'What?' He scrubbed his fingers across his chin and pulled the bed covers back across him.

'It's Open Day! And I was supposed to bake a cake!' The sinking feeling intensified. 'And I've got to run the bake stall at eleven o'clock. Oh, Alex! What shall I do?' She had leapt from bed and was hurriedly hunting through her wardrobe for something to wear. Alex forced himself fully awake.

'Buy one,' he remarked laconically. 'Who cares if you slaved over it or someone else did? As long as it raises some money.'

'But what will Amanda say?' she wailed and Alex laughed. He found it a pleasure to watch his wife scurrying around naked, hurriedly washing, brushing her teeth, collecting clothing. Things wobbled that he hadn't realised wobbled before. Wobbled charmingly. And what Amanda had to say mattered less than nothing to him.

'Who cares? Look at Amanda. She's one of the prim, duty-bound, bossy and interfering wives that people dreaded of old, except these days she has no power just because her husband is senior to me. No one cares what she has to say or think. If she wants to do all of this, then fine. But you don't have to. Nothing's going to happen to my career just because my wife forgot to bake a cake!' He laughed again and Kate paused in zipping up her jeans and tucking the pink cotton shirt in.

'Really?' she asked.

'Really,' Alex assured her. 'So relax.'

'Easy for you to say. You don't have to deal with her,' Kate murmured, slipping her feet into soft leather loafers, throwing a pink cashmere cardigan over her shoulders and coming over to kiss Alex. 'Now, I must fly. I'll see you there, all right?'

'Relax, my love.' Alex calmed her again. 'Oh, and don't forget about the parade at one o'clock, if you can make it.'

'Yes, yes, I'll be there.' She smiled distractedly and disappeared out the door.

By the time she had hurried to Stewart's supermarket and bought the best cake she could find, along with a cake stand and some cling film, and driven back to the camp, it was nearly quarter to eleven. She wondered whether to put it on one of her own china plates, to make it look more home-made, but realised she might lose the plate forever that way. Who cared if people knew it was bought, she reminded herself firmly? Alex didn't.

Swiftly she pulled it out of its wrapping, placed it on the silver foil cake stand and wrapped the whole thing in cling film. Lemon sponge with old fashioned lemon icing just like she was forced to make at school years ago. No one would ever guess. She breathed out with relief, hurriedly locked the car and set off to find the bake stall.

Amanda was there before her, her long nose lifted at just that particular angle that let everyone know exactly who she was. Dressed in low pumps, a Liberty patterned skirt, a starched blouse with the collar wings turned up, much like a seagull in flight, Kate thought, with the inevitable husky, pearls and alice band, Amanda was enough to set one's teeth on edge. Well, hers anyway. And even worse, Kate thought, Amanda's clear, commanding voice could be heard organising even the placement of the baked goods on the stall exactly as she wanted them. What a gauntlet to run with a store-bought cake, Kate sighed to herself.

Gingerly, she tried to ease her own meagre offering onto a corner of the stall without anyone noticing. 'Ah!' Amanda, noticed immediately. 'Good, Kate, I was beginning to think you weren't going to turn up and I'd have to fill in for you. We've already had one no-show this morn—' She broke off as she picked up Kate's cake and looked at it. 'Good heavens! Have you bought this?'

Kate flushed. 'Um, well, I'm afraid so. I had guests staying, you see and I quite forgot until this morning. Still, I don't think many people will either notice or care, do you?'

'Well,' Amanda sniffed, 'this is meant to be a fresh bake stall – you know, home-made baked goods, so I do really think you could have let me know if that was going to be a problem.' She grimaced at the cake and gave a pained smile to the two women beside her. Kate didn't recognise either of them and flushed even more awkwardly. 'Still, it's done now, I suppose. Charlotte? Do you think you could try and make this look a bit better?' Amanda handed the cake over to one of her cohorts who smiled condescendingly at Kate.

Kate looked at her watch, her eyes pricking with angry, mortified moisture. Still five minutes to go. She turned away abruptly as Amanda launched into an attack on another plate of pastries. 'Look at this! Jam and cream *millefeuille*! I always thought *millefeuille* had crème patisserie in it. Who on earth made these? Or perhaps they're bought as well!' With red slashes burning brightly across her cheeks, Kate blundered into the crowd and was almost immediately cornered by Laura, entertaining several of the good-looking young captains and subalterns. Kate breathed deeply and forced herself to smile.

'Hallo Laura, I'm glad to see you at least are not wearing Liberty and pearls!' She kissed Laura warmly, admiring the skin-tight jeans, cowboy boots and suede jacket. Not a frill or alice band in sight. In fact, Laura looked sexy, ravishing and completely unarmy-wife-ish. Kate grinned, her humour restored, as Laura introduced her to the surrounding gaggle of young men.

'Henry, Tony and Will, meet Kate. No last names, please.

Far too boring and far too difficult to remember since they all seem to be double-barrelled! What's up, Kate, you look thoroughly pissed off?'

'Oh!' Kate blew out her cheeks in exasperation. 'I don't really want to be difficult or indiscreet, but a certain person who organises bake stalls has got thoroughly up my nose. And I'm due to take it over in five minutes! I shall be lucky not to hit her with one of her home-made rock cakes,' she ground out furiously and the young men burst out laughing. They weren't sure who Kate was, entirely, although they knew they'd glimpsed her at the Ladies Dinner Night. Whoever she was, they thought, she was quite stunning. They beamed at her.

'So? Don't turn up. Say you got held up, had an emergency, felt sick, heck, I could come up with a dozen valid excuses.' Laura yawned. 'Besides, if she's annoyed you, annoy her right back. It's a free country.'

'Don't tempt me. I mean, honestly, just because I didn't bake the cake myself – say, why aren't you doing a slot?'

'Because I never turn up,' Laura laughed and slid her arm through Henry's. 'Not when there's so much else more interesting to do! Nor do I bake cakes or even buy them,' she added meaningfully. Henry laughed, his ruddy fair-haired looks and clear grey eyes obviously appealing. The other young men immediately seconded Laura's suggestion.

'Come on, let's go and see round the stalls and try out all the rides and then have lunch up on the battlements,' Will insisted and took Kate's arm. 'You don't want to turn into a boring duty-wife, now do you?' he urged. Kate, still deeply hurt and angry at Amanda's humiliation of her, was tempted.

'I have to be at the parade at one,' she temporised. The

others nodded. 'Of course. We all do.' She hesitated, glancing back over the throng to where the bake stall was doing a thriving business and Amanda could be seen thrusting her way past people to look for Kate.

'Oh, all right then, but quickly, she's looking for me,' Kate agreed hurriedly, grinning with pleasure like a truanting schoolgirl as they all ran laughing and scurrying through the crowd, their heads bent low. Will had his arm proprietorially around her shoulders and his vivid good looks and the mischief in his eyes did as much for her spirits as did the thought of annoying Amanda. They disappeared from sight as Amanda craned back and forth, her clear voice calling Kate to heel.

The morning became one of light-hearted fun, flirting and behaving in quite a silly fashion, Kate thought to herself, but, oh, she hadn't had a chance to be silly in far too long. It made her heart feel light and her soul soar. They went over the displays, admired mortars and milan missile launchers and clambered over armoured personnel carriers for a while, each young man in charge of one display or another proudly introducing them to their men and enjoying a light-hearted mockery from the NCOs, who clearly knew a great deal more about it than they did.

Then they roared around on bumper cars and flopped all over the bouncy castle before settling down for a much needed drink at the 'pub' that had been erected. Kate sat, surrounded by her admirers and several others who seemed to have become part of their noisy crowd even though she hadn't been introduced to them and had no idea of their names. She saw Suzy wander past with Joss, and waved, but they didn't seem to notice her.

For a moment a slight shade was cast over the morning.

Was she behaving badly? Had they really not seen her or were they slighting her for not doing her bit? And where was Alex, after all? She really ought to be trying to find him.

Distracted, she found the banter around her suddenly less amusing. In fact, she began to notice that one particular man was continuously making rather uncomfortable innuendoes. Her smile became strained. 'So . . . how come we haven't seen you round here before, then, Katie my girl? Where're you been hiding yourself, sweetheart? 'Cos I'd've noticed a lovely little stunner like you, I'm sure,' he was asking and Kate focused back on him.

'Oh, because I haven't been here. I only arrived about a month ago.' She smiled politely but without her previous warmth, hoping he would sense her withdrawal. But he had been drinking beer steadily, as had most of the others, and was oblivious to her discomfort.

'Really? So you're new to camp following, are you, love? Well, you can come to me to learn the ropes any day. I'd be happy to teach you, wouldn't I, lads?' A couple of his mates nudged each other and sniggered. Kate flushed.

'I don't really think—' she began, but suddenly an arm was going round her and she stiffened angrily as she turned to see who it was. Alex smiled sleepily into her eyes. 'Hallo, my love. Enjoying yourself here with Whitey?' He seemed amused and Whitey was quite unabashed.

'Oh no, boss, don't tell me she's yours!' he complained. 'I might've bleeding well known.'

Alex grinned. 'Tough life, isn't it? Besides, your Susan's looking for you. I saw her a couple of minutes ago and said I'd pass on the message.'

'Oh, ta very much, sir!' Whitey grinned mischievously at Kate, who, with Alex's presence beside her, had relaxed enough to admire Whitey's bravado. 'But don't you forget, Katie love. I'm the one you want when the Persil packet's in the window. After all, me and the boss go back a long way together. Share and share alike . . . I'll tell you all about it sometime, shall I?' He laughed cockily at Alex who jabbed a thumb at him with long-suffering humour.

'Hop it, now, before I find an excuse to give you thirty days. And tell Susan you were helping entertain my wife. I'm sure she'll be understanding when she hears . . .' He steered Kate away from the others towards the parade ground, laughing at the obscene comment Whitey lobbed over his shoulder. Kate felt thoroughly flustered.

'What on earth did he mean about the Persil packet?' she demanded uneasily and Alex kissed her hair.

'My poor innocent! You won't like it,' he warned. Kate looked at him enquiringly. 'All right then,' he continued. 'In the past, when a wife on the patch was having an affair and wanted her lover to know her husband was out, she placed a packet of OMO washing powder in the window. OMO – Old Man Out. But that became such a cliché that any wife even buying OMO at the Naafi was suspect. So, Persil took over . . .' He grinned as he saw Kate flush.

'You mean he was offering to have an affair with me?' she asked indignantly.

'An affair? No. The odd bonk? Well . . . not really. Just teasing. That's Whitey's way. As he said, we go back a long way together and when I was a very junior lieutenant, we got into a few scrapes from which he extricated me. He's a good bloke and Susan, his wife, is great. She keeps him in check.'

'She'd need to, cocky beggar! I'd like to meet her. Perhaps I could learn something,' Kate laughed. 'Oh dear, I'm afraid

I've let you down badly, my darling. I didn't turn up for the bake stall—'

'So I heard,' he agreed feelingly.

'Oh lord, how?' Kate was horrified he'd heard already. Perhaps that was why Suzy and Joss hadn't noticed her? On purpose?

'From Amanda personally, I'm afraid. I went to collect you and found her foaming at the mouth instead.' He laughed delightedly. 'I had a terribly hard time keeping a straight face and agreeing that you were "most remiss"!'

'I was what?'

'You heard. And Suzy was trying so hard to placate Amanda—'

'Oh my God! Suzy knows! Was she furious?'

'Not in the slightest. Why should she be? She's perfectly aware of what a tyrant Amanda can be. We heard all about you buying your cake and Suzy remarked that it was a brilliant idea and she'd do the same next time. Particularly as it was one of the first ones sold. Then she walked off, sniggering into Joss's shoulder. Amanda nearly had apoplexy.'

'Oh, I can't bear it!' Kate groaned. 'I shall be the laughing stock of the patch. Why on earth did I listen to Laura?'

'Ah, yes, I did rather wonder! But, more to the point, did you enjoy yourself?'

'Thoroughly.' Kate smiled reluctantly. 'Much, much more than if I'd been running a cake bake.'

'Then, that, my darling, is all that matters to me.' He kissed her again and held her tightly to him. 'I don't want or expect a dutiful, conformist wife, despite what you might hear from the Amandas and Hughs of this world. I like you just as you are and I like it even better when half the men are thoroughly jealous that you're mine and not theirs. Now,' he glanced at his watch, 'we better get over to the parade ground. We're running late.'

'We're about to be later still,' Kate warned, nudging him. 'Here comes Hugh and he doesn't look a happy bunny.'

'Does he ever?' Alex forced himself to give a welcoming smile. 'Hallo, Hugh, on your way to the parade too?'

'I'm looking for Laura,' Hugh announced peremptorily. 'I understand from Amanda that Kate,' he glanced coldly at Kate, 'went off with Laura this morning when she should have been on duty and then drew in rather an unsuitable crowd of admirers. You've been drinking, I gather, Kate, and being rather overfriendly with some of the men.' He stiffened as he saw Kate's mouth quiver with suppressed laughter. 'I just hope you didn't encourage Laura into similar behaviour. And I must say I'm astonished to find that Laura isn't still with you – or does extricating silly females from embarrassing predicaments only extend to your own wife, Alex? Even after she led mine astray?' But that last comment was too patently absurd for Alex to swallow and he shook his head in disbelief at Hugh.

'You are truly incredible sometimes, Hugh,' he said with a snort of laughter. 'It was all innocent fun and besides, Laura has never needed anyone to "lead her astray", as you put it, least of all Kate. Rather the boot on the other foot, if you don't mind my saying—'

'Actually, I do!' Hugh cut across Alex furiously. 'How dare you insinuate—'

'Oh? But it's all right for you to blatantly say as much of Kate? Grow up, Hugh and get your own house in order,' Alex snapped, in a tone that left Kate appalled and Hugh silenced. 'Laura was, last time I saw her, somewhere in the vicinity of the pub. Why don't you go and look for her? Now we're late, so, if you'll excuse us?' And Alex strode on, leading Kate away from Hugh at a pace that nearly had her running beside him. 'Bloody man! I could do him a permanent injury! In fact, if that report I saw is put forward, I bloody well just might . . .' she heard him mutter and sighed deeply to herself. Clearly her morning's light-hearted fun had misfired.

Emma, watching the parade form from the stands that had been set up around the square, had seen the altercation although she had been too far away to hear what was being said. She raised a hand and beckoned Kate. Alex helped Kate up into the stands before disappearing off to take his place to one side of the parade.

He wasn't actually a part of the display, which was comprised of only one company and the regimental band, but it was his job to see all went smoothly and to deal with any problems. And when the Lord Lieutenant reviewed the troops with the colonel, Alex had to trail along behind looking stern and deferential at the same time, Emma whispered to Kate, who had no real idea what Alex's job entailed.

'He's Joss's right-hand man and also the man with the big stick, where the men are concerned. He jails them and prosecutes them if they've been bad,' Emma explained. 'That's why his own behaviour has to be holier-than-thou. Hell of a job, adjutant. But important and very interesting, I gather. They hear things no one else knows until weeks later, if ever. Postings, confidentials and so on.'

'Was Fergus adjutant, then? Before Alex?'

'Yes, but not with this battalion. He did an eight-month fill-in job with the 2nd battalion after he'd been their

Operations officer and then took over B company here. That's his company out there about to be reviewed.' Emma nodded down at the parade ground and Kate, focusing in, noticed Fergus standing to one side talking with his company sergeant major. Alex strolled over and joined them, the three clearly intent on the job before them.

With the cold wind whipping at their hair, their hats beneath their arms, their khaki dress uniform and shiny black crossbelts, they looked young, dashing and heroic, Kate thought with a fond smile. She saw Emma smiling too.

'They become different people down there, don't they?' she whispered as they began to form up. 'Half gods, half very mortal men.' She shivered suddenly as a cloud flitted across the parade square and plunged everything into shadow. Just how mortal, she wondered, would they be if the Peace didn't hold? She didn't want to find out.

'What was Hugh on about?' Emma asked, suddenly remembering the angry scene. Kate rolled her eyes. 'Oh lord, I might as well tell you before you hear about it anyway. I've been a bad girl . . .'

Laura, swinging one long, booted leg with the other perched on a bar stool, a beer bottle in her hand, looked thoroughly at ease beside Henry. Rather too much at ease, Bill thought with half hurt and half irritated jealousy as he watched them laughing together. He had come looking for Laura when he'd seen Hugh stomp past moodily in the other direction, but now he was unsure if he wanted to talk to her or not. He stood, being buffetted by the crowds surging past, watching them.

In fact, he thought uneasily, he was unsure about a lot of things. Did Laura love him? Would she be faithful to him, if somehow or other things worked out? And was she worth risking his career, his pride and his own personal integrity for, when, the minute his back was turned, she was busy flirting with someone else? Perhaps doing more than just flirting? He glowered at Henry's easy, smiling face.

If Henry wasn't careful, Bill thought with a burst of furious jealousy, he might just find himself on the dud end of the next exercise. And then Bill was instantly appalled at himself, at his thoughts, at the way jealousy could corrode both his friendships and working relationships before he even knew where he was.

He shook his head, reeling with uncertainty, and wandered off down the street. Was this how Hugh felt all the time? Gutted, disorientated, wondering if people were sniggering behind his back, twisted with rage? Suddenly, Bill felt truly sorry for Hugh. He'd stay away from Laura, he vowed, breathing in deeply the fresh salt-laden air gusting in as the day turned overcast and chill. He'd clean up his act, start seeing other, unmarried girls, try to get his life together. And Laura could find some other poor sod to dangle from her strings. His jaw tightened and he walked on firmer and surer now. The parade. He ought to be there. He doubled his pace.

'Do you think you should have upset Hugh like that?' Henry asked tentatively, his brow crinkling with uneasiness. He was only recently promoted to captain and he would much rather not offend a senior major if at all possible, he thought. Least of all over his wife. Besides, everyone knew Laura was just a bit of fun. No one wanted to risk their careers over her. He leaned back on his chair, leaving space between them. Laura eyed him ironically.

'Losing your nerve, Henry?' she drawled, deadpan. He flushed.

'I wouldn't want your husband getting the wrong idea,' Henry shrugged deliberately. 'Besides, we both know you're just kidding around, don't we, Laura? A bit of a laugh with yet another lad, nothing more.' He glanced at his watch idly and then sat up hurriedly. 'Oh my God, I should be at the parade! It started ten minutes ago. Got to go, Laura.' He grinned, flashing even, white teeth at her, and winked. 'See you around.' And Henry swilled back the last of his beer, catapulted out of his chair and disappeared rapidly through the crowd.

'The last of the great heroes,' Laura jeered, eyeing the rest of the company at the bar. Several men eyed her back with interest. But, to be honest, her heart wasn't in it. She had hoped Bill would come by to see her, notice the crowd of admiring men around her and want her all the more. Or failing that, that Hugh would have, at least, insisted she leave with him. Instead, he had merely told her sharply that her behaviour was not becoming and she had told him to take a hike. Which he had. And that was rather unsettling altogether.

Hugh would never normally leave her, least of all in the company of other men. So what had changed? She shivered in the breeze, glanced coldly at the one man who was bold enough to approach, and stood up.

'I'm going,' she told him abruptly. He stood back, shrugging his shoulders, hands held palm upwards, a cocky grin slipping slightly.

'It's a free country, love,' he commented inoffensively and Laura laughed harshly to herself. Wasn't that what she had told Kate? But it wasn't, not really. Not for her, anyway. She pushed through the crowd. Time to go home.

It wasn't until much later that evening, after they had returned home from the Open Day, that Kate finally set about tidying up after their guests. It was late and she was tired, her hands clumsy as she emptied ashtrays and opened windows. She was stripping the beds that Nicky and Serena had used when a small, spiral notebook slipped out from beneath one of the pillows. Damn, she thought to herself. Now she'd have to send it on to Nicky or she might descend on them again and Kate couldn't think of anything she would like less.

Idly, she flicked through the notebook, wondering which of the girls it belonged to. And then, frowning slightly, she took it over to the light and read the lightly pencilled notes again.

'Is there life in the army still?' it began, rather condescendingly, Kate thought. Not Nicky's handwriting. Must be Serena's, then. She read on. 'Or are they all leading lives of such stultifying boredom, with no real wars to fight, that they have to pick fights with local inhabitants instead? (Discuss pub punch-up, man run over, etc – show soldiers as having been trained to kill, dangerous people now with no real role in life anymore. Bullying mentality. Discuss Hungerford, etc.)

'Having stayed with the adjutant of the Duke of York's Own Light Infantry, one of the smartest line regiments in a rapidly dwindling and increasingly redundant army, I can now tell you just where most of your hard-earned tax money is going. On financing his life-style.' A gasp escaped Kate before she read on, increasingly unnerved.

'Midas must have been his middle name (talk about silver framed wedding shots of large estate, family portraits, general air of sophisticated living, etc), yet he still had the effrontery to talk about his men (poor, downtrodden, overworked, bored, etc) in tones of contempt as he jailed them for dope smoking (who doesn't these days?—even the adjutant admitted he did himself), etc . . .'

Kate stared at the lined paper, her mouth slightly parted. What was it Serena had said she did? She was freelance – what? Freelance gutter press, by any chance? And what did she think she was doing? Twisting everything, writing outright lies, even? Did she think a newspaper would buy such an article without substantiating the facts? And then Kate realised that she was the one being naive. Of course they would buy it. The scandal would be a two-day wonder. And Alex's career would be ruined. Just like that.

But what could they do to prevent it? Apart from throttling the bloody girl, Kate thought furiously. How could Serena? And, more importantly, how could Nicky or Tim have brought her along with them, when it was obvious now that this was her intention even before she stepped through the front door? Bitch! Kate ripped the pages from the notebook and crumpled them in her hand. Bloody bitch!

Alex, walking in to the bedroom, found his wife mangling the pages tightly in her fist and swearing furiously. The flimsy army curtains billowed, unnoticed in the chill evening breeze.

'God, it's freezing in here, Kate. Shut the window, will you?' He paused. 'What's up?'

'This! Oh God, Alex, that bloody girl – here, read this.' She held out the pages and Alex straightened them out and slowly read them through. His face grew tight.

'Wonderful!' Long fingers scrubbed at already tired eyes. 'Just what we need. The men'll love being cast as sad and pathetic psychopaths, and this'll do great things for my career, I can tell you. Not to mention the regiment's name being dragged through the mud, yet again. Truly incredible!' He sat down heavily on the bed with a disbelieving snort.

'I'll sort it out, somehow, Alex,' Kate began, her eyes pricking with guilty tears. 'It's all my fault for insisting they come and stay and I could kill myself – no, I could kill bloody Serena and bloody Nicky too. She clearly knew what was going on. That's why she kept giving all those funny looks . . .' Kate paused. 'Thank heavens we didn't discuss anything about the SAS or 14 Intelligence or anything . . .' Alex glanced sharply up at her.

'You haven't been . . . ?' he began, but Kate cut across him.

'No, no, don't be silly. I wouldn't dare. It just occurred to me that I hear all sorts of things here, when your army buddies are around, that the press would love to know and write about. And you all discuss it so normally, as though it's just another day in the office – which, of course, it is to you, I know, I realise that . . . but, still . . .' She paused, her thoughts becoming tangled. 'Anyway, I'm just glad that I was always too careful to discuss any of it with my family, or anyone else for that matter. And then, when nothing has happened, nothing really important, anyway, someone, some complete outsider chooses to write lies that make it sound as though you're a hypocritical tyrant and worse!

What on earth are we going to do about this?' She tossed the offending notebook across the room. Alex lay back on the bed.

'Perhaps I could put out a contract on her?' he joked, half-serious. 'Get one of my psychopathic soldiers to bump her off in all the free time he clearly has?'

Kate smiled ruefully. 'Fat chance. It'd go wrong and she'd write an exposé about that!'

'What about your mother?'

'I don't think she does contract killing, actually Alex.'

'No, no,' Alex smiled tiredly. 'Could she bring pressure to bear on Nicky?' He stared up at the ceiling. 'And perhaps Nicky could influence Serena?'

Kate shrugged. 'We could try, I guess. And what about your journalist friend? The one who works for the *Telegraph*. Any chance he could help?'

'He certainly owes me,' Alex agreed. 'I could give him a bell and see what he suggests . . . Oh, damn!' He hit the pages with the back of his hand. 'I just can't believe it! Damn it, Kate,' he sat up wearily. 'Now do you see what I meant when I said I didn't like them? There's always been something a bit suspect about the twins and their buddies. And in this job, you just have to be careful about who's listening to what. One bad report, one lousy comment in the press and that's it, you're finished. So, next time, do me a favour and just listen to me, will you?'

Kate pulled a face and turned away. But she couldn't argue. This time Alex was right.

Chapter Nine

Hugh didn't come in for supper. Laura had been home for nearly three hours and still there was no sign of him. And this made the third time in a fortnight. She shrugged, making herself a sandwich instead and settling down in front of the television with a book, a magazine and the remote control. Her boots were kicked off to lie haphazardly across the faded persian rug and she lay out along the sofa with a sigh of satisfaction. How nice if Hugh never came home, she thought. Why couldn't some terrorist oblige her, just this once?

Not that she actually wanted another man in his place, right at the moment, she amended. Bill was in her bad books. She hadn't seen even a glimpse of him all day, and he had promised to find her and give her lunch. The suspicion that he was tiring of her gave her a cold, snaking feeling in her belly.

She was tired of all the other men, fooling around, flirting, but none of them having the balls to stand up to Hugh. Men!

Huh! She aimed the remote at the television and changed channel several times rapidly.

She didn't care where Hugh was. Probably out supervising the dismantling of all the stalls, she thought contemptuously. That would be about his speed. He liked to be in charge of petty little things. Major Control Freak. She shifted in annoyance, unable to quite find a comfortable position. So much for Hugh's Big Day.

She wished, suddenly, that she had a dog. A nice, happy, tongue panting, tail wagging retriever. Someone to lie on the sofa with and cuddle but not have to take up to bed. Someone who unfailingly thought she was wonderful. Someone who was always there for her, no matter what. Yes, she thought. She needed a dog . . . or a baby. But that thought was instantly dismissed. She didn't want Hugh's baby and Bill wasn't about to cuckold a brother officer, she could tell.

In fact, Bill had rather a lot of scruples altogether. Pity Hugh didn't throttle her more often. That was the most reaction she had ever had out of Bill. Pity someone didn't throttle Hugh. Or worse . . . Perhaps, just perhaps Bill wasn't going to be the answer she had been looking for? And, she had to admit, she was tired of cold climates and duty and correct form. She was tired of a lot of things. Time to rethink, perhaps? She sighed and punched the pillow on the sofa. Where was Hugh?

Outside, the evening lengthened out into darkening shadows.

'Can't you do something, Mother?' Kate demanded, sitting cross-legged in her dressing gown on the bed, hunched over the receiver. Dimly, she heard her mother protest.

'I don't know! But this wretched girl wouldn't have come here in the first place if you hadn't asked it. As it was, Alex and I had a furious row about it because he can't stand Tim and Nicky – no, he can't, and I'm afraid I now agree with him totally . . .' She paused, listening to her mother's mild soothing tones, her peaceful world obviously still undisturbed even by Kate's demands.

'No, you know we'd never met Serena before . . . Oh my God, you're joking!' Kate closed her eyes, wondering how it was her mother could have neglected to mention the particular tabloid that Serena often worked for on a freelance basis. Well, at least now they knew just how bad it was. 'No, Mother, I really don't think appealing to Serena's better nature would work . . . no.' Kate glanced at Alex, sitting propped up against the pillows, going through their address book to see who they knew and who could help. Their friend from the *Telegraph* had already proved a wash-out. He looked up, his eyebrows shooting skywards at the thought of Serena having a better nature.

Kate's mother, slightly eccentric and stylishly vague, continued to witter in Kate's ear about Serena's articles, Serena's friends (Nicky amongst them), Serena's likes and dislikes, high levels of comfort and low levels of work respectively. Clearly her mother liked and approved of Serena, Kate thought. This was going to be even harder than she had thought.

And tomorrow was the Ball and she had to help with the flower arranging in the morning, especially in view of her own bad behaviour today. No, they had to get this sorted out tonight.

'So, do you have their telephone number in Waterford,

Mother?' she cut across her mother impatiently. 'Could you get in touch with Nicky?'

'But of course, darling. They're staying with good friends of mine there,' Harriet Gordon announced, complacently. 'I arranged it personally.'

'Oh, wonderful! I'm sure Serena's planning an article destroying them as well at this very moment. Your friends and family *will* all appreciate you, Mother.' Kate was sarcastic and her mother paused.

'Do you think so? I don't imagine Jeremy would like that very much.' Mother sounded worried for the first time, Kate noted with satisfaction.

'Bound to be. She seems incapable of realising how disloyal it is to accept someone's hospitality and then write vitriol about them. Is Jeremy someone well-known, by any chance?'

'Jeremy Spender . . .' Mother's voice sounded faint. Kate grinned. How typical. Jeremy Spender, one of the more notorious playboys of the seventies, who had retreated from the public eye after a rather exhibitionist affair with a minor royal, would be a real coup for Serena. People still wondered about him. Some, rather cattily, said he was still living on HRH's money, but of course, Mother said, that wasn't true. It was their mutual great-aunt who had left him sufficient funds to live rather well in Ireland for the rest of his life, not that tedious woman. Mother clearly had a soft spot for Jeremy as well.

'Well, Serena's going to make a killing out of this holiday, isn't she? Perhaps she's going to write an article about you too, Mother? How the snobbocracy live, perhaps?' Pausing to let this sink in, Kate ventured, 'I do think perhaps you'd better see if Nicky has something on Serena that could influence her. Better that than all of us appearing in the tabloids, don't you think?' She heard her mother sigh rather loudly.

'Oh, very well. I can quite see it could be embarrassing and poor Jeremy would never forgive me. He was rather looking forward to having some company, apart from that apathetic wife of his. The son's away in Australia, I gather, so he was quite pleased at the thought of the twins coming over – but Serena is obviously not to be trusted. How tedious . . .' Mother paused. 'I'll give you a call tomorrow, shall I? Let you know how it goes?'

'I think I'd rather hear tonight, Mother, if you don't mind. We do need to sort this out rather quickly, you know. I'll expect you to call in about half an hour, shall I? Or would you rather I called you?'

'Oh, Kate, you are really being rather dull about all this, don't you think?' her mother complained.

'Half an hour, Mother. If you don't mind?' Kate smiled as she put the telephone down. 'Gotcha,' she said aloud.

Stepping out of the glare of The Laughing Donkey's lights into the near pitch black of the country lane, Bill collided with Fergus, who had come to an unexpected halt. Bill lost his footing, stepped sideways into a damp flower-bed and felt his suede brogue sink heavily into mud. He cursed.

'Shh,' Fergus warned him abruptly. 'Look!'

Bill peered into the gloom. 'Can't see a noddy. What's up?' The night was sweet and fresh, smelling of damp earth and growing things. The first real thaw that spring. Bill shrugged as Fergus gripped his arm and pulled him into the deep shadow of the inn's wall.

'There, over by that far cottage. Who does that look like to you?'

Bill peered, dimly saw a couple embracing beside a car, and sighed. What on earth was Fergus getting so het up about? 'No idea. Why?'

'Recognise the car?'

'No . . .' Bill glanced over it idly. Then, suddenly, he looked harder at the couple. Both short, middle-aged, he thought. The man looked squatly familiar. Surely not? 'At least . . . no, it can't be . . .' He turned to smile quizzically at Fergus. 'I mean, who'd have him?'

'Don't know. Can't imagine, either. But that's Hugh's car. I'd recognise the bloody thing anywhere.' It was a rather large, tan Mercedes of uncertain age that Hugh tended to leave parked across two spaces at a time. Since Fergus's parking space was adjacent to Hugh's, it was understandable that he should recognise the car.

'So . . . what's sauce for the goose . . . ?' Bill grinned, feeling relieved suddenly. It was one thing to have been responsible for perhaps destroying a marriage where the husband still cared, but quite another when the man also strayed. In fact, for most of the evening Fergus had been giving Bill rather a hard time about his behaviour with Laura and he had promised Fergus that it was all over, that he was tired of it and feeling wretched. And now, salvation! Hugh was playing the game too. Bill felt as though a huge weight had been lifted from him.

'Who is she? One of the other wives? Or a local?' Fascinated, Bill leaned on Fergus's shoulder only to be shaken off roughly.

'Don't know and don't care. Their marriage is not really my business, nor, so you said earlier, is it yours,' Fergus reminded him sharply. 'The man's a complete knob but he'll get his come-uppance one day, that's for sure.'

'What goes around, comes around?' Bill asked, enjoying his clichés thoroughly. 'I'd love to believe it. In fact, I'd happily do him in if I thought I could get away with it. Clobber him over the head one dark night . . . Oh well, just a thought! Come on, let's go home or Em'll start wondering where you are.'

The couple in the shadows carried on oblivious to their audience and only started apart when a car sped past them, spraying them with water from a puddle. Hugh shook his fist and cursed loudly after it.

'Lord, I hate flowers that won't behave!' Kate threw the offending carnation down. 'And I hate carnations as well.'

'They last well,' Emma replied calmly, twitching her third table arrangement into place and putting it carefully to one side. Kate was still on her first. She tugged at the greenery and tried to hide the bald spot unsuccessfully.

'Yes, but they're thoroughly naff. Oh, hell!' Another piece of greenery broke off. 'Who on earth ordered them?' Kate glowered at the yellow and white carnations filling several buckets near them. Emma, neat and precise as she placed her foliage in exactly the right formation, glanced across at where Amanda was cheerfully tackling one of the very large arrangements.

'Guess,' she murmured. 'Suzy's not great with flowers and Amanda is – needless to say – very experienced. Lots of church flower arranging, I imagine. Besides, there was a very limited budget. So, Amanda said she'd order what was needed and show everyone how to arrange them.'

'You don't need showing. You're good at it.' Kate peered

at Emma's efforts. 'In fact, you're a lot better than Amanda. Why aren't you in charge?'

'Because I've no desire to deprive Amanda of her moment of glory when everyone arrives tonight, gasps at the display, and asks who did it all. Besides, if you offer once, you're suddenly put in charge of it for ever more. I don't mind occasionally but I don't want to do it on a regular basis.'

'Too true! Oh, hallo Olly . . .' Kate paused as a toffee-haired toddler lurched over to her, tripped on several branches and sprawled headlong. Kate caught him just in time. 'There, that was nearly it! Do you think if I did up your shoe it might help?' Oliver burbled happily, urdle, urdle, urdling back to Kate, only a couple of words making vague sense to her.

She sat him down in her lap, did up his shoe buckle firmly, set him back on his feet and sent him tottering back towards his mother, his fat fist waving in the air as he closed his eyes tightly with pleasure and grinned toothily. 'Urdle-urdle-urdle . . . !' he shrieked happily.

Several other young children and babies were spread around the mess drawing room or 'ante-room', as it was known, chasing various sizes of dogs who tussled over rawhide bones, flowers and a couple of velvet cushions. The mess staff tried, in vain, to keep them all in check as the mothers carried on with their flower arranging and gossiping, for the most part oblivious to the mayhem around them. Occasionally a sharp, 'No, Sophie, don't pull Adder's ears,' or, 'Jemma, be nice and share your toy with Toby,' could be heard, but otherwise the children blundered on with only the dogs to keep them in order.

Kate, watching it all with incredulous laughter, turned back to Emma, only to see her wan and dark-eyed.

'Oh Em, I'm so sorry.' Kate was appalled at her own insensitivity. 'I just didn't think. Are you all right?'

'Yes, yes.' Emma forced herself to smile, to grip one hand tightly in the other so that it didn't shake. 'Sometimes it just gets me down, that's all. Don't worry, I'm fine.'

'How's it going with the doctor? Did you get that appointment brought forward?'

'Um, yes, but only by a fortnight. Still, these things take time. They want us to go away for a week or so, to just relax, so we're off as soon as Fergus gets leave. As if I can relax! It's just . . . well. You know . . .' Emma paused and cleared her throat, frowning slightly. 'I just, still, feel like I shouldn't have lost the first one, wouldn't have if . . . if I hadn't fallen . . .'

'I didn't realise you had,' Kate ventured, wishing she could say the right thing, anything that would help.

'Oh yes, I overbalanced when someone pushed past me on the stairs up to Fergus's last office. You know, those concrete fire escape ones.' Emma drew in her breath to continue. 'I fell the entire flight before I could stop myself and I landed heavily on my side and stomach. I was black and blue. The doctors say it's unlikely that caused the miscarriage because it didn't happen until over a week later but, I'm sorry, I do think so.' She glared fiercely around, as though daring anyone to contradict her. Kate wasn't about to.

'Oh, Em! Oh, my God! I'm so sorry. I had no idea. I don't think anyone does.'

'No, well, we didn't tell anyone. At the time we were rather in shock and then, well, what was the point?'

'Did Fergus – I mean, who was it that toppled you? I expect he feels terrible . . .'

'No, not really.' Emma snorted angrily. 'I don't think he

realised at the time, he was so intent on pushing past and going about his business. Later, when Fergus confronted him about it, he denied it, said I was making it all up. Fergus nearly lost control and hit him, but I managed to calm him down. I really don't think Hugh believes he did anything. And as I said, what's the point? The baby's dead. Nothing could bring him back.' She stared down at her hands.

'It was a boy?' Kate ached with sorrow for Emma.

'Yes. Nearly four months old. I thought I was home free.' Emma gave a shaky laugh. 'Sometimes I wake up in the night and I'm confused still with sleep and I think he must be next door in the nursery. And then I remember.' She glanced up at Kate. 'And then I want to go out and kill Hugh.'

It was said calmly and matter-of-factly, but there was a thread of hate there in her tone that made Kate shiver. Suddenly she remembered the Dinner Night and Emma's expression as she watched Hugh. She leaned forward and held Emma's hand.

'Don't. He's not worth shrivelling yourself up inside over. Just look forward to the next one.'

'That's what I told myself, at first,' Emma agreed. 'But now there doesn't seem to be a next one. And Hugh owes me a life. That's how I'm beginning to feel.' She smiled a hard, twisted little smile.

'From what I hear from Alex, you'll have to get in line to bump Hugh off. There are several others ahead of you, for one reason or another . . . So, I repeat, don't let the bloody man get to you. You will have another baby. I know you will.'

'Um, yes, I suppose so . . . Oh, look, here's Laura. Don't tell her. She doesn't know. No one does except you and that's how I'd like to keep it.'

Just at that moment the mess staff brought in a large urn of coffee and two vast trays laden with cups, saucers, heavy silver EPNS milk jugs and sugar bowls, and plate-loads of biscuits. The children scrambled rapidly towards them and were caught and restrained by their mothers until the coffee was safely out of reach and the biscuits passed around. Sergeant Hoskins, in charge of the mess staff, brought Emma a cup himself, smiling broadly at her as though they were best friends. And, it seemed they were, Kate discovered, listening to them chat away about family and animals and past postings.

Emma had been a child, her father the colonel, when Kevin Hoskins had been the colonel's driver. They knew each other well, Emma asking about Jenny and the children, Sergeant Hoskins asking about the old colonel and his lady. They settled down comfortably to discuss which O levels the eldest Hoskins child should choose and Kate slipped away to join Laura.

'What brings you here?' she asked idly, helping herself to a cup of coffee. 'I thought you didn't do flowers – or cakes, or anything.' Kate was feeling suprisingly penitent about the previous day's jolly. She might not care for Amanda personally but she could see that someone had to do these jobs and that it was only fair if she helped out a bit.

'I don't,' Laura shrugged, 'but I was feeling lonely, so I thought I might drop by and see if I could lend a hand.' She dropped her voice, 'Amanda's not speaking to me.'

'Nor to me,' Kate sighed. 'I do feel rather awful, actually, so I'm trying to make amends. You too?'

'Um, a bit, I suppose.' Laura nodded reluctantly. 'And I also thought it wouldn't hurt if Bill saw me doing something for the battalion. I think he's avoiding me, actually.' Kate glanced at her, noting the pale face and slightly depressed hunch to her shoulders. This wasn't like Laura at all.

'It was becoming a bit noticeable, I'm afraid,' Kate told her, 'so I expect someone's had a word and warned him off for the moment. Besides, he's probably worried about Hugh's temper. Taking it out on you, I mean.'

'I don't think Hugh really cares anymore, actually,' Laura said with baffling calm. 'He didn't come back last night until the early hours and when I came into the kitchen this morning and asked where he'd been, he just looked at me in complete silence and carried on eating his toast.' Laura pulled a quizzical face. 'Something tells me he's got someone else.'

'Hugh?' Kate snorted in disbelief.

'Why not? I mean, I must have found him attractive once, somehow or other, or I wouldn't have married him. Maybe someone else fancies him now. Stranger things have happened, you know. Perhaps he'll be the one asking for a divorce and I'll be the one left with no one who'll have me?' She laughed a little self-consciously, and again Kate thought, how odd, this isn't the Laura I know. This Laura seems much more vulnerable, more – likeable. Kate passed her a cup of coffee.

'Nonsense. Endless men are lining up to throw themselves at your feet. I refuse to listen to such drivel. Now, come on, let's go apologise to Amanda. I think we owe it to her. After all, she ended up doing three hours, in all, on the bake stall. Not really fair.'

'Um, well, no thanks. I may feel sorry, but there's a limit to how much grovelling I'm going to do. I'm going to have a chat with Em.'

'Laura?' Kate paused uncertainly. 'Uh, just – be careful

with Emma, won't you? She's feeling terribly fragile about the baby. Try and cheer her up, talk about something light-hearted. Not Hugh, if you know what I mean . . .'

Laura looked surprised. 'Right, okay. I'll see what I can do.' And she wandered off, coffee cup in hand, towards Emma. Kate watched them both with worry. And then, with a sigh, she went to make her peace with Amanda.

Chapter Ten

When Kate got home, at last, the telephone was ringing. She fumbled with her keys, yanking at the door until it finally gave and threw down her bag and parcels as she reached for it. For a moment she thought it was too late.

'Hallo? Hallo?' she said breathlessly.

'Kate?' There was a long pause and Kate suddenly realised it was Nicky calling. She breathed in sharply.

'Yes, Nicky, it's me.'

'Oh, uh, you spoke to your mother, did you?'

'Yes. I gather you feel you can influence Serena enough not to write her spiteful little article. Is that true?'

'Oh, yes, yes, that's no problem. I've got her cold on several rather touchy subjects. She won't publish, I promise.'

'Good.' Kate paused with relief. 'What on earth made you bring her to us, Nicky?' she asked, puzzled. 'You must have known what she'd try and do.'

'Well, no,' Nicky faltered, 'not really. Or I just thought

it'd be a bit of a lark. I didn't think she'd try and ruin Alex's career! I mean, I thought Serena was just, you know, poking a bit of fun at a stuffy institution.'

'And now?' Kate asked icily but Nicky was going off at a tangent. One that clearly mattered to her.

'Besides, Serena's met Kit Spender – Jeremy's son. He came back unexpectedly early from Australia. Anyway, they went off somewhere together early this morning . . .' Nicky's discontent was obvious. 'So, I wouldn't worry. She doesn't want to rock any boats at the moment. Your mother spoke to her last night, and I think offered to smooth things over with Jeremy as long as Serena behaved herself. Not that disappearing with Kit is exactly behaving – I mean, he's always been my particular friend, you know, and the way she muscled in there, tossing her hair and fluttering her eyelashes . . . Anyway, it's all very boring but I'm sorry if we messed you about.'

Kate grinned to herself. Nicky would never have bothered to ring and apologise if Mother hadn't insisted, she thought. Mother had surprising clout when she could be bothered to exert it. 'You did, Nicky, and very badly. I think you owe Alex the apology, though. It was his career on the line and in case you hadn't noticed, it does rather matter to him! Why don't you ring later, around six, and talk to him then.' She sounded cool and remote.

'Well, all right,' the reluctance was obvious, 'if you think I should.'

'I do. Especially if you want your car back sometime. Otherwise you might just find a stray tank has run over it.' Kate was firm. 'Anyway, I've got to run. Speak to you later. Bye.' Good, she thought, putting down the receiver. That was one problem sorted out. If only Emma's and Laura's were as easy. She sighed and carried the shopping into the kitchen and began to unpack.

It was four o'clock. Plenty of time to sit and soak in a bath and have a long glass of wine before getting ready for tonight, she thought with pleasure. Idly, she wondered where Alex was. Working, no doubt. When wasn't he?

And then she realised that she hadn't checked to see if his dinner jacket was clean and pressed or if he had a shirt ironed. Knowing Alex, neither, she thought with a sigh, and then he'd hop around in a panic trying to do everything at once with only ten minutes to spare. Better if she went and sorted it out now. Humming to herself, she climbed the stairs.

They were due at seven for drinks and it was just past that as the Kennedys left their house. Fergus hesitated as he helped Emma into the old Volvo estate they had bought in expectation of there being a larger number of them in the near future. Emma's large skirts were folded and packed into the foot space, springing back again where the net underskirts refused to lie down.

Fergus made sure she was settled comfortably, shut the door and went around to his own side of the car. Settling in heavily and pulling the seat belt across him, he glanced at her again, seeing the paleness that make-up had done nothing to alter, the contained pain. He breathed in deeply.

'I'm thinking about leaving,' he said baldly. Emma, shocked, turned to look at him.

'Leaving . . . ?' Her eyes were wide. 'The army?' Not for a moment had she even thought he meant leaving her. Fergus and all his friends constantly discussed 'leaving', and everyone knew just what they meant. 'But you love it. Why?'

'So we can have a decent life together in one place, have several children and see them grow up around us, not shunted off to boarding school, or dragged from one garrison town to another. So you can have a house you cherish and a garden where you'll stay put long enough to see one of the roses you plant actually flower. Oh,' he sighed, 'and for me too, I suppose. I'm not sure if there's much future left in the army. Not with all these cuts going on.

'You know, several of my men aren't even going to make it through the Junior NCO's cadre before they're axed? All that bloody hard work and commitment for what? Treasury-driven cuts that'll have to be reversed the moment things go wrong and then we won't have any trained troops. It's enough to make you sick.'

'Oh, sweetheart,' Emma reached over and smoothed the dark brown hair, with its first flecks of grey, back from his forehead, 'I know. I know how you feel but don't rush anything, all right? We've still got to do this stint in Belfast, no matter what. Why don't you wait and see how you feel about it all when we've been here longer?' She caressed the creases around his eyes, the smooth, hard plane of his cheek. His skin was a deep, wind-blown brown from all the time he had spent out of doors readying his men for the cadre.

He looked so handsome to her, in black tie, the snowy folds of his shirt contrasting against his weathered skin. Still very much the good-looking, considerate man she had married. She put both arms around him and kissed him, feeling him pull her in tightly against him.

'I love you, Emma,' he murmured, gruffly, 'and I can't bear to see you so unhappy. Tell me what I can do.'

'Oh, darling, I know, but I can't help it. And there's

nothing you can do. I just . . . I wanted our baby so much. I loved him. And Hugh killed him. I can't forgive him for that. I just can't.' She turned to Fergus and saw he was as devastated as she. 'I don't know what to do about it. If only I could get pregnant again and have something to look forward to . . .'

'You will, sweetheart, you will. You just have to let yourself relax,' Fergus coaxed.

'I try, but then I see Hugh swaggering by or I hear from Laura that he's done something else unspeakable, and I feel all the rage inside me boil up again . . . Why on earth couldn't he be axed, with all these cuts? Or sent to Bosnia and blown up on a mine-field? Why always people you like? Never the toads like Hugh?'

'That's another good reason for me to leave, then.' Fergus said grimly. 'So you won't have to see his bloody face ever again. I'll sort it out, darling. Don't you worry. I'll take care of things,' he soothed and stroked her hair, brushing the hovering tears carefully from her lashes so that her mascara would not streak. 'Shh,' he cradled her against him, 'shh.'

Sergeant Hoskins was standing by the door of the Officers' Mess, directing several of his staff to take coats and wraps, offer champagne or Bucks Fizz, and show guests the seating plan for dinner. Once they knew where their tables were, the guests wandered through into the ante-room where people were gathered beforehand for drinks.

A huge flower arrangement in an antique blue and white porcelain bowl filled the circular hall table, and around it, carved into the old mahogany of the table were the names of all the officers who had passed through the mess since the Peninsula Wars. Several guests lingered, admiring it, tracing the names of famous Generals and the occasional Field Marshal who had carved their names as young subalterns. The table was history in and of itself.

Laura didn't pause. She smiled at Sergeant Hoskins briefly, collected a glass and sailed on through in search of Bill. Hugh grunted angrily, ignoring everyone around him, and followed after her, unaware of the cold, hard stare the sergeant gave him. Hugh was rarely aware of anyone but himself and certainly never considered the mess staff. If he could have read Sergeant Hoskin's mind, it would have shaken him deeply. Instead, Hugh was thinking about Laura.

He had no desire to be with her that night, he realised, but he would not allow her to humilate him again. So, much like a determined terrier worrying over a bone that he no longer wanted but refused to allow any other dog to have, he trailed after her, glowering furiously. Her shocking pink mini-dress, draped over one slim shoulder and revealing long, long legs, flitted amongst the dark jackets of the men, forever, elusively, out of reach.

Everyone was there. Suzy and Joss were holding court near the blazing fire, the huge mantelpiece banked with flowers and greenery, as they entertained the more senior guests and several of their own who had come to stay. Dressed in black velvet sweeping down to the ground, with unexpectedly large diamonds draping her bosom and sparkling in her ears, Suzy looked both pretty and regal at the same time.

Joss smiled at her, admiring the effortless way she had organised both the evening and the guests they had staying. She was a good girl, he decided, and looked pretty wonderful tonight. She caught his eye fondly. This would be their last ball while he commanded the battalion. Rather a poignant moment for him. She smiled with understanding and, reaching out, gave his arm a quick squeeze.

Amanda, dressed in brightly checked Thai silk with a black velvet bodice and huge silk leg-of-mutton sleeves, her hair drawn up into a roll, was wearing pearls, of course. No one had ever seen her wear anything else. Jewels were too gaudy for her pale skin, she explained with a brittle laugh and besides, she loved her pearls too much to ever take them off. The fact that she couldn't afford real jewels and wouldn't dream of wearing fakes was not mentioned. The pearls faded into insignificance in the glamour of the evening but Amanda was happy enough with all the praise the flowers were attracting.

Emma, revived after a couple of glasses of champagne, was flushing prettily with the attention of several of the younger officers who all adored her and hoped they would one day find someone as lovely and sweet as Emma herself. Tightly boned into dark green silk, huge skirts sweeping out from a tiny waist, and her bodice and arms covered in dark green lace, she was causing quite a stir. Emeralds, that had belonged to Fergus's grandmother, glinted at her ears but she wore nothing at all around her throat, the dress decoration enough itself. Fergus stood protectively beside her until it became obvious to him that he was no longer needed and then he melted into the throng.

Bill was part of a rowdy crowd near the french doors leading out to the marquee where dinner would be served. His normally tousled hair had been slicked back wetly and his face was brown and creased with laughter as usual. Smart wing-collars slightly impeded his head-turning ability as he casually scanned the crowd for Laura, caught sight of her briefly and immediately looked away. Out of sight, he told himself, out of mind. But the thumping of his heart, the deep hollow feeling in his stomach, refused to be quietened. He glanced back again, frowning.

Kate, entering at that moment, saw Bill's face and read it easily. She nudged Alex beside her. 'Bill's pining, I'm afraid. Look,' and Alex reluctantly agreed as he followed her gaze.

'I was hoping he'd come to his senses where Laura's concerned. That's a pile of trouble just waiting to come down on his head, that whole affair.'

'Poor Bill. And poor Laura. What a mess!'

'What? No "poor Hugh" as well? Shame on you, Kate, your good nature is slipping.'

'After what Emma told me, all I can hope is that Hugh takes a short walk off a long drop!'

'And I'll happily add the final push,' Alex replied icily.

He couldn't help searching for Laura himself amongst the dark jacketed throng and, having located her, mentally comparing her flamboyance to Kate's quiet elegance. Each to their own, he thought, but could not in any way find the clashing exuberance of the red hair and pink mini-dress enticing, nor the wild character either.

He glanced down at Kate, silver blonde hair flowing over her bare shoulders and her body draped in an ice blue silk slip that followed gentle undulations to her ankles, hinting rather than proclaiming her sexuality. Aquamarines, set in a chunky, modern choker and earrings, reflected in eyes as blue as cornflowers. Alex found her far more to his taste and wondered briefly if he was in danger of becoming smug in his happiness with Kate. But he couldn't help it. He kissed her fingers lightly.

'I suppose we should mingle?'

'With this many gorgeous men around? Of course we should mingle, Alex!' Kate teased him and slipped from his side to join a group nearby. Alex sighed, shrugged and turned good-humouredly towards another. Thank heavens they had no guests to entertain this time, he thought. At least they could leave when they wanted – or stay until breakfast at dawn. He swallowed the champagne quickly and reached out a hand at a passing tray, smiling at a mess waiter. 'How are you all coping, Corporal Riley? Not too many hysterics in the kitchen?' The corporal grinned conspiratorially.

'Don't eat the first course, sir. It fell on the floor and had to be scraped up. Just a word to the wise, sir.' They nodded at each other and passed on.

'Alex? I thought that was you! I hear you're about to take over a company. Well done!' Alex's previous colonel reached out a proprietorial arm and patted Alex's back. 'Come and tell me all about it.'

'That's not all I'd like to discuss, actually, sir. I've got a bit of a problem with a report Hugh's drafted . . .'

And Kate, glancing around, saw Alex deep in conversation and oblivious to the stir in the women around him. He was generally oblivious, Kate realised with fond amusement. Only the really pushy or the truly stunning seemed to pierce Alex's armour. She wondered briefly which she was. Maybe a mixture, she hoped? Because there was no doubt in her mind that, from the moment she was first introduced to Alex, she had wanted him for her own. And been determined to have him. She turned back into the crowd, smiling wryly at herself.

The carved ice waterfall in the centre of the buffet tables, banked with flowers and a crystal pavilion was causing a huge amount of excitement as they all filtered into the marquee looking for their tables. Half lobsters, stuffed with crab, roast beef, pinkly glistening in wafer-thin folds, carved turkeys and game hens, terrines of baby vegetables and salmon roulades, pâté de fois gras and baskets of freshly baked rolls and endless platters of other culinary delights bore testimony to how hard the chefs had worked. Kate drew in her breath in astonishment. She had never, ever, seen a display like it.

The pillars that supported the green and white striped tent were wrapped in garlands of yellow and white flowers and the starched white damask-draped tables each bore sparkling silver candelabra with dark green candles, snowy folded napkins, gleaming silver and crystal and yet more flowers. It was a staggeringly impressive sight. Oohs and aahs of delight echoed around the marquee.

'Enjoy it while you may,' Emma whispered in Kate's ear, having come up behind her unheard. 'The catering staff are going too, you know. A civil firm's taking over. And they won't be able or willing to do this sort of presentation. So this will be one of the last you'll ever see.'

'But it's only my first,' Kate protested. 'How unfair! What happens to all the chefs then?'

'Same as all the rest – redundancy and dole queue if they can't find work quickly. Pretty grim for them and maybe for us too, who knows? Ah well, let's enjoy this one, shall we? Ooh, look, aren't these wonderful!' And Emma idly poached a tiny asparagus quiche from the spread and popped it in her mouth. 'I must say, I'm absolutely starving looking at all these goodies. Come on, let's go and find the table fast and hope we're some of the first ones to be called,' she urged, sweeping down the narrow passages between the tables with her enormous skirts. Kate followed, eyebrows raised. Emma seemed much happier suddenly, she thought, as though something had been resolved in her mind. Or perhaps it was just the champagne?

There was a jazz band after dinner and a disco down in one of the sitting rooms for the more lively and fit, the walls draped artistically in arctic camouflage nets. Alex and Kate emerged after twenty minutes, exhausted from the strobe lights and determined to find a quiet corner outside to enjoy the stars together. It was not to be. They came to an amazed halt outside the french doors, surveying the scene with laughter.

'I can't believe they've got a bucking bronco! Who on earth ordered that? I'll bet there'll be some split trousers tonight!'

'Lucky it's not mess kit. No one would even manage to climb on that thing, let alone ride it. Oh look, typical! There's Henry, playing the rodeo rider for all the girls to ooh and aah at!' Kate followed Alex's gesture and was amused to see that Henry's trousers were, indeed, split, revealing multi-coloured boxer shorts and a flash of inside thigh. His invited guest for the night, wearing a very short gold lamée dress, was cheering him on from the sidelines.

'She's not wearing anything under that dress. Have you noticed?' Amanda could be heard demanding of some poor long-suffering guest. 'Not even tights. I really don't think dresses like that should be allowed. And look at that tattoo on her shoulder!' Henry's girl screamed with laughter as Henry went flying, nose down, onto the mattresses around him and Amanda huffed noisily and retreated inside again. Alex grinned at Kate.

'I think what Amanda really means is, girls like that should not be allowed. And she may have a point. That dress could cause a riot. But Henry likes his girls – raunchy, shall we say? Oh no,' his tone changed from indulgent amusement to foreboding, 'look, Laura's climbing up. Hugh'll have a fit.' But there was no arguing with Laura, for all Bill was trying. She shook him off, kicked her shoes loose and, tossing her pink chiffon scarf over his head, climbed nimbly into the saddle and brought her long legs up into jockey position. She wrapped the reins around her hand and looked calmly at the bronco's operator, nodding her head just once.

There was something remarkably competent about the way Laura sat the bronco as it began to tilt, gently at first and then increasingly wildly. She seemed to float above it, one long arm held out above her head to balance herself, as she gave the performance of the evening. Every eye was riveted upon her, not all oblivious to the way her pink mini-dress had risen up her smooth thighs. The cheers became louder with every passing second.

After five minutes of keeping her seat, despite the wild gyrations and every trick the operator could think to throw at her, the beast came to a gentle halt, to thunderous applause. Laura threw one leg over its head and slid gracefully down to the ground and into Bill's arms.

She laughed delightedly and kissed Bill blatantly on the lips before he could move back. Around her there was a sudden collective indrawing of breath. 'Oh Laura, sweetheart,' Bill murmured, catching her hands together in his and pushing her away, 'what are you thinking of?'

But before he could lead her into the shadows and out of the view of nearly half the mess, Hugh had surged forward, gripped him by the shoulder, and swung him around. Laura was flung to one side as Hugh backhanded Bill soundly across the face and Bill sagged back onto the grass. There was a stunned silence around them and then Alex and Fergus threw themselves forward, each to restrain Bill before he could climb to his feet and grapple Hugh. From the look on Bill's face, they were only just in time.

Hugh stared down at Bill in disgust.

'Oh, very convenient, Ovington! But then, we all know you're all bluster and no show, don't we?' Hugh wiped his hand down his trouser leg and started to turn away, eyeing Laura with fury but not making any attempt to help her up or take her home with him.

'You're dead, Hugh,' Bill ground out furiously as he shook himself to free his captors. 'Just you wait! You're dead!' But Alex and Fergus hung on grimly, dragging Bill away before Joss could notice the fracas. Hugh sauntered off, smiling tightly to himself.

'God, what an evening,' Alex sighed as he climbed into bed beside Kate and snuggled in against her. 'Bill must be mad. He'll get transferred, just you watch. And it certainly won't be a promotion. More like watch-keeper in South Georgia, I expect. Joss won't stand for that sort of thing in the battalion. And as for Hugh . . . God knows what'll happen there. I've never heard of anything like it!'

'Laura precipitated it, didn't you notice? I mean, she did it deliberately.' Kate's tone was dry. 'I think she felt Bill was cooling off and if she didn't do something to make it impossible for him to back down, she'd lose him. So she made it obvious to everyone, so that even Hugh couldn't ignore it anymore.'

'So now Hugh'll divorce her and what . . . ? Is Bill going to marry her? Is that what she thinks?'

'Could be.' Kate shrugged. 'I don't know. Laura doesn't confide a great deal. At least, not to me. Maybe to Emma. Speaking of which, did you see how much happier Em was looking? As though, well . . . could she be?'

'What?'

'Pregnant, Alex!'

'I thought she wasn't . . . you know . . . ovulating?' Alex heard Kate sigh beside him.

'Um, you're probably right. I just thought she looked – better, relieved or something. But it was probably just all the drink that loosened her up a little.' Kate sighed again. 'Actually, that's a point. She wouldn't be drinking if she were pregnant, would she? Oh well . . .' She paused. 'I do hope Bill doesn't do anything silly.' She rolled against Alex and wormed her way into the crook of his arm. 'You don't think he will, do you?'

'Bill? Quite possibly.' Alex sighed. 'He's a bit volatile to begin with and no one would take a slap in the face like that happily. I wanted to jail him, to keep him safe, but Henry promised to keep an eye on him instead. Besides, I really have no authority to do such a thing and it would make it all official that way . . . Christ, I hope he doesn't go after Hugh . . .'

'He won't, darling, I'm sure.' Kate kissed Alex's cheek and turned off the light. 'He's not totally insane, and neither is Laura. It'll all be fine in the morning, you'll see.'

They lay comfortably together in the dark, drifting gently towards sleep until Alex's bleeper made a shrill noise from the dressing table and Alex groaned. Kate kept her eyes shut, ignoring it, while Alex called in. Then with an even deeper sigh, she heard him say, 'Right, I'll be there in fifteen minutes. Is the girl all right? And you've got Tomkins locked up, I hope?' He listened, sighed again, and replaced the receiver. Turning to look at Kate, he shrugged.

'One of the boys beat up his girlfriend for playing around on him. Her parents are demanding to see me, right now. I'll have to go in.' He grimaced, leaned over and kissed Kate, and started to dress.

'Do you think it's something in the air over here?' Kate asked idly, her eyes still shut. Alex grunted.

'Just good old sex, as usual.'

'Chance would be a fine thing!'

Alex grinned. 'Keep that thought in mind. I'll be right back!'

Chapter Eleven

In the chill night air, Hugh's footfalls could be heard distinctly, chipping at the hard surface of the back lane between the camp and the officers' quarters. The sound echoed in the stillness of that particularly dead hour between two and three in the morning when few, if any, were abroad. There were none that morning. Hugh shivered.

He had wanted to leave earlier but refused to lose face. So he had stood at the bar, drinking one whiskey after another, staring down anyone who glanced at him, nothing making much impact upon the fog of anger swirling in his brain. No one had approached him. No one had sought to take his arm and cajole him to go home, to calm down, to sleep it off. Once they might have done but Bill was popular in the mess and Hugh was not.

He didn't know where Laura was. Home perhaps. Or, more probably, still pouring out her miseries to Emma yet again. Hugh's hand clenched involuntarily. How was he expected to feel, knowing Emma knew all their personal secrets, that his wife was indiscreet about every embarrassing detail of their daily lives? He wasn't sorry Emma had overbalanced and fallen. Stupid, interfering, patronising bitch that she was, she deserved everything she got. Hugh gave a throat-clearing sound of disgust, his breath fogging out in the clear night air for a moment.

Half the stupid notions Laura had were of Emma's making, he had no doubt. And that bloody Fergus looking down his nose all the time, threatening him for having knocked his wife down when he hadn't touched the bloody woman . . . well, barely. Could he help it if the stupid woman didn't think to hold on to the railings? It hadn't been on purpose. And he still wasn't sure the fall had caused the miscarriage. Not his fault, that was for sure! For all they were trying to blame him.

Not to mention Alex . . . the look in his eyes these days, such contempt, such disgust. How dare he! Who did he think he was? Hugh cleared his throat at the rising bile. Well, perhaps, by now, Alex knew about the complaint he, Hugh, had made about Alex, his sloppy habits, his casual attitude, his high-handedness. Oh yes, that report could do a lot to damage the blue-eyed boy's sky-rocketing career!

Rage curdled sickeningly in Hugh's stomach and he had to pause and throw up into the bushes. He wiped the back of his hand across his mouth and lurched on again, breathing deeply through his nose to still the nausea. He wouldn't think about Alex, thrusting his way ahead, getting promotions early, just because he was the right sort, had married the right sort, the sort the regiment liked. He wouldn't end up a passed-over major, oh no, but . . . if that report got through all right . . . Who knew? Hugh spat again.

Bill, he didn't really care about. Bill was just a stupid pawn of Laura's, thoroughly twisted around her crooked little finger but he had overstepped the mark tonight, Hugh thought savagely. That cosy little trio, two of them smug with their perfect little wives and one trying to take another man's wife away and everyone condoning it, looking the other way! It was unbelievable!

Bill would have been shipped off to the Falklands or points further south if it had been anyone else's wife, but no, it was only Hugh. Hugh who wasn't good enough for the regiment, who didn't fit, whom everyone looked down on. So, go ahead, take Hugh's wife. What the hell!

He lurched again, looking up at the dark cavern of sky overhead, branches etched, one blackness over another, as they stretched to touch each other along the avenue of trees. Staggering around in a circle, head thrown back, his eyes focused on one particular star. It blurred and danced in his vision. Well, fuck'em, he thought with rage. He'd lay a formal complaint against all of 'em in the morning. Colonel Joss too! Maybe he was passed-over, maybe he wasn't the same sort, he thought with corrosive self-pity, but he could still make their lives hell.

Joss couldn't look the other way then. And he'd start divorce proceedings. He didn't need Laura anymore. Not now he'd found Jenny. Jenny, Jenny . . . she was the woman for him, not some stupid, strident, wild bitch like Laura. Bill could have her, if he wanted, if he was mad enough to take her on. But not before he, Hugh, had made sure Bill's career was over. Joss couldn't walk away from this one. Oh, no! He'd go over Joss's head. Go to the brigadier. Or higher if necessary. Hugh laughed as he spun around.

And then he came to an abrupt halt, rocking from side to

side as he peered into the gloom. 'Who's there?' he called harshly. 'Come out, I can see you! Come out and show yourself!'

There was nothing, just the swaying of the trees in the wind, the dark undergrowth shivering lightly. He grunted and turned around, moving on again down the lane, still stumbling from time to time. Maybe he wouldn't go home, he thought suddenly. Why go home? What was the point? He'd go to Jenny.

Nice, comfortable Jenny who understood him so well and thought he was wonderful, looked up to him, did everything he said without question. Jenny, whose no-good husband was away on duty all night, he'd made sure of that! What a shame he couldn't have taken her along to the ball, she'd have loved that . . . but that would have caused a terrible stink, finished his career for good . . . not that Laura hadn't already done her best there!

Yes. He halted again. He'd go to Jenny's house. It wasn't far. Just a couple of streets away on the far side of the patch. No one need see him, if he was careful. Sod Laura, he wasn't going home to her!

He spun around to retrace his steps and cried out suddenly in startled fear. And then a blow came whistling down, brutally clubbing him across his face and the stars seemed to spin out and explode in the darkness. He sank to his knees. Dimly he saw the arm raised again and beyond it, lit slightly by the moonlight, a face he knew but twisted with such rage and disgust that fear crashed through him, thundering into his chest as he gaped upward in astonishment and horror.

He frowned and cried out desperately, 'No! Don't, please!' but the arm was already coming down and his words never made it from his mouth, ending instead, abruptly, as the blow ended all thought, all life . . .

Hugh stared sightlessly up at the branches and sky above, a look of shocked surprise on what was left of his face. The only sound was the gentle crunch of footsteps moving quickly away and, then, just the sighing of the trees in the wind.

An early morning jogger found the body. One of the NCOs, hoping to clear his head and refresh himself before work, came upon the dew-sodden bundle at just a few minutes past six in the morning. He recognised Major Mallory instantly, despite the blood obscuring the face, the mouth open with a shocked, fish-like expression, the eyes staring glassily upwards. Major Mallory was well known and well disliked by most of the NCOs and men who had worked with him in the past. Corporal Evans stood still, looking down into Hugh's face. He didn't attempt to touch him, to feel for a pulse. He knew a dead body when he saw one. Then he turned and sprinted for the guard room.

By the time Alex was roused at 6:20am, the body was roped off and a guard of four soldiers placed to prevent anyone from tampering with it or the surrounding area. Already the police were on their way and Joss, the RSM, and Alex were roused and informed. Alex groaned, the phone cradled against his ear as his fingers scrubbed the sleep from his face. 'Oh, Jesus, no,' Kate heard him whisper into the receiver. She sat up abruptly, a feeling of foreboding rippling through her as she saw Alex close his eyes.

'Anyone see anything? No, I suppose not. All right,' he sighed, 'yes, I'm on my way. Give me fifteen minutes. Thanks, Sergeant Riley.' With a groan, Alex replaced the phone on the beside table and flung back the covers. The chill air struck his bare legs and he shivered. Glancing over at Kate as he reached for his trousers and hurriedly pulled them on, he wished desperately that he could just lie back down in the billowing warmth of the duvet, bury himself against Kate's smooth body. He felt sick from too little sleep and too much alcohol, let alone this discovery.

Instead he stood up and stared at the gaunt face reflected in the dressing table mirror. The dark blue eyes were cold and still.

'Hugh's dead,' he said tersely. 'Murdered somewhere out in the lane in the early hours. Bludgeoned across the head. Corporal Evans just found him.'

Kate covered her face with her hands, her breath suddenly sucked away with the horror of it all. She had seen Hugh only a few hours ago, walking around, ranting, his usual bragging self. And now, suddenly, he was no more. Just a thing. A body. And soon that would go in the ground and he would be no more. She shook her head, numb with shock, cradling the pillow in her arms for warmth. Her eyes searched Alex's questioningly.

'Bill? My God, it couldn't have been, could it?' she whispered.

Ashen-faced, Alex shook his head. 'No. It wasn't Bill. I know Bill. He wouldn't do this. He wouldn't.' But Alex's fingers were trembling as he tried to fasten his belt and he had to hold them out and steady them with conscious will.

'Are you all right, Alex?' Kate's brow puckered with worry. 'You look terrible . . . what time did you finally get back last night? I'm sorry, I fell asleep . . .'

'I'm not sure, really. Late, anyway . . . maybe two, two-thirty. And I went down the lane too, but by bike. Maybe

Hugh was already lying there in the undergrowth, dead, and I just passed him without noticing . . .' Alex shook his head.

'My God! Then . . . you could have seen the murderer! Did you notice anyone?'

'No. Not a soul about.' Alex shivered again. 'I guess I should be glad it wasn't me . . .'

Kate looked at him slowly. 'You don't think this was a random killing, do you? I assumed . . . you know, that it had to be someone with a grudge against Hugh.'

'Probably. It's too early to say. I'm just glad I went by bike. The guard room will have me booked out and the guards at this gate will remember me coming in. The whole journey couldn't have taken more than two or three minutes . . .' he trailed off, giving her a wry grimace. 'It's unlikely I could have killed Hugh in that time and still made it back here. At least, I hope that's what the police will think.'

'You really think you'll need an alibi?' Kate was aghast, her eyes widening as she grappled with this new angle.

'I think everyone's going to need an alibi, quite frankly, since just about everyone loathed Hugh.'

'Not enough to kill him! That's a bit extreme, isn't it?' Kate had sat up, clutching the covers to her naked body and her hair fell forward over one shoulder. She was oblivious to how seductive she looked. Alex smiled awkwardly and twitched the covers over her, not wanting to be distracted.

'Of course it's extreme. But so is living in these hot-house conditions, everyone on top of each other, working, living, cheek-by-jowl, everyone on edge as the Peace gets more and more fragile . . . It's causing enormous strain even between close friends. With someone as difficult and obnoxious as Hugh . . . well, it looks like someone's control finally snapped.' Alex sighed and turned away.

'Does Laura know yet? Oh, lord, I should go around and stay with her. Make sure she's all right.' Kate stumbled out of bed, hunting wildly for something to throw over her nakedness, oblivious to anything but the need to see Laura. Alex shrugged.

'Suzy will go, with the padre. To tell her. But Laura won't care,' he replied curtly. 'She'll be relieved, I expect. As long as Bill doesn't get charged for it, that is. Who knows, maybe she did it herself.' He briskly scraped the stubble from his chin, cursing when he nicked himself, and then plunged his face and hair into the basin of water.

'Don't be ridiculous, Alex! Hugh was strong – a woman couldn't have done it! And Laura wouldn't!' Kate snapped quickly in reply, but inside herself a small voice was wondering just that. She watched Alex give her a half-smile, wearily towelling himself off and slicking back his hair with his brushes.

'He was drunk, Kate. I'd say anything's possible right now.' He sighed. 'God, what a mess! Hugh struck Bill in front of fifty or more witnesses last night and Bill said "You're dead, Hugh." You remember?' He grimaced at Kate, seeing her eyes widen in recollection. 'And this morning Hugh is just that. Dead . . . Even if Bill didn't do it, he's going to have a hell of a job getting out of this one. Oh, shit! This is really all we need with the Peace as shaky as it is . . . and Bill's the Ops officer!' And with that Alex grabbed his combat smock and threw it on, kissed Kate briefly and was gone, thundering down the stairs two at a time. Kate heard the front door slam behind him.

But Bill certainly wasn't the only one to threaten Hugh's

life, Kate remembered guiltily. Emma had said Hugh owed her a life only the afternoon before. And Fergus looked at Hugh as though he could easily kill him for Emma and the baby's sake. How many others felt the same way for one grievance or another? There was a rumour that one of the NCOs had, in the past, ground up shrimp and put it in Hugh's food while on exercise, knowing full well that Hugh was allergic to shellfish . . . Bill, Laura, Emma, Fergus . . . Lord, even Alex had made remarks about knocking Hugh off in the past, particularly if that damaging report came out . . . so how many others in the battalion could join the list of possible suspects? And how was the battalion going to survive tearing itself apart in its search for the killer?

She sat at the dressing table, staring blankly at the face before her, mechanically brushing her hair while her mind scurried around in circles. Was a wife considered a good enough alibi? Because most of the suspects would have only that.

She put her brush down, fiddling with the crystal stopper of the perfume bottle, tap-tap-tapping it as she mentally relived the hours before Hugh's death. But nothing stood out, nothing occurred to her – except for the fight between Hugh and Bill. Afterwards, Bill had disappeared with Henry – to nurse his grievances, no doubt. And Laura had left with Emma and Fergus. And perhaps an hour after that, she and Alex had gone home. Leaving Hugh alone at the bar . . .

She jumped in alarm as the telephone shrilled beside the bed. Kate hesitated between running after Alex, in case it was for him, and answering it. Finally, she shook herself, and went to pick up the receiver. 'Yes?'

'Kate? It's me, Emma. You've heard?'

'Yes, Alex is on his way over right now,' she sighed.

'Oh, Emma! I just can't believe it! Does Laura know yet?'

'I expect so . . .' Emma's voice sounded hesitant. 'I thought she might like us to go over, but I don't want to intrude. What do you think?'

'I think if she wants to see anyone, it'll be you.' Kate shrugged, before volunteering, 'But I'll come too if you like – and go away again if she doesn't want me.'

'Would you, Kate? Thanks! Look, I'll see you outside in five minutes – if that's long enough? They may shut off the phones, to stop people spreading the news until more is known and Hugh's family are contacted, so don't be surprised if you get cut off shortly. It's fairly standard practice when there's a death in the battalion. I'm surprised they're still on, in fact. Fergus will have them shut off any minute, I expect.'

'Fergus?'

'Yes, he's Ops 1.'

'Really? I didn't know.' Operations 1, in charge of the security of the camp and ready to be deployed in two hours in case of trouble, in case the Peace came crashing to an end. Each of the companies rotated through the four states of readiness. Fergus was it, right now. And so Hugh was also his immediate responsibility. Kate nodded.

'All right, I'll go now. Oh! One last thing . . . Does anyone know if Bill . . . you know . . . has an alibi?' There was silence for a moment and Kate wondered what Emma was thinking. Was she glad Hugh was dead? Did it make up for the baby? Or was she as sickened as everyone else?

'I don't know. But Bill didn't do it. I know that,' Emma replied firmly. She sounded much like Alex, Kate thought. Almost sure. Almost . . .

'No, of course not. But he'll have to prove it—' But suddenly Kate's telephone line went dead and she stared at it in confusion for a split second before realising what had happened. Which was all for the best. What was the point in speculating when no one knew anything yet? Quickly she gathered up a sweater and slung it over her shoulders. Time to go.

Laura's house had three cars drawn up outside and the lights were blazing in the windows. Emma pulled a face. 'Maybe we're intruding . . . ?'

'Then let's ask,' Kate replied firmly as she raised her hand to knock sharply on the door. 'They'll send us away if we're not wanted or needed, but at least Laura will know we came.'

Reluctantly, Emma nodded and when the door was answered by Father Ralph, the padre, they were quickly ushered in. 'Good girls! I'm so glad you've come! Laura's in need of some company, and she said a few minutes ago that she wished you two were with her.' He hesitated for a moment before clearing his throat and continuing. 'I'm afraid I must be going and I think Mrs Mailer-Howatt would rather leave Laura in good hands. She really shouldn't be left to – to . . . grieve, alone, at this time,' he murmured as they stood in the hall.

Emma smiled quickly, nervously, nodding her head, agreeing. But Kate wondered if the padre was as naive as he pretended. Something about those shrewd, light grey eyes made her suspect otherwise.

They followed the padre into the sitting room where Suzy sat beside Laura on the sofa. She glanced up with quick relief when Emma went forward to put an arm around

Laura. Laura, still in her dressing gown, her face smudged with mascara stains, was sitting cradling a cup of tea in her hands. She smiled dimly at Emma and Kate, and swallowed hard.

'Hiya. I hoped you'd be round. Kind've hard to take in at the moment.' She giggled uncertainly, as though embarrassed, then sipped at her tea again. With her fiery head bowed like that, it was impossible to gauge her mood. Happy, relieved that Hugh was no more? Shocked and grieving for the man she had once loved? Or simply indifferent? Laura gave no hint, hugging her secrets to herself as she hugged the mug of tea.

Suzy caught Kate's eyes and fractionally raised her eyebrows. Kate nodded.

'Well,' Suzy began brightly before remembering she should tone it down a bit, 'if there's anything I can do, Laura, just let me know. I'll drop by again later in the day. But I think you'd probably prefer to be with Emma and Kate, just now, wouldn't you?'

Suzy had half-risen and hesitated as Laura seemed to dredge inside herself for the polite words of release. Eventually they came.

'Yes, of course, Suzy. I'm fine, really,' Laura looked up, tucking a wild, escaping strand of hair behind her ears as though to damp it down. 'Thanks for coming by. I'll speak to you later. And you, Father Ralph.' She looked away, wary of his eyes. 'Thank you for – for, um, breaking the news. You were very kind.' Smiling uncertainly at no one in particular, she lapsed back into the numbness of a moment ago, hunched forward over her tea.

Kate saw the others to the door, thanked them, and let them out. How strange, she thought to herself, as she returned to the sitting room. Laura had never done anything with propriety in her life and now, on Hugh's death, when she could with most justification have gone to pieces, she remembered her social graces perfectly. Kate couldn't help glancing at Laura speculatively, wondering just how numb she actually was.

But Emma was gently taking the cup from Laura's hands and offering to fill it again and Laura was shaking her head. Kate forgot her momentary disquiet as Laura looked up at them both and gave a terrified look.

'Bill didn't do it. I know he didn't. But . . . he'll be blamed, won't he? I mean, he said he would kill Hugh, didn't he? Last night? You remember that, don't you? So he'll be blamed.'

'Not necessarily,' Emma soothed. 'He may well have had lots of people around him all night. Remember, Henry promised to keep him safe. Or . . . perhaps he was doing something, making a telephone call or . . . whatever, where they can verify the time. I'm sure they'll sort it out. No one thinks Bill did it, do they, Kate? We don't!' Emma said it so fiercely that it was obvious she wasn't sure herself.

'Well . . . no, of course we don't!' Kate tried to be convincing. 'Everything will work out just fine, you'll see.' She came and sat down opposite the other two women, smiling, awkward, her fingers plaiting together.

The room was shabby but comfortable, sagging sofas and old rugs giving it a charm that was distinctly masculine. Kate assumed Laura wasn't interested enough to put her own stamp on the room. 'Have you been in contact with Hugh's parents? Or is the padre doing that?'

'No, they're, um, sending someone – one of the other company commanders, I expect. It's not something you can tell over the phone. But I'm not close to Hugh's family. They don't like me . . .' Laura trailed off awkwardly. 'So I don't expect they'll want to see me.'

'What about your family? Do you want to contact them, ask your mother or someone to fly over?' Kate urged, but Laura shook her head violently.

'God, no! What use would they be to me now, my father telling me it's all my fault and my mother not daring to say a word? No, I'd much rather stay with one of you two, if I could, until this is all over . . . Then I'll probably go away somewhere . . . I'm not really sure where just yet.' She looked distrait at the thought, knowing she couldn't go to Hugh's family home, knowing there was nowhere else for her to go, not when Bill still hadn't committed himself. Emma patted her hand awkwardly.

'I'd have you to stay with me, Laura, but I'm supposed to go away with Fergus on leave, though . . . um, maybe we'll . . . we'll cancel now . . . I'm not sure. Maybe we won't be allowed to go. I'll have to talk to Fergus . . .' She glanced at Kate, half pleading and Kate felt she had no choice but to rise to that appeal. Emma needed to get away, the doctors had said, somewhere peaceful with Fergus for a break. And Fergus would need a break after Ops 1. Neither of them should have this tragedy dumped in their lap at the moment.

'Well, we're here, so come and stay with us, Laura,' Kate announced firmly and brightly. 'We'll cosset you through all this and then you'll have ample time to make any decisions you need to. Stay as long as you like.' She smiled widely at the other two, hoping Alex wouldn't disown her. He didn't much care for Laura. But what else could she do?

Laura sniffed, and smiled back. 'Thanks, Kate, that's

very good of you. I promise I won't stay long.' And again, Kate thought, uneasily, this isn't like Laura. So polite, so self-effacing. The Laura they all knew didn't care what anyone thought. So why, suddenly, was Laura being so . . . so . . . Kate grappled in her mind for the exact word but it escaped her. All she knew was that something strange was going on that had nothing at all to do with the shock of Hugh's death. Or did it?

The press was having a field day. There had been a dearth of sensational news in the last few days and this story had just about everything a red-blooded tabloid journalist could wish for: a smart regiment based in Northern Ireland; adultery; officers feuding and coming to blows; a husband murdered; a lover held for questioning; a wife who was no better than she ought to be; and plenty of eyewitnesses to attest to the ugly fracas at the Officers' Ball – it was all too good to be true and the press descended in droves.

Alex wished desperately that he were not still Adjutant and could just hide his head like the others. Two more weeks and he would have been home free and a company commander. Instead, he and Joss were in the firing line.

Reluctantly he had rung the Army Press Office to be briefed on how to phrase the statement they would release shortly, and how best to handle the press who were busy clamouring outside the front gates of the camp, trying to find access in any way possible.

If a terrorist wanted to choose a time to mortar them, now would be perfect, he thought ironically. Who wanted to shoot a terrorist when there was the off-chance it was only a huge telescopic lens being pointed at you instead? Better brief the men again on the rules of engagement contained in the Yellow Card, just to be on the safe side. No one wanted another Clegg.

And then he glanced out of the window to see Bill, accompanied by Fergus, being escorted into HQ to give his statement. Bill looked tired, hungover and badly crumpled as he loped along beside Fergus. As they all did. Alex scrubbed his face again with long, bony fingers, trying to force some energy into his brain. He felt numb instead.

It had taken time to find Bill, let alone rouse him, since he hadn't been in his room in the mess or anywhere in the mess at all. In fact, it was nearly eight in the morning before he had been discovered sleeping over in one of the quarters set aside for young unmarried officers who wished to live out of the mess.

Bill and Henry, Will and Tony, it transpired, had spent the rest of the night sitting up playing poker until nearly three in the morning when they had, one by one, fallen asleep in a drunken stupor. Alex thanked God for once that Bill could be relied upon to behave badly. At least this time he had an alibi and witnesses to back him up.

Hugh was probably dead by four – or so the battalion doctor has whispered in Alex's ear, although variations in temperature and body weight could change timings slightly. But the civil authorities had taken over now and they would have to wait for the results of the official autopsy to be sure. Nothing was confirmed yet, nor would be for some time.

Except that Henry had woken and tried to rouse Bill from his own bed at four-thirty and, having failed, slept on the floor beside Bill all night until woken at eighty by a pounding on the door. Henry was adamant that Bill was legless and quite incapable of moving during the night. In fact, it had taken a great deal to bring him around at eight.

So, it looked very likely that Bill was off the hook. Alex sighed with what he knew was merely a temporary relief. Because if Bill didn't do it, then who *did*?

'It could have been anyone,' Laura argued stubbornly, sitting at Kate's kitchen table and nursing a stiff gin and tonic. 'Let's face it, Hugh was fairly universally loathed. He's been disgustingly unfair in the last month or so to several of his men, sending them off on unnecessary exercises, jailing them for petty offences, docking their pay – enough for any of them to gladly do away with him.

'And then . . . there's the matter of Emma and the baby . . .' She glanced up at Kate's surprised face. 'Oh yes, I know about that. Hugh ranted on about it. I felt quite sick – didn't have the nerve to discuss it with Emma. So, Fergus might well have felt he had good reason . . .' She grimaced. 'Even Alex was angry enough to threaten him not so long ago. I remember it distinctly. Something about a report . . .' Her green eyes slanted across at Kate. 'So Bill is certainly in good company.'

'As are you,' Kate added tartly. She hadn't liked that sideways glance. No doubt Laura had been quick enough to tell the police all this. She had already been interviewed and Kate had been intrigued to see Laura was wearing remarkably subdued and proper clothing. An ankle-length draped skirt in a pale patterned blue and a long cream twinset and simple strand of pearls made her look both alluring and innocent at the same time. She hardly looked like an adulteress and the DCI who had interviewed Laura had been suitably impressed.

Laura's red hair was drawn back into a barrette, she wore plain pearl earrings, and her make-up was minimal. Just enough for her to look beautiful but still frail and distressed. The DCI had even patted Laura's hand consolingly as he left. All rather dubious, Kate thought again and then chided herself for her cynicism. But she couldn't help wondering if the DCI had noted the flaming red hair – or was that just an old wives' tale?

Kate had stood outside in the hall, drinking yet more coffee, while the interview took place, close enough so that she could be of use, if needed, distant enough to give some privacy. But she had still heard enough of Laura's version of events to raise her eyebrows sharply.

Laura, it seemed, had not wanted to go on the bronco at all but been encouraged by Bill. When she had finally been allowed down again, Bill, slightly overcome with drink, had kissed her cheek in congratulation at having stayed on the bronco to the end.

Bill did admire her, yes, but had always been a gentleman. Unfortunately her husband had been insanely jealous of all other men and Laura had only to smile politely at a man for Hugh to accuse her of much worse. Kate had coughed into her coffee at that point, earning a look of disillusion from the constable in the hall. Clearly he thought her less than charitable. And Laura's version had continued unabated.

Hugh had hit Bill, and Bill, angry and drunk, had threatened Hugh but everyone knew it was just an idle threat. Bill would never do anything like that, Laura insisted vehemently, even if he was a bit volatile from time to time. (Here, Kate pursed her lips tightly in disapproval.) Laura, embarrassed and upset, had gone home with the Kennedys and not seen either Bill or her husband again. At six-thirty the following morning, the padre and the colonel's wife had come to tell her of Hugh's murder.

And, of course, she was devastated but she was sure that Bill had nothing to do with it. Even drunk, as he was. No, no, it could have been anyone.

Which was what Laura was repeating now as she sat at the kitchen table and stared moodily out at the muddy field that passed for a garden, the hedge shivering in the wind gusting off the lough. Kate nodded.

'Even a total stranger, nothing to do with the battalion at all,' she added hopefully and again Kate nodded. The lane that passed between the camp and the far quarters was outside 'the wire', or perimeter fence, and anyone could travel it. There was a long silence.

'Hugh didn't leave much, I'm fairly sure. He didn't have much and the house belongs to his family. So I'll have to go home for a while, I guess. Rethink things, see how – how Bill feels . . .' Laura trailed off, glancing at Kate sideways from beneath lowered eyelashes.

'I think they'll send him away somewhere for a while, you know,' Kate began awkwardly. 'Somewhere – unaccompanied.'

'Like Benbekula for a year, you mean? To cool his heels and teach him a lesson? Yes.' Laura paused coldly. 'I expect you're right. But I can wait a year, if necessary, don't worry . . .'

'You'll feel better about everything once you get away, Laura. Get a wider perspective on it all, not just this tiny inbred view from inside the wire,' Kate urged suddenly and impulsively. 'You and Hugh were no good together, and while no one in their right mind would ever have wanted this to happen, well, in some ways . . . it's a release for you, isn't it? A chance to start again, start over. Find the right person for you this time, and . . . and maybe Bill isn't it.

Maybe army life really isn't for you . . .' Kate trailed off, feeling she had perhaps overstepped the mark beyond which Laura was currently willing to go. But she was surprised by Laura's next words.

'Yes! Oh, yes! Don't think that hasn't occurred to me.' She smiled triumphantly up at Kate, her face glowing with that knowledge. 'I'm free of that bastard and I don't really care who did it. There were so many candidates . . . I don't even want to know. I'm just glad. I'd like to shake the murderer's hand!' Then the light seemed to die out of her again and she withdrew into herself and wrapped her arms around herself defensively. 'Don't tell anyone I said that. Not anyone, Kate. You promise me?'

Kate shrugged awkwardly. 'All right, I promise. But most people will know anyway. You and Hugh were hardly on good terms . . .'

'That doesn't mean I killed him!' Laura flashed back and Kate blinked as Laura's tone changed, became hard and cutting. 'That's what you're wondering, isn't it? Wondering if I crept out and smashed his head in while he was drunk? It's what everyone's wondering. Well . . . I've thought about it.' Laura licked her lips. 'Oh, yes, I've even dreamt about it, every tiny little detail, but . . . I didn't do it. I don't have the guts or the stomach to do such a thing.' And she drank deeply from her glass while hunching away to stare out the window again.

Kate didn't move. She couldn't think of anything to say. But a small voice inside her niggled that Laura was a tall, strong woman and she had ridden that bronco with an ease that showed a cool nerve and an iron will. Perhaps it was an unlikely murder for a woman to perform, bludgeoning a man to death, but, as Alex said, Hugh was very drunk . . . Unable to help herself, Kate shivered.

Laura watched that shiver in the reflection of window and pursed her lips carefully.

Chapter Twelve

Alex switched the overhead light off and climbed into bed beside Kate, pounding the cool, starched pillows into a suitably comfortable back-rest and picking up his book. The bedside lamp draped a pool of soft light over them both and he sighed with relief. What a day.

Kate snuggled in against him and laid her golden head across his chest. He stroked it idly.

'So? Tell me,' she urged. She felt him hesitate.

'The funeral's to be held on Friday. Hugh's father's requested a quiet family affair in their own village. No army, no friends, just family.'

'And no Laura?' Kate sat up in surprise.

'Laura will go, obviously. She'll accompany the – Hugh, on Thursday, stay the night in a hotel nearby, be driven to the funeral – we're providing a car and driver for her – and then catch a flight back home the following day.'

'She's agreed to all this?' Kate asked. Laura had alternated between agreeing and being adamantly against going to the funeral, even to simply pay her respects. Kate had pointed out how odd it would look if she weren't to go and Laura had gone sullenly silent on the subject.

'Yes. She had a long chat with Joss and that's what was decided. The police see no reason to detain Laura at the moment.' Alex's eyebrows lifted slightly at Kate's moue. 'Do you?'

'Not really, no.' She shook her head. 'She just . . . no, it's nothing I can put my finger on. She's just . . . being odd – for Laura, I mean. So polite, so . . . decorous. All her emotions shut off and hidden away. It isn't her at all. Gives me the willies!'

'So . . . nothing concrete, anyway.' Alex smiled grimly. 'They're going through Laura's house with a fine-tooth comb but I very much doubt there's anything there to hint at who did it. So they're letting her go off on the understanding she might have to fly back should any developments arise.

'And, let's face it, I shall be glad to have her away from Bill,' Alex continued, sighing. 'No good can come of them seeing each other at the moment.'

'You don't like Laura much, do you?'

Alex hesitated. 'We've never really hit it off, no. But that doesn't mean I'm accusing her of Hugh's murder. I just think Bill can do better and if he's kept away from her, he'll begin to realise that for himself. Besides,' he pulled Kate back against his chest and continued stroking her hair, 'I really would like to have the house back to ourselves. It's a bit cramped with Laura's black moods at the moment.'

'Alex, her husband's just been murdered!' Kate protested. 'Of course she's going to be in a black mood!'

'That's not the reason and you know it. She's glad he's

dead.' Alex sounded disgusted. 'No, she's just brooding because she can't see Bill and she doesn't want to go to the funeral. Joss insisted. Besides,' Alex's voice became lower still, 'there's no money. The regiment's paying her fare home.'

'Which makes it even more unlikely she'd have done him in, doesn't it?' Kate persisted, trying to overcome her own doubts as much as Alex's.

'Perhaps. But Bill comes from a very old, very wealthy family. He may only be the second son and not inherit either the title or estate, but he's got a private income that means he doesn't need to work a day in his life, if he doesn't choose to. The fact that he prefers to is entirely to his credit.' Alex picked up his book and turned to the last chapter. But Kate was not to be silenced so easily.

'And you think Laura saw this as a means of entrapping Bill? Getting him to commit to her?'

'Oh, I don't know . . .' Alex sighed heavily. 'I just intend to keep Bill confined to his office and his room until Laura is safely away. And I depend upon you to keep Laura away from the camp – if you possibly can.'

'And if I can't?'

'Let me know and I'll have Bill locked up,' Alex said grimly.

'You know, Emma looked pretty odd today, too . . .' Kate continued awkwardly. 'As though she knew she should be shocked and sad, but was really thrilled instead. Very creepy, to be honest. Not that I blame her . . . It's totally understandable . . .'

'But horrible to be looking at all your close friends, suddenly wondering if they're wearing some sort of mask and underneath it is someone you don't know at all . . . someone capable of beating a man's skull in . . .' Alex clarified for her.

'Yes! That's exactly it. I feel . . . sick! I don't know what to do, everything I say or do makes me wonder if someone is suspecting me, so I end up feeling furtive and stupid. And I didn't even have a grudge against Hugh at all! Not a personal one, anyway.'

'Poor sweetheart!' Alex bent down to kiss her head. 'I know how you feel. The whole battalion's on edge, what with the police interviewing just about everyone and pointing fingers and trying to dredge up dirt, and I'm both the adjutant and a suspect. Very odd!' He gave a snort of derision before adding quietly, 'Fergus looks like hell, as though he's eating his guts out about something . . .'

'You don't think . . . ?'

'God, I don't know what to think. Both Bill and Fergus saw Hugh with another woman a couple of nights back. They didn't recognise her—'

Kate shifted sharply in his arms to look up at him eagerly, 'But that's what Laura said! She thought Hugh was seeing someone else! Maybe it's this other woman's husband?'

'Maybe . . . But no one else seems to know anything about it and Laura's denied any such thing to both Joss and the police, probably because it gives her a very good motive for doing Hugh in, otherwise. So unless the woman comes forward herself, I very much doubt we'll ever know . . .'

'Poor Laura.' Kate sighed. 'What an end to it all.'

'Poor Hugh. He doesn't even get the military funeral he'd have wanted. I've argued every which way with his father but the man won't have it. So Hugh goes in the ground without the fanfare he, of all people, would have expected. I find that very sad.'

'The whole thing's sad.' And Kate snuggled tightly into Alex's arms. 'Promise me you'll never let our marriage go sour like that?'

Alex smiled and stroked his wife's cheek gently. 'That's an easy one to keep.' And then, unexpectedly, the image of Joanna flashed through his mind, accompanied by the worrying news in the *Belfast Telegraph* about her exhibition arriving at Ross's Gallery shortly. He shook his head to clear it. He was well rid of Joanna and she couldn't do anything to hurt his marriage now. It was too late. He picked up his book again.

The interest would have died down, inevitably, as some other sensational item of news took over, had there been no progress on the case. And, despite interviewing several people who were known to dislike Hugh and bear him a grudge, the police had got no farther within the battalion. No one was willing to point fingers at anyone else, everyone seemed to have the time in question accounted for, even if it only meant they had been at home in bed, and the battalion closed ranks to protect itself. There would be an internal enquiry, everyone knew, but no one was going to offer information to outsiders.

But, quite by chance, Hugh's wallet and signet ring were discovered in the possession of a local thug who was being investigated on drugs charges, and the case became newsworthy again.

The local lad denied killing Hugh, said he had just robbed the body, but, as he was well known for his violent attacks in the past, the police were unimpressed by his refusal to co-operate. He was charged with murder, remanded for justice, and once again the interest flagged.

The press contented themselves with writing unflattering exposés on the army, the regiment, the battalion, the commanding officer and all the officers in general. They wrote particularly flamboyant pieces on Bill and Hugh and Laura, with little attention to the facts, and everyone kept their head down and got on with the job in hand.

And Alex thanked every saint going that Serena had not been permitted to write her article. That would have been the final clincher.

A fortnight passed. Emma and Fergus went away for ten days and then returned, happier and more relaxed than anyone had seen them in a long time. Laura departed tearfully, with Hugh's body, telling them all she would be back. Few believed her. Bill was told he was to be sent to Bosnia on mine-clearance duty as soon as someone could be found to replace him. The press faded away and the Peace faltered on, giving moments of alarm and moments of boredom. Everyone sighed with relief.

And then the twins came back for their car.

'They're not staying.' Alex was adamant. Kate and Emma stood in the kitchen, preparing a tea tray, while Fergus, the twins and Simon were left in the sitting room, striving valiantly to keep the conversation going between them. Alex, on the pretext of carrying the tray through from the kitchen, had gripped Kate's elbow and stared her in the face. 'You promised, remember?'

'Oh, I know, Alex but their ferry isn't until tomorrow morning.' Kate looked harassed. 'Where are they supposed to stay?'

'On the street for all I care. What's wrong with a hotel, for a change?'

'Emma?' Kate turned to plead for help. 'What would you do? I mean, it wasn't actually the twins who were to blame, really. It was Serena—'

'They're trouble, Kate!' Alex cut across her insistently. Emma looked uncomfortable as Kate reiterated her question. 'Well . . . ? Would you turf them out?'

'Oh dear, it's very awkward, isn't it?' Emma began reluctantly. 'I can certainly understand that they're family, Kate, but . . . let's face it, they set out to try and ruin Alex's career, which amounts to the same as trying to ruin both your lives, really . . . I'm sorry, but I agree with Alex. Let them go and find a hotel or somewhere . . .'

'There!' Alex was triumphant. 'You see . . . and you can't find someone fairer or more decent than Emma . . .' At which, Emma blushed cruelly red, the colour then fading rapidly to a blotched white. Kate stared at her, brows knitted.

'Well, then *you* must do it, Alex, because I can't!'

'Fine, that's no problem. Just as long as you back me up. All right?'

'Um, I know this is probably irrelevant . . .' Emma hesitated. 'But why are they going from Larne in the first place? Why aren't they catching the Belfast to Liverpool ferry tonight instead? It would save them a ten-hour journey down from Scotland tomorrow, and they could sleep on the ferry instead of finding a hotel . . . and then you could get rid of them without actually having to cause offence!' She seemed to have recovered her colour and be in control of herself once more.

Kate looked at her in astonishment. 'That's brilliant, Em!

Why on earth didn't we think of it? Alex, do you think it's too late to try and change their tickets?'

'It'll cost them extra . . .' he warned. 'But it's worth trying. Emma, if they accept, remind me to buy you a present of your choice.' He grinned and kissed her cheek, before picking up the tray and walking briskly back into the sitting room.

'We've had a thought . . .' he began. But instantly he was aware that the atmosphere was unreceptive. Fergus was standing, stiff-backed and defensive, by the fireplace and Simon was tittering, hyena-like, into his goatee while both the twins looked like predatory birds circling a wounded prey as they leaned forward on their chairs. Fergus greeted Alex's return with scarcely concealed relief.

'Your cousins seem . . . avidly interested in the . . . in Hugh's death,' Fergus remarked shortly. 'Perhaps you'd like to fill them in? I'm afraid I have to be going.' He smiled insincerely at the others, murmuring '. . . to have met you. Goodbye.' And then he walked out abruptly.

Alex stared at the twins coldly for a moment before putting down the tray and following Fergus to the door. 'I take it, the twins have been digging for dirt,' he remarked calmly to Fergus, who glanced at Alex's wryly amused face. For a moment Fergus seemed about to leave without comment but then he shook his head lightly, his stiffly-held body relaxing.

'Shovelling it, more like. Are they always so ghastly?' Fergus didn't attempt to lower his voice and it boomed clearly through the house. Alex grinned.

'Totally. And they shan't be getting a bed here tonight, I can promise you. What did they say to get your back up?'

'What didn't they! Wanted to know if I'd done it! Or if you had! Unbelievable . . .'

'Not if you know them as well as I unfortunately do. And what did you tell them?'

'Bugger all! Outsiders can just sod off, as far as I'm concerned. Maybe this local thug did it, maybe he didn't . . . but I'm not going looking for the culprit, I can tell you. Hugh deserved everything he got!'

Emma appeared in the doorway of the kitchen, Kate hovering behind her. 'Fergus? Are you all right?' The alarm and agitation in Emma's voice surprised Fergus.

'Fine, darling, just fine. But I think we should be going, don't you? Leave Kate and Alex to their charming guests . . .' He grinned his apology to Kate. 'See you later.' And then he ushered Emma past the others and out the door, leaving Kate frowning awkwardly at Alex.

'What happened?'

'The twins happened,' Alex replied sourly.

'Shh! Keep your voice down!'

'Why? They don't bother to be polite, why should we? Come on, let's go and tell them the good news about the ferry.' He smiled a thin, determined smile that made Kate's heart sink. But, almost more than that, she was worried by the way Emma was behaving. Almost, as though, she thought . . . that Fergus might have done it? No, the idea was absurd. Kate glanced at Alex but could read nothing more than pleasure on his face at the thought of telling the twins where to go. With a sigh, she followed Alex back to the others.

'Morale's pretty low at the moment,' Fergus commented, a week later, as he drove quietly and firmly down the Bangor road, ignoring the chivvying of other cars behind him trying to pass at points where the two lanes simply weren't wide enough. 'I presume you've noticed?'

Alex nodded glumly. He stared out of the window as the last of the expensive suburban houses, hidden behind massive yew hedges, petered out and countryside took over.

Behind them in the car, the women were discussing their plans for their business and Alex, lowering his voice, murmured to Fergus, 'It's damned hard to keep the men motivated when they're supposed to be in a high state of readiness at all times and nothing's happening. They're fed up and it's not really surprising. Besides, this business with Hugh's still hanging over everyone.'

'Enough to make anyone jumpy,' Fergus agreed. 'Not least since that guy they've locked up for it is still protesting his innocence. What if it wasn't him? What if it was someone in the battalion? Practically in the family! That's what everyone's thinking.

'My only consolation is that if it had to happen, at least it was to someone who was universally disliked,' Fergus added, 'and won't be missed.'

'Maybe so, but Joss's career may be blighted over it. Doesn't look like he's fully in control if he allowed the sort of in-fighting and affairs that the press made out were going on. Besides, none of it's much of an excuse for doing Hugh in, in the first place,' Alex remarked pointedly, ignoring Fergus's snort of disgust. 'Let's hope it was the local lad and leave it at that.'

Behind them, Emma suddenly snapped, 'Oh, do stop talking about that man, will you? He's dead and gone and it's all over. I don't want to have it all rehashed during our first lunch out together.' She seemed to take a deeper breath and force herself to be calm as the others lapsed into uncomfortable silence. 'Sorry.' She patted Alex's shoulder. 'Just a bit shaky about it all still. Is Bill going to join us later, or not?'

'Not. He's still moping, poor pet,' Kate added and the two men shook their heads uneasily. Bill was depressed and unwilling to listen to reason, so he was shunning his old friends for the moment.

Fergus swung into the driveway of the Blackwood golf course and meandered up the road towards the clubhouse past rolling meadows of green and smooth fairways beyond. The first daffodils were sprouting green stalks through the turf and the sun shone more brightly than it had in weeks.

Shanks Bar and Grill, supposedly one of the three best restaurants in Northern Ireland, was by the left of the clubhouse, and they pulled up outside expectantly. Very few of the battalion had had the time or leisure to explore Ulster yet but everyone had unanimously suggested Shanks for a casual Sunday lunch. The four climbed out of the car and looked around with pleasure.

'Be nice to come out and play a round some day, if everything stays calm,' Fergus commented, glancing over the course. No one even noticed the tag to his words. That was how everyone spoke. 'Nice to do this – if the Peace holds.' 'Nice to do that – if things don't break down.' No one even suggested trips down to the south around Newry, Armagh and Crossmaglen. That was still declared bandit country and out of bounds to the men. And the women had no real desire to go on their own.

Crossing the border into the south was completely forbidden. The men had to go across to England and then back across to Southern Ireland, rather than go through those dangerous lanes at the border. The battalion had already done repeated tours in Northern Ireland in the last twenty-five years of the Troubles, and both Alex and Fergus – and Bill too – had done a six-month 'unaccompanied' down in the border area. None of them had any strong urge to go back.

'Looks so calm and tranquil, doesn't it?' Emma commented. 'I keep pinching myself that I'm actually in Northern Ireland, half the time.'

'Until you take a wrong turning and end up going through some inner city estate with multi-coloured kerbstones and twenty-foot-high murals of paramilitaries in balaclavas, armed to the teeth.' Kate grinned. 'Then you know just where you are!'

'I'm a better map-reader than you,' Emma laughed back. 'I stay well out of those areas, thank you very much.'

'Well . . . I didn't exactly intend to go down the Falls Road, I admit, but I got forced down it by getting in the wrong lane on the West Link. And I have to say I was sweating furiously, my fingers clenched on the wheel, expecting to be stopped and dragged out of the car like those two poor soldiers—'

'Oh, don't! I don't want to hear about that again.'

'Well, the point is, yes, I did see all the murals and I did see the Sinn Fein headquarters and all that, but it was so surprisingly small and shabby and – ordinary. I just couldn't get over the fact that all that trouble has come out of such innocuous little areas.'

'And just how long did it take you to come to this conclusion?' Emma asked with a smile.

'About three blocks when I managed to make a left and get the hell out of it.' They all laughed at Kate's admission.

'Just don't go down into the estates if you can help it. You'd stick out like a sore thumb and I don't really think you'd be welcome. Okay?' Alex counselled and Kate nodded firmly.

'Not to worry, my love. I don't really intend to go back if I can avoid it. There wasn't much to entice, to be honest.'

Laughing, they entered the restaurant and gazed around at the large paned windows that overlooked the rolling green course, beyond which distant groups of golfers strolled between holes or stared into the distance in the hope their ball had not gone in the lake after all. The décor inside was modern and light but welcoming. Several tables had children seated at them and the general feeling was relaxed and friendly. Emma stroked a baby's head as she passed his table and the infant beamed up at her.

As they were being seated, a man at a far table rose uncertainly, looked across at them, and then finally came across.

'Kate? Kate Gordon?' He hesitated, unwilling to intrude until Kate, glancing up, exclaimed with pleasure.

'Richard! How lovely to see you again. And here of all places! Darling?' She turned to Alex. 'Do you remember when I redid that entire mansion block in Kensington? That was Richard's project. He owns the Western property group. Richard Christie, my husband Alex Aldridge.'

She waited while the two men smiled, Alex rising to shake hands with Richard, and then she completed the introductions for the Kennedys. Richard was urged to join them and after hesitating politely, he gladly sat down at the table.

'I'm only over for a few days, to be honest, and I don't know many people here yet, so I was just going to eat on my own. So . . . you're a married woman, Kate? I had no idea! When did that happen? Surely it wasn't that long ago that we did that project together? No more than a year?' He seemed almost unable to keep his eyes off her. Kate, embarrassed, looked down at the table.

'About eleven months, actually. I knew Alex then but things moved forward a bit more suddenly once it became clear he was being posted across here.' Kate waved her hand around vaguely and gave an awkward smile. She had always sensed Richard was interested in her on more than just a business footing and the quickly concealed disappointment in his eyes reinforced the feeling. But he was carrying on calmly enough.

'Ah! Yes, I thought so when you first came in. Which regiment?'

'The Duke of York's Own,' Alex replied quietly, wishing the man would keep his voice down.

Richard laughed beguilingly. 'Oh yes, I've heard or rather read about every sordid detail in your battalion's lives. Bad news about that murder, wasn't it? The Republicans must be laughing their heads off,' he teased, his eyes shrewd and amused as he watched them all. He was a tall, rangy man, with a high-cheek-boned, tight-skinned tanned face from which his very short fair hair had receded slightly.

Emma found him devastatingly attractive and could quite understand Kate's pleasure at his sudden appearance. Older than their two husbands by a few years, he gave the impression of being very much his own man. And wealthy as well it seemed.' Emma sighed. Kate did have all the luck.

'They'd be fools if they weren't,' Alex was replying wryly. 'But I expect we're still fairly welcome compared to the lot before us, anyway. So, what brings you over here, Richard? Business?'

'Yes, naturally.' Richard smiled broadly. 'We're renovating one of the older, more established hotels, bringing it up to date to take advantage of all the businessmen flooding in to Belfast lately.'

'Really?' Kate glanced at Richard beneath her eyelashes. 'And who's doing the decorating side?' She saw Richard's eyes slide over to her, focusing intently for a second before grinning.

'Well, now that you mention it . . . I had thought to bring in a local firm but I haven't found one I like just yet. I don't suppose you're still in the market . . . ?'

'Oh yes, very much so! Emma's my partner over here.' Kate smiled with triumph. And Alex, glancing between the two, wondered whether Richard was referring to Kate's professional skills or otherwise. He smiled with thinned lips as Richard raised a glass to Kate and then belatedly to Emma.

'Then, I think we're in business. We've certainly worked well together in the past and I don't see any reason why we shouldn't in the future. Why don't you come by my hotel tomorrow and we can sort out the details?' Richard suggested lightly. 'And now, let's order shall we? I'm suddenly starving. And I think we should have some champagne to celebrate, don't you? Oh, by the way,' he grinned at the other two men, not quite patronising but definitely displaying his tail feathers, Alex thought coolly, 'this is on me, I insist.'

Fergus smiled smoothly, barely glancing at Alex as he thanked Richard. But Alex had caught that flicker and knew just what it meant. The man was after Kate and everyone at the table was aware of it.

* * *

Alex, driving around the estates, plain-clothed, in an unmarked RUC car, his loaded gun down by his leg, tried to concentrate on the job in hand. But, no matter what, his mind kept drifting back to the lunch the day before. By now Kate (with Emma, he desperately hoped) would be in Richard Christie's hotel room, discussing the deal. Alex frowned, staring out the windshield at the green and orange painted kerbstones, his mouth firmly pressed shut. Davey, the RUC man beside him, glanced across at Alex, wondering just what was up.

'There's been some action round here in the last few days,' Davey commented, nodding his head towards a particularly notorious inner circle of the estate. He halted the car for a moment, while Alex and the two other RUC men in the back seat memorised the layout. Then he took a quick left, leaving the cul-de-sac sharply as another car came up behind him. It was nothing, but Davey was taking no chances.

'What sort of action, exactly?'

'Arms movement, we suspect. Also a couple of kneecappings. Drugs-related, we're told.' Davey saw Alex give a thin smile.

'Nothing else?'

'We're waiting to hear. Your I-Corps boys should know pretty soon, they tell us.' Alex merely grunted. Bunch of bloody old women, they always gave gloom-and-doom intelligence reports, he thought. But then, he sighed to himself, that was their job. To suspect the worst. And, let's face it, they were probably right.

They drove on in silence for a while, circling back onto the Falls Road, down the Shankhill and back round again, looking, memorising, letting Alex get the feel of the place if he suddenly had to deploy his men out on these streets. A half hour passed in desultory conversation and then, as they began to ease out of the Red Area into Central Belfast, they were gradually hemmed in by more and more traffic until they were at a standstill. Not far away, the Europa hotel seemed to leer amusedly at Alex.

Trust Richard bloody Christie to stay there, Alex thought with irritation. The most bombed building in Belfast had had a complete refit and was the hotel where President Clinton had stayed when he made his historic visit. The visit they were all pinning their hopes on to achieve peace.

Alex hoped Richard was not enjoying his stay and would take his business elsewhere. But he knew that was unlikely. Richard had found Kate again, and this time, Alex suspected, he would try his best not to let her go.

The sun beat down on the windscreen, almost blinding them, and the heat built slowly within the car. But they couldn't wind down the windows or unlock the doors. Not with loaded weapons in the car. Alex drummed his fingers idly on the dashboard, glancing around, wondering what it would be like if all hell broke loose again. Bloody, he suspected. A lot of casualties. He shuddered at the thought.

He'd seen it all before, down in the Border area. In fact, that was where he had got the scar on his cheek-bone. A bomb going off prematurely in a field had blown bits of stone wall in all directions, cutting and bruising the patrol he had been out with and leaving him with a cheek cut down to the bone. But nothing worse on that occasion. He'd been lucky then.

And then, abruptly, his attention was jerked back to the present by the sound of screaming. Looking up, he saw a woman was crying out as she ran along the pavement, holding a shawl-wrapped bundle in her arms. Screaming, hysterical, howling up at the sky. Dimly the words filtered in to them. Her baby, she screamed, her baby had stopped breathing.

Alex shifted quickly, unlocking his door and slipping out before the others could react. Dimly he heard Davey tell him not to be a bloody fool, but by then he had reached the woman in a few strides. He looked around desperately at the gridlocked traffic. The baby, blue-tinged and limp, lay still in the woman's arms. Alex looked into her pleading eyes and saw a terror that left him hollow-bellied.

She looked away from him, spun around inside the wall of shocked bystanders, pleading for help, but no one moved. They gazed silently and with horror. Alex groaned and then made his decision.

The Royal Victoria Hospital couldn't be more than six blocks, he thought quickly as he snatched the baby from thc woman, shouting at her to follow him as fast as she could. The baby felt so light, so tiny cradled in his arms that he could barely believe it was a child and not a doll. And as he set off at a desperate pace, dodging and weaving through the crowds, yelling hoarsely at them to get out of his way, he knew he was entering the Red Area and he groaned again.

He was a British soldier, alone, unarmed, in one of the worst Republican areas of West Belfast. Fair game. But what choice did he have? The baby couldn't wait for an ambulance to try to force its way through. It lay limp in his arms as he ran on, gasping for breath himself, pushing himself harder and faster than he knew he should. But there was no alternative.

The hairs on the back of his neck were standing up by

the time he neared the hospital, sullen, angry faces clustered on street corners, staring at him as he ran through them. They knew who, or rather, what he was. They knew a soldier, plain-clothed or not, when they saw one. Grudgingly they parted to let him through, murmuring amongst themselves.

The mother had fallen far behind and Alex could not wait. He ran on into the casualty area, calling hoarsely for help, his sides heaving, the breath left in him barely enough to explain. Whisked from his arms, the baby was placed on a stretcher, a bag and oxygen mask placed over its tiny face. With one person holding the mask and the other pushing the stretcher they disappeared at a run down the corridors, and Alex stood leaning weakly against the wall of the Emergency Room, gasping for breath.

It wasn't that he had run far, just that he had sprinted the whole way and his oxygen-starved body was clamouring for relief.

Slowly, his vision cleared and the shuddering gasps subsided. He looked around slowly, feeling the eyes focused on him but, as he turned, they seemed to slide away, refusing to confront him. He would have to stay there, he realised, until Davey could catch up. Even so, he felt exposed, vulnerable. No soldier was allowed at the RVH without an armed escort, even now. And he was alone. He wiped the sweat from his eyes and wondered about the baby.

Chapter Thirteen

The minutes ticked by as he leaned against the wall, watching the emergency room warily. But interest in him had subsided as their own ailments took over again, crying children, shouting women, silent men all awaiting their own turn. Several of the nurses watched him, half-unnerved at his presence there alone, but finding him interesting for more than just his profession.

They whispered amongst themselves, giggling nervously, as they flashed glances over at the tall, lean figure standing against the wall and back to each other, pursing their lips teasingly at each other, flashing their eyes. They noted how the dark hair was brushed back by his hand, revealing the face in all its planes and angles, how the blue eyes searched the room, narrowed and wary. They took in his tension, the grim, unsmiling mouth and felt a frisson of excitement shiver through them.

Alex kept watching the glass doors, waiting, hoping Davey would realise where he had gone. Every time the door opened, he tensed. And every time it was yet another admission with a broken wrist, a slashed leg, a pain in their chest . . . Alex watched the clock and wondered yet again about the baby.

The mother suddenly appeared, wrenching the door open and thrusting herself into the room with fear etched in her face. Alex pushed himself off the wall and walked forward to meet her. A couple of men were with her now, he realised, but she shook herself free of them as they attempted to restrain her, and ran over to Alex.

'My baby?' she gasped, breathless with anguish, and Alex took her hands between his own. Despite the heat of the room, they were cold and unyielding.

'They took him in. I haven't heard anything yet.' He looked towards the desk again, and the woman immediately dropped his hands, forgot him, as she approached the admissions desk.

'You've got my baby,' she started, half belligerently and the nurse glanced up quickly.

'The one that man brought in?' She gestured to Alex. The woman nodded curtly. Behind her, the two men had come up to flank her. Neither of them glanced at Alex beyond their initial stare. But Alex had recognised one of them and he stepped back sharply and glanced once more at the glass doors. The name escaped him but the face didn't. The man was a player. Alex felt his mouth go unpleasantly dry.

But he couldn't help trying to hear what was being said. The nurse was calling through now and after a brief delay, when Alex thought the mother might collapse and the two men beside her took her arms and held her between them, the nurse looked back at them speculatively.

'He's alive. Your baby's alive,' she smiled, and the woman's face crumpled in relief. Tears welled and began to slide unchecked down her face. She slumped against one of the men, who put an arm around her waist and held her tightly as the sobs came now, jerky and uneven with the release of an unbearable tension. He patted her head awkwardly. But the nurse was continuing, leading the group over to one of the orderlies, 'He was breathing by the time he was admitted. I gather that man ran with him and the doctor feels the jogging must have stimulated your baby to breathe again. We're not sure yet if any damage was done but the doctor thinks it unlikely. A baby can stop breathing for much longer than an adult without it causing future problems . . .'

As she ushered the family away, one of the men glanced speculatively back at Alex. He didn't smile. He didn't offer thanks. But, for a moment, their eyes locked. Then he turned the corner and was gone, and Davey was walking in through the glass doors. Alex breathed deeply and went to meet him.

'You're a bloody idiot!' Joss snapped coldly. He sat at his desk, his forearms resting on the flat surface, his fingers steepled together. For a moment Alex felt like a subaltern again, standing in front of his colonel, waiting to hear his fate. He stood stiffly, not quite at attention, not quite relaxed either. 'I don't know what you could have been thinking. Entering a Red Area is a courtmartial offence and no one should know that better than you, Alex!' Joss continued and Alex frowned.

'I didn't have a choice, Colonel. The baby had stopped breathing. It was blue!'

'I know, I know. I've heard all about it from the RUC and

the hospital and what you did – does you credit. The baby is alive due to you and I'm sure the family is suitably grateful, but . . . Jesus, Alex! You could've been shot and brought the whole Peace process down with you.' Joss was appalled at the risk Alex had taken. Alex was silent.

'I know you think I'm being hard,' Joss looked up shrewdly, 'and I know you think you did right. Possibly you did. But that's only because it worked. You were balancing that baby's life against your own and God knows how many others if the Peace failed because of you. It's not a risk you should have taken, but . . . it seems you did.' Joss shook his head. For a long time, several aeons it seemed to Alex, Joss was silent as though contemplating his choice of action. Then, finally, he sighed and looked up at Alex again.

'However, in your favour, we've had a telephone call from the mother, asking that you be thanked. Since we know she comes from a well-known Republican family . . . well, hearts and minds, Alex, hearts and minds . . .' Joss rose and came around the desk, holding out his hand. 'I personally think you're a damned brave man and with any luck the press'll have something nice to say about us, just for a change.' A crease of his cheek was the most Joss would permit himself in the way of a smile.

'Almost as good as the kitten patrols in Cross, sir,' Alex added, suddenly almost giddy with relief. Joss's forehead puckered.

'What was that? Don't remember hearing about it . . .'

'Oh, when we were in Crossmaglen a couple of years ago, the place was infested with cats and endless litters of kittens. The previous bunch used to drown the kittens but my boys were too soft-hearted, so they used to stuff them down the front of their smocks when they were going out on check-point duty, and stop cars and offer them kittens. Did no end of good all round, actually. And we found homes for a lot of the little beggars.'

Joss laughed, unable to help himself. 'Well, that's the way to disarm then. Never mind peace talks. Just hand out kittens and save babies. Come on, let's go have a drink. Then you can go home and tell Kate what a bloody hero you are,' he added sardonically.

'She's more likely to knock me flying, I suspect,' Alex grimaced, relief that Joss was not going to continue the 'bollocking' almost as palpable as the relief he hadn't been shot. Joss laughed again.

'Not Kate. You're a lucky man there, Alex. She's made of the right stuff.' Which remark only made Alex remember Richard Christie. The dull weight that thudded into his stomach reminded him that his luck might be about to run out.

'Come on, a bottle of bubbly to celebrate the fact you're still alive seems a sensible idea.' Joss glanced at his watch. 'And it's after five. Good! Nice to have something to celebrate after the last few weeks of hell.' He rubbed his hands together with satisfaction, enjoying the thought of the news he would have for the brigadier. 'Let's go, shall we?'

It was nearly seven before Alex managed to escape the mess and, despite the fact that he had several times attempted to contact Kate by telephone, he had yet to find her in. The driveway stood empty when he drew up, the house unlit. He stood hesitating in the hall, looking around for a note. But there was nothing. Reluctantly he entered the kitchen and looked up Emma's number. But Kate wasn't there, Emma had told him, sounding surprised. And Alex hung up, feeling awkward that he should have exposed himself to Emma. Quietly he switched on the lamps and went upstairs to get changed.

When Kate finally arrived home, nearly half an hour later, Alex was sitting silently watching the news in their sitting room. He didn't go to meet her, waiting instead for him to seek her out.

'Alex? Alex!' Kate's voice, high and joyful, preceded her into the room, as she hurriedly peeled off her jacket and glanced around in surprise. 'Didn't you hear me calling you?'

'No,' he shrugged. 'I was watching the news. Why?' He didn't get up to kiss her as he normally did, merely taking another sip of beer and returning his attention to the television. 'Have a good day with Richard?' he enquired coolly, without looking at her.

Kate frowned. 'A good morning, yes. We've got the job and it'll be a real in to the market here. The hotel will showpiece our ability better than any private house.' Her smile faltered. 'Why? What's the problem?'

'Nothing,' Alex said after a pause. 'So, where've you been since then?' He swivelled his eyes, so still and deep, to look up into Kate's outraged ones.

'I came home and spent part of the afternoon discussing things with Emma and calling Milly for contacts. Then, after I'd tried, without success, to get hold of you, I went out to Bloomfields to do a large shop. That's what's littered all over the kitchen floor at the moment. Would you like a detailed description of who I saw and spoke to while in the supermarket?' She slammed out of the room, returning to the kitchen to unpack.

Alex continued to watch the news, feeling churned up

inside in a way he hadn't felt before. He loved Kate desperately and he needed her. But he wouldn't beg for her.

She did not return. Finally, with a sigh, he got up and followed her into the kitchen. He stopped her as she brushed coldly past him to put away some tins, taking them from her hand and putting them down on the table. Then he folded her into his arms and held her tightly.

'I'm sorry,' he breathed into her hair as he clasped her and felt her relax against him, wrapping her arms around him in return. 'I know I'm being a fool, but I can't help being jealous of that bloody man,' he murmured and Kate pulled back slightly to look up into her husband's pained face.

'You've no reason to be, you know,' she chided gently. 'I like Richard, I work well with Richard, but . . . I married you. I love you.' And, looking at him, at the worry in his eyes and the firm, resolved curve to his lips, she thought, there was no one else who could ever steal her away from Alex. No one.

'I know.' He kissed her. 'I know. I can't really excuse myself. I've just . . . had a bad day, and when you weren't here when I got home and there was no message . . .' He didn't elaborate on his day. Now was not the time, he felt. Kate patted his cheek tenderly.

'My poor darling. I did try to call, several times. I last tried just before seven when I left the shops . . . But you weren't home and you weren't in your office . . .'

'No,' he agreed. 'I was having a drink in the mess. I tried you here several times too. We've obviously been playing telephone tag. Ah well, I guess it's just one of those days . . .'

'Umm . . .' Kate eyed him doubtfully. 'Well, you're going to have to get used to me seeing Richard without flying into a jealous fit each time. We're going to be working together on this project for several months in all and who knows, there may be others after that . . .' Kate wriggled herself free to stack the tins in the cupboard.

'As long as he remembers you're not still in the market.' Alex walked over to the sink and stared out at the falling dusk. Outside the trees were still bare, the garden lit with the halogen lights of the perimeter fencing. It half lit his face as well.

'Oh, that! A chance remark that you took the wrong way, Alex!' Kate laughed over her shoulder scornfully, not seeing Alex's face, the darkened eyes.

'Did I?' Alex sighed. 'Well, we'll see . . . Now, what's for dinner? I'm starved.'

She frowned around at him. 'Typical man! I've been working all day too, you know. And this contract will be quite lucrative, I'm sure. So . . . how about you cooking dinner for a change?' She smiled as she heard Alex mock-groan.

'We'll do it together. How's that for a deal?' he compromised, turning back to her. Kate shook her head.

'Grounds for divorce. Okay, move over, I'll cook – this time . . . So,' she glanced up idly at Alex's face, wondering a little at the lines of strain she could see around his mouth, 'do you want to hear about my day? Or would you rather tell me about yours?'

'Let's hear yours.' He smiled. She was obviously bursting with pride to be back in business again. He hoped Richard wouldn't do anything to spoil that. But, somehow, he had the feeling that Richard thought Kate was on offer along with her designer skills, or rather, he felt he should expect to receive both in the contract. Alex hoped Kate wasn't going to be made very unhappy.

* * *

'They've had to let him go,' Joss murmured to Alex over coffee in the mess the following morning. 'Insufficient evidence.'

'But . . . he had Hugh's wallet and ring!'

'Shh, not so loud. We don't want this getting out just yet if we can help it. I *know* he had the wallet and ring, but it seems he was accounted for during the crucial two hours of Hugh's death. So . . . it looks likely he was telling the truth and did just lift them from Hugh's body some time just before six.'

'Which leaves us precisely where, Colonel?'

'I think you know the answer to that, don't you, Alex? Up shit creek without a paddle. So, just keep an open mind and an open eye, all right?' Joss moved away, clapping Henry on the shoulder and moving him into a corner for a private chat. Alex wandered over to the heavy mahogany side-table where coffee was left laid out each morning at ten-thirty. To do so he had first to step around and over several dogs, children and chairs.

This morning some of the wives seemed to have chosen to put in an appearance. Alex heard something to do with 'SSAFA Wives Club' mentioned while he smiled politely and offered his own just-poured cup of coffee to Amanda.

Amanda smiled archly back. 'Thank you Alex, you are a sweetheart! How are you finding your new job? Quite grown up suddenly, isn't it all? Good heavens, I remember you when you were a newly arrived subby, all fresh-faced and bumptious! How time flies!' She laughed, a little trilling sound that Alex found tedious. Quite how her husband, Philip, had borne with her all these years . . . but then, Alex shook his head at himself; she was basically a good person and tried very hard to do her best for Philip. Pity it was so obviously a waste of time.

Philip would go no higher than second-in-command within the battalion. Future jobs would shift him laterally, perhaps into something with the TA. Perhaps out of the army altogether. A shame when he was such a good man, and such a good soldier. But exams mattered these days and Philip hadn't passed the crucial ones. Alex tried to remind himself of this when Amanda got on his nerves.

'And where's Kate this morning?' Amanda was asking, annoyingly. 'I'm sure I mentioned to her about this meeting and that we do need all the support we can get.'

Alex sighed, weighing his words and then deciding to be blunt. 'Kate works, Amanda. I'm afraid she doesn't have time for your committees . . . Ah, Bill, wait a second, would you? I need a word. You'll excuse me, Amanda, won't you?' Alex moved deftly to one side with barely a smile and caught Bill by the elbow.

'What is it?' Even to Alex, Bill sounded distant and faintly belligerent. Alex pulled him over by the door, casting careful glances around the room.

'A word in your ear,' he murmured softly. 'The police've let their suspect go. So, watch your back and go over your alibi again. Right?'

'I didn't do it, Alex,' Bill ground out fiercely in an undertone that held a mixture of pain and frustration. 'I wish you would believe that.'

'I bloody know that or I wouldn't be warning you now, mutton-head. If I thought you'd done it, I'd let you go to the dogs. So, get that lazy brain of yours in gear and start thinking who could have, before this all becomes public knowledge. The police are, as of now, looking for someone to put away. Make sure it's not you. All right?' Alex shook Bill's arm in exasperation. 'And do stop being so pathetic over Laura. If you still care after six months' mine clearing, then she's the girl for you. If you don't, this gives you the breathing space you need. Oh,' Alex drew back again for a moment, 'by the way. You didn't hear any of this from me and I'll skin you alive if you pass it on to anyone – anyone at all. You understand me, Bill?'

'Yes.' Bill grinned faintly, his handsome face lightening slightly. For the past few weeks since Hugh's death, he had felt as though he were in a fog of depression. It was good to know some friends still believed him innocent. 'And thanks, Alex. I'm sorry if I've been a bit . . . what was it? Mutton-headed . . . ?

'You have,' Alex's cheeks creased, 'but then, we've all been through it. However, I'd say your time's now up. Start waking up, all right?' He gripped Bill's arm and shook it slightly.

'Right. Oh, um, I heard about what you did yesterday – the baby,' Bill clarified when Alex looked blank. 'That was good going. The men are pretty pleased over it all. Think you're a bit of a hero . . .' Bill gave a lop-sided grin. 'It's done no end of good for morale.'

'Joss thinks *I* was a mutton-head, actually.' Alex grinned ruefully. 'I suspect he's right but, damn it, if you'd seen that baby, you'd have done the same.' He shook his head and then he moved on, pausing to chat briefly with Fergus, exchange a joke with Will, scratch Toby, the Border terrier's ears. He glanced once, assessingly, at the colonel but Joss was oblivious to his manoeuvre, still going over something with Henry.

Thank God he wasn't adjutant anymore, Alex thought.

Or he couldn't have said a word, even to Bill. He really shouldn't have anyway . . . Christ, he hoped Bill was discreet. He put down his coffee cup, glanced at it suddenly as a thought occurred to him, sighed and then wandered out into the sunshine to return to his office.

That was something else he had to deal with shortly, he realised with a faint sinking feeling: the company coffee morning to introduce Kate and himself to the men's wives and deal with any problems that might have arisen since the battalion had moved to Northern Ireland. It wasn't that he minded; in fact he looked forward to getting to know everyone, but . . . he knew he was going to be in the firing line over the post not being delivered while the men were away on exercise, for one thing . . . and he had so much else on his plate, not to mention Hugh's murder . . . Better get his sergeant major to organise something with the cook house for next Tuesday. And warn Kate! She should love this one . . .

But Suzy was before him in annexing Kate for yet another duty evening. Emma fought to keep the dismay off her face as Suzy popped in unexpectedly as Kate was laying out her design boards on the dining-room table and Emma was shuffling expertly through material sample books. They both looked up in surprise as Suzy cooeed from the kitchen door, and then glanced quickly at each other. Emma shut her eyes briefly. She knew what it would be about. Kate, thinking it nothing more than a social call, greeted Suzy with more genuine enthusiasm. At least, momentarily . . .

'Hello! What are you two up to?' Suzy bustled in, trim in navy jeans and a crisp blue-and-white striped shirt under a short red Austrian jacket, pearls and smart loafers. While not setting the world on fire with the originality of her dress sense, Suzy always looked smart and neat, the way a good colonel's wife ought to, Kate told herself, amusedly. She kissed Suzy's cheek and invited her in.

'We've got a design job,' Kate announced proudly and Suzy's face fell slightly.

'Oh? Really? What? The pair of you?' From the hesitation in her voice Emma, at least, recognised that Suzy had come on a duty-begging mission and was not best pleased to find two of her recruits busily occupied elsewhere. Kate nodded.

'Um, yes, Emma and I have gone into business together and we've brought off a bit of a coup . . .' As Kate continued to explain, gesturing to the boards and showing Suzy the intended colour scheme for the show suite, Emma watched them both with amused resignation. There was no doubt that Kate was a whirlwind of efficiency and organisation when she wanted to be, nor that Suzy could be too. But someone was going to have to give way on this and Emma wondered which one it was likely to be. Somehow, she suspected Suzy, with years of experience at cajoling people into doing jobs they really didn't want to do, would carry the day.

For a moment her mind drifted away from the other two. The doctor's office had rung earlier, asking her to come in for another scan. She hoped they'd be able to see the problem this time. Yet another scan, yet another discussion, probably more pills and more suggestions – and what good was any of it doing? None at all, it seemed. Her only consolation, and she mentally chastised herself for it but couldn't help it, was that she didn't have to see Hugh swaggering around anymore. Which was a dreadful thing, to be pleased someone was dead, murdered. She knew it was wicked. But, somehow, she couldn't feel differently. A life for a life. Perhaps now she could get on with her own?

She focused back, with a shake of her head, on the discussion the other two were having. '. . . So, you see, we've booked the hotel and the food and everything but we haven't sold enough tickets to cover the costs. Initially I was told we could count on at least 150, but we've barely got a hundred wives signed up and despite all Sheila's appeals, no more have come forward.' Suzy looked at Emma equally appealingly.

'It just looks so bad if there aren't enough wives there and I know the Wives' Committee isn't aimed at officers' wives, but I really need all of you to help me out this time. It's only one night . . .'

'Of course we'll come,' Emma announced, glancing at Kate. Kate's face was set into awkward, pained agreement. She nodded her head.

'Yes, of course, Suzy. We couldn't leave you to deal with it alone. Um, who's Sheila?'

'The RSM's wife.' Suzy sounded surprised that Kate didn't know. Kate smiled thinly. 'Oh, yes, of course,' she murmured. RSM, she reminded herself, meant Regimental Sergeant Major, the most senior soldier in the battalion and God to all enlisted men beneath him – and to many of the subalterns too. His wife would, naturally, head the Wives' Committee along with Suzy. God, what a minefield it all was, trying to remember who was who, whose wife was what, and to do all that was required of you without seeming like a sycophant at the same time.

The thought of a dinner at £25 a head in a large (and let's face it, she thought dismally, naff) hotel with more than a hundred women she had never met and who would all know vastly more about her than she would know about them, horrified Kate. But Emma was taking it calmly enough and Suzy was preparing to leave now, her task accomplished, so Kate stood, smiled and saw her out.

She returned to the dining room with a stony look on her face. 'I'm not in the army, am I, Emma?' Emma smiled and ignored the question but Kate was serious. 'No, I mean it, Em. We've got a job that we're working hard on and that could bring in big money. We're both married and expected to continue running our husband's homes with minimum disruption despite having a job. And on top of all that, we now have to spend money and time socialising with a bunch of people we don't know and who won't want to know us, just because our husbands happen to work together in the army. And yet you just smile serenely and agree. Why?' The exasperation was plain in her voice. Emma looked at her steadily.

'Oh, Kate . . . just accept it, will you?' For the first time, Emma sounded irritated. 'This is the way things are. There are a few – very few – duties that are asked of us, and we have to just get on with it, whether we like it or not. I expect in civilian life wives have to entertain or go to company functions. It's much the same.'

'Not if their husband owns the company,' Kate muttered darkly, thinking that Richard's wife would never be expected to do so. Emma shrugged.

'We're talking reality here, all right? Okay, you can buck the system and complain furiously about the injustice of it all – much like Laura did,' she added ominously, 'but it won't do Alex any good. He'll never actually be told to get control of you, but there'll be subtle hints that he should.

And even more subtle hints that if he can't manage his own household, why should he be put in charge of others?'

'I thought you said, when I first arrived, that there was no such pressure?' Kate demanded, outraged. 'That it didn't make any difference to a husband's career?'

'Yes, well,' Emma yawned, 'you were newly married and probably didn't need to hear the realities of life just at that moment.' Briefly, Kate remembered Laura's scorn at what Emma had had to say back then. She grimaced.

'I see. Is there anything else you're holding back from me? Any other minefields I should know about?' She sat down abruptly and took a large sip of coffee. Emma gave her a rueful smile.

'I'm sorry, Kate. I know it's hard to adapt sometimes but it gets easier and easier over the years until you don't even remember what it was you used to kick against, it all seems so natural. And, let's face it, poor Suzy's in a bit of a fix. You'd give up an evening to help out a friend in need, wouldn't you? So what's so different?'

'Oh, I don't know,' Kate groaned. And then she paused. 'Well, no, that's not quite true. I guess what's really scaring me is . . .' She hesitated, looking at Emma awkwardly, 'whether I'm going to get on with them, whether they'll like me or just think I'm some stuck-up—'

'Who? The soldiers' wives?' Emma asked in incredulity.

'Yes! Yes, dammit! I wasn't brought up in this system like you were. I haven't breathed in all the subtleties since I was a child, and my father was never a colonel, so I haven't the foggiest how to go about it all. I get all awkward and tongue-tied and they think I'm being difficult . . .'

'When did this happen?' Emma laughed.

'Oh, when I was newly engaged to Alex and had to go to

some dreadful boozy piss-up at the end of an exercise. I've never felt so stupid and out-of-place in my life!'

'Good lord, what a fool Alex was to take you to something like that! I'd've refused point-blank if Fergus had asked me, or else come down with violent and communicable bubonic plague!' She laughed again, softly. 'Oh, Kate, this won't be like that at all. Everyone will be trying to please everyone else and no one will dare get drunk – well, very few, anyway – because Suzy will be there and no one will want to make fools of themselves in front of her. No, it'll be stiff and proper and you'll just have to try hard to talk babies – that's always good common ground – or jobs or something until everyone loosens up and starts dancing.'

'Dancing? With who?'

'Each other,' Emma shrugged. 'Not much else you can do when there are no men invited.'

'Oh, great! I'll bet the waiters have a good old smirk! Do I really have to dance?' Kate asked plaintively. 'Will people be upset if I don't?'

'Listen, the other girls'll be far more terrified of putting a foot wrong than you.' Emma shook her head. 'You really are amazing sometimes. Anyway, come on, we need to get back to work.'

Which slightly mollified Kate and allowed her to file the date in the back of her mind and get on with the job they had. Richard had asked for the mock-up boards by the end of the week since he had a meeting of the hotel management, investors and various other big-wigs who would have to be sold on the idea of using their design firm on the following Tuesday. That way, if he didn't like the layout, they could improvise something else in time. But it was going to be tight, she thought, frowning at a wallpaper sample she had in mind for the bathroom. Very tight. She hoped Alex wasn't expecting much to eat over the next few days . . .

Chapter Fourteen

Emma left at five, promising to return the next day as soon as Fergus had left for work. Kate, unused to pandering to a husband quite as much as Emma seemed to, carried on working. She would send Alex out for a take-away, she decided, pencil in mouth and several different swatches in hand. Now that the ban on soldiers entering the nearby town after six in the evening had been lifted, there was no reason why he couldn't go to look for a Chinese or Indian meal. They hadn't had a take-away since they'd arrived. It would make a nice change. Besides, she grinned to herself, they might have to try out each and every one of the fast food places this week!

Alex, however, hadn't quite planned the evening that way. He walked in at six with Bill in tow. 'Darling? I'm home. Bill's with me. Any chance there's enough for him to eat with us tonight?' He peered into the kitchen, then the sitting room, finally tracking her down in the dining room. She looked flustered and tired, he thought, her hair pulled back into a ponytail and no make-up. Wearing jeans and a white T-shirt, she looked about sixteen. With misgiving, he noticed the slight pucker between her dark brows.

'Hello, Alex, hello, Bill.' Kate wiped her face smooth and forced a smile. 'How are you?' She kissed them both and tilted her head to one side, her hands spread out wide. 'As you can see, you've rather caught me on the hop. I've been working all day and I haven't even thought of supper – in fact, I was hoping you would pop out for a take-away? If Bill doesn't mind . . . ?'

She wouldn't have given it a thought when she had lived in London and Alex had unexpectedly turned up with a friend in tow. A take-away was fine, then. But she could tell instantly from the slight burn on Alex's cheeks and the clear, steady gaze he gave her, that he *did* mind and was embarrassed by her inhospitality. Obviously being a wife meant catering every night, she thought with growing irritation.

'Surely there's something you could throw together, Kate, isn't there? You always have the fridge packed with food.' Alex's tone was still light but there was something there that Kate knew was more than a suggestion. Her tiredness made her cross.

'Maybe there is, Alex, but I've got a lot on, as you can see. But, if you two would like to "throw something together" tonight, that would be a godsend.' But that suggestion was obviously even worse. Alex's face became devoid of emotion and Bill, on the pretext of just popping out for a second, made himself scarce.

'For Christ's sake, Kate,' Alex ground out in hushed tones, glancing over his shoulder to make sure Bill was out of earshot, 'this is the first time Bill's been out of the mess since Hugh's murder and he needs to be welcomed, not told to go and get a take-away or cook his own meal. You're embarrassing me! Just,' he gestured abruptly at the chaos spread out over the table, 'clear this away, will you? Richard bloody Christie can wait, can't he?'

'No, he can't, Alex!' Kate's cheeks were burning crimson. 'There's a board meeting on Tuesday when Richard and I will put forward our plans for the design to be reviewed—' But Alex wasn't listening. He had caught the word 'Tuesday' and was instantly up in arms.

'Tuesday! Oh, no, I'm sorry but you'll just have to cancel. Richard will either have to reschedule or manage without you, I'm afraid—'

'Cancel? You must be joking! You don't cancel board meetings, Alex! And I'm afraid I have every intention of being there—' Kate began stubbornly.

'I've scheduled the company coffee morning for then. The leaflets have already gone out to every household and the cookhouse—'

'I don't give a damn about your bloody coffee morning, Alex,' Kate glared. 'This is my business you're interfering with—'

'Can you imagine how it would look if you weren't there?' Exasperated, Alex took a couple of quick steps back and forth, his fingers raking the hair back from his weary face. 'All the other wives would think you were too stuck-up—'

'Well, maybe I am!' Stung, Kate flared up. 'Maybe I have other, better things to do with my time—'

'What's got into you?' Alex looked around the room as though seeking the cause of Kate's rebellion. 'Christ, ever since Richard Christie came on the scene you've become bolshie and difficult. You're never here when I need you—'

'Oh, this is so damned unfair of you, Alex!' Kate's voice had risen to a shout and Alex snapped coldly for her to keep her voice down.

'Why the hell should I? I'm sure Bill's heard raised voices before.'

'Yes, and look where all Laura's wild behaviour and rebellion has got *him* . . .'

'I am *not* being either wild or rebellious, Alex.' Kate fought to hold onto her temper. 'I am a career wife and you agreed, damn you, when we got married that I could—'

'I didn't agree to you swanning around with some man who's trying to get you into bed—'

'Oh?' Kate's voice became sarcastically sweet. 'Is that what all this is really about? Your inferiority complex where Richard is concerned?'

'On the contrary! This is to do with *my* career and you not making me look a fool in the battalion—'

'I don't have to, Alex,' Kate snapped coldly. 'You're already looking like a bloody fool.' She swept past him into the hall where Bill was awkwardly hopping from one foot to the other in an agony of embarrassment.

'Oh, Bill,' Kate gave him a quick hug, tears hovering on her eyelashes, 'I'm so sorry you had to listen to that. It's nothing at all to do with you, I hope you know? It's just . . .' but words failed her and she ran past him and up the stairs, slamming her bedroom door behind her. She flung herself on the bed and wept angrily and inconsolably.

Alex, after a few deep breaths, came out of the dining room stony-faced. Bill held up his hands. 'Alex, I'm sorry. This is obviously a bad time . . . I'll just go back for supper in the mess.'

'And I'll come with you, I think.' Alex collected his stick and gestured to the door.

'I'm sorry, Bill,' Alex said finally, as they walked in silence up the road.

Bill shook his head. 'Don't be stupid, Alex. Kate had a perfect right to want to continue working and not cook us supper . . .'

'I wouldn't have minded if I thought it was just that,' Alex agreed wearily. 'But ever since that man came back into her life . . .' He trailed off and stared blankly into the evening light. 'Never mind. It doesn't matter. Just . . . don't go mentioning this, will you?'

'Of course not. Wouldn't say a word.' Bill glanced questioningly at Alex's set face and hesitated. 'Um, you don't think, maybe, that you're overreacting a little? Kate adores you and you're newly married. Why should she care about some other chap?'

'Because Richard Christie has set out to woo Kate with his money and influence and by offering her her old life back – and if he has to do it by stealing her from me, then he will.'

'And has it not occurred to you . . .' Bill angled his head to one side, his eyes deceptively lazy; he swished his stick at a weed, '. . . that you're playing right into his hands?' He saw Alex falter and glance quickly at him, obviously arrested by the thought. 'Well?'

But Alex was still too angry to see reason. 'Damn bloody Richard Christie to hell! I need my wife at that coffee morning and I expect her to be there.'

Oh dear, Bill thought, as he sighed and walked on beside Alex. This is all going to end in tears . . .

* * *

Kate was asleep by the time Alex returned home. For a while he had contemplated sleeping in the mess. But he had realised that to do so would cause comment. So, late, and in that state of angry alertness when no amount of alcohol downed would make any difference whatsoever, Alex let himself into the bedroom and saw Kate lying quietly beneath the bedclothes. Her cheeks were blotched and stained with tears and her hand clutched a mangled and soggy handkerchief of Alex's. Alex felt his anger evaporate instantly.

Poor darling, he thought, crying herself to sleep while he was out boozing with the boys. Maybe he was overreacting as Bill had suggested? But . . . what was he supposed to do? He was married and everyone would expect Kate to be there. People would be slighted if she didn't make an appearance. And it was too late to try to reschedule it because the flyers had gone out and there were too many people to try to rework just because his wife had another engagement. Couldn't she see that?

Besides, he might be a fool about a lot of things, but he knew he was right about Richard. That man was doing his best to lure Kate back into the world she had shared with him before and if he could just make Kate realise that . . .

Suddenly, he wondered if Kate had read the piece in the *Belfast Telegraph* about Joanna . . . That Joanna was bringing her exhibition to Belfast did not altogether surprise Alex. She was a vindictive woman and would want Alex to know just what he had lost when he married elsewhere. But it also occurred to Alex that Kate might be desperate to show that she was just as talented and just as able as Joanna to provide a financial boost to his own salary. He groaned at the thought and Kate, stirring, blinked up at him. Her initial quick smile faltered and died away as she remembered.

She didn't say anything, simply turned over and pulled the bed-covers up around herself. Alex's sympathy ended abruptly. He turned and retreated down the hall to the spare bedroom, undressing quickly and sliding into the single bed. Damn Kate, he wasn't going to go begging her forgiveness like some sulky child. She could stew for a few more hours. It might bring her to see the other side of things for a change.

But in the morning Kate remained in her bedroom until after Alex had slammed out of the house and she angrily related the evening's argument to Emma an hour later, without having changed her mind in the slightest. Emma closed her eyes briefly.

'Oh lord, Kate! I think Alex *is* jealous, yes. You could see that last Sunday over lunch. But he does also have a point about the first company coffee morning. He really does need your support there.'

'Then he should have checked with me first before scheduling it for next Tuesday. What, does he think I'm free whenever he chooses to crook a finger?' Kate passed Emma a steaming mug of coffee and a couple of biscuits which, as always, Emma declined. For once, Kate indulged herself and crunched the digestive angrily.

'I know that was foolish of him and I'm sure he's cursing himself that he didn't ... but now he's stuck! I'm sure Richard could handle the presentation on his own, couldn't he? Or I could?' Emma raised her eyebrows tentatively.

'No, not really. You're not experienced enough and they'd eat you for breakfast. Possibly Richard could do it, but that's not the point! I am not some chattel of Alex's to jump to attention every time he snaps his fingers! If I turn up at these army dos it's because I love Alex and want to help him, not because it's my duty!' Exasperated, Kate didn't even notice Emma's faint purse of her lips. Emma shrugged.

'Well, if you love him, then you'll put your pride to one side and help him out,' Emma urged.

'I don't see *him* putting *his* pride to one side—' Kate argued stubbornly.

'No, but he's a man—'

'So what, Emma!' Kate hunched away from Emma's hand on her arm. 'Don't go telling me men have more professional pride than women, please! I'm just so angry, I could spit!'

Emma sighed. 'That much is obvious,' she retorted. 'Look, it might help things if you keep it in mind that the reason Alex didn't eventually marry Joanna is because she thought her work was more important than the sum of them. Don't make that mistake, Kate,' she warned in a serious voice.

Kate looked at her oddly. 'Don't you realise that Joanna is half the reason I'm so determined to get this business up and running. We've been handed a real plum by Richard – and I'm supposed to throw it away? Because of Alex's coffee morning? Alex admires how well Joanna's doing, don't you worry . . .'

'Admires, possibly. Wants his wife to compete? I very much doubt. He loves you, Kate. He needs you. Don't be silly over all this.'

'I'm not being silly. Alex is the one who's got it into his head that I'm about to run away with Richard, for God's sake. And if he keeps this sort of behaviour up, I might just! At least then I wouldn't have to attend any wretched coffee mornings.'

'Oh, Kate, be careful . . . you never know how precious what you have is, until you lose it.' Emma was filled with foreboding but Kate simply tossed her long mane of fair hair over her shoulder and leant over the boards.

'Tosh! Come on, we're wasting time that we don't have. Let's get back to work.'

When Emma returned home that evening at five, as usual, leaving Kate to work on, she wondered whether she ought to pull out of the partnership. She and Kate clearly had such different ideas about family and home. Kate really was a career girl and as single-minded as any man when it came to her business. While, she, Emma, simply wanted a little work on the side to fill in the hours when Fergus was out and to bring in some extra cash. Perhaps she ought to offer to be Kate's P.A. instead? She grinned as she realised that wouldn't work either. Kate could then demand she stay late and finish the job in hand.

With a sigh she set about supper. That morning she had left some meat in a slow cooker so that it would be tender by the time she got home. She intended to bake a steak and mushroom pie, so she set about flouring the table and rolling out the pastry. Thoroughly absorbed in her task, and enjoying it as she hadn't enjoyed anything all day, she didn't notice Fergus had come in. He put his arms around her and kissed her neck with a loud, smacking sound.

'Hello, gorgeous, what's cooking?'

Emma turned and flung her floury arms around Fergus's neck. 'Your favourite, my love, steak and mushroom.'

He kissed her long and hard until she squirmed away.

'That is, if you let me go long enough to make it,' she added with a breathless laugh.

'Um, um! That's why I love you. Your mother must have whispered something about the way to a man's heart.' Fergus teased, letting her go and walking over to raid the larder instead. He opened a packet of crisps and hunted for a beer in the fridge, offering one in a glass to Emma but drinking his own straight from the bottle. In his camouflage combats with loose smock, he looked even more burly than usual. Emma dimpled as a stray and rather provocative thought passed through her mind. She shook her head to clear it.

'Yes, well, maybe Kate's mother should have whispered the same to her,' she added wryly. 'She seems to have missed that lesson.'

Fergus raised his eyebrows. 'Ah! Yes, Alex has been going around like a thundercloud all day, I must admit. What's happened?'

Emma filled him in on the feud while briskly rolling out her pastry and fitting it over the meat-filled dish. From time to time she glanced up at her husband and he nodded to let her know he was listening still.

'So, you see, neither one's willing to budge. Both have a point but both are being pig-headed as well. And I can't get Kate to see reason, so maybe you could with Alex?'

But Fergus was shaking his head. 'No, I can't go interfering, Em,' he stated categorically. 'If Alex had wanted me to know about it, he'd have discussed it with me, griped the way Kate did to you. Then I could give advice. But . . . he'd be mortified if I just butted in with suggestions on how to run his own marriage. You must see that?'

Emma sighed and gave an uncomfortable smile. 'Yes,

of course, you're right. I just hadn't thought it through properly. And, of course Alex would be too proud to go discussing it – except with Bill, perhaps, since he was actually there and heard it all. Anyway, I offered to go to the board meeting in Kate's place but she says I'm not experienced enough to field their questions and it would be better that neither of us went and Richard handled it alone, if the worst comes to the worst.' Emma grimaced.

'Were you hurt? Is your nose just a little out of joint?' Fergus smiled tenderly at his dark-eyed wife.

'Well, just a little, yes. After all, I am a solicitor – well, was – so I do think I could have done it. But, anyway,' Emma shrugged and gave a rueful smile, 'I must admit I was glad to come home and be Mrs Homemaker again. If that's what being in business does to a marriage, I'd rather forgo the pleasure!'

'Amen to that! Besides, your little-ones-to-be will take up all your time, won't they?'

Fergus put down his beer and put his arms around her, holding her close to him. Neither of them had to say anything. They had worked it out over the last few years and knew exactly how each other felt. Instead they enjoyed the feel of each other, the warmth of skin, the touch and taste of familiar territory. With a sigh, they broke apart again.

'Oh, by the way, just to change the subject.' Fergus returned to his position leaning against the kitchen cabinets. 'I'm going up to have a look over Belfast on Friday by helicopter.' He smiled. 'Should be fascinating, looking down on all those trouble areas—' He broke off as the telephone shrilled in the next room, and grimaced as Emma nodded her head at it.

'Will you get it?' Her hands were even more floury as she

held them up. He sighed and loped off to answer it. Emma heard the ringing stop, then a long pause and then finally, Fergus returned holding the mobile receiver, a strange look on his face.

'It's Laura, calling from Kenya,' he whispered. 'So hurry up and take it, will you?' Emma's eyebrows shot skywards. Hastily she rinsed her hands. 'What's up?' she mouthed at Fergus as he continued to hold his hand over the receiver.

'The police've been on to her to tell her they've let their suspect go. She's been trying to get hold of Bill with no success, so she rang here to find out what's going on. I told her we had no idea.' He held out the receiver as she dried her hands and reached for it, her mind suddenly in turmoil.

'Hello? Laura?'

Chapter Fifteen

Bill had taken Alex's suggestion, that he start using his lazy brain to figure out who killed Hugh, to heart. He had spent most of his free time since then cataloguing everyone who was known to have had a grievance against Hugh, where they had been during the crucial two-hour slot of the murder, and the likelihood that they could wield something heavy enough with which to smash in a man's head. That let out most women, he realised. Besides, it didn't really seem like a woman's preferred method.

The difficulty was that most of the suspects had no real alibi other than being home in bed, with only their wives or room-mates to testify to that. Two sergeants, a corporal, four privates (at least – possibly more he didn't know about), three or four officers (depending upon how literally one took a threat) and a couple of wives – Laura and Emma, for starters. How on earth was anyone supposed to sort that out? Obviously the police weren't having much luck. Added to which, there was the booking-in and out system from the main gate.

He understood there had been no sign of a murder weapon in the vicinity of the body, neither had any forensic evidence turned up that could be separated from the scores of people who passed by that lane every day. In fact, Bill concluded with not a little relief, there wasn't much hope of ever finding out who had done it. As Laura had said, it could have been anyone.

Idly, he put himself in the place of the murderer. All right, he (and Bill concluded it must be a 'he' since Emma was surely not physically strong enough, and Laura – well, he refused to believe it was Laura) must have been at the mess and seen how drunk Hugh was. Perhaps he had followed Hugh from the mess, not really sure what he was going to do but hoping something might come to hand – no, no, that was all wrong!

Anyone who followed Hugh from the mess with murder on his mind would have taken a weapon with him, ready to use, surely? So . . . what? Bill looked around the ante-room, speculatively.

The only idea that sprang to mind was the poker. After all, you could hardly walk off with one of the bronzes or some of the silver without someone noticing! There were two fireplaces in the long ante-room, one at each end, with massive brooding portraits of Peninsular war heroes over them. Bill prowled forth from his easy chair to check them. The first fireplace certainly had its full complement of fire-dogs, brush, shovel and poker. In fact, they needed a good going over with Brasso. He ought to have a word with the mess staff about that.

He shrugged and walked down to the other end of the room. Obviously he was wrong. There must have been something else – but, suddenly, he paused, glancing around.

He leaned down and hunted amongst the wood basket but no, it wasn't there either. He stood up in some surprise. The second poker was missing.

'Sergeant Hoskins?' As the sergeant passed by, Bill beckoned him over. 'I say, you haven't seen the poker, have you?' he asked in a low, puzzled voice. Sergeant Hoskins eyed Bill impassively.

'No, sir, haven't seen it in days. Mind you, sir, it's been so mild for the time of year, we haven't needed both fires in the evenings. I'll ask Sergeant Riley to look for it, sir, shall I?'

'Oh, well, no, don't fuss. I expect it'll turn up and, as you say, we hardly need it at the moment. Thank you, Sergeant.' Bill dismissed him and wandered out into the front hall in a daze of speculation. So, he, the murderer, had grabbed a likely weapon, and, concealing it against himself, set out to follow Hugh home. At the darkest, loneliest place, between the camp and the quarters, he had struck. And then . . . done what with the murder weapon? Flung it far into the bushes? No, the police had scoured the area. Taken it home and disposed of it later? Possibly. But, think what a risk to be seen flinging a poker away, or even carrying it out of the house again!

No, if he were the murderer, he would have taken it home with him, washed it carefully and either hidden it in the house until things had calmed down and he could return it quietly to the mess, with no one the wiser – or, perhaps buried it? No, the next family to live in the quarter might dig it up accidentally and then the fat would be in the fire. Just hide it and forget about it? Or take it away with you when you were next posted and then dispose of it, far away from all suspicion? That would be the safest option, surely?

Bill walked out into the evening, beneath the huge cedar tree that overshadowed the mess, and stared quietly up at the dusk drawing in. Laura couldn't have done it, he reasoned with delicious relief, because she had gone home with Emma and Fergus, and she could hardly have hidden a poker in that dress. And she couldn't have returned, either, without having been spotted.

So who was around at the time that Hugh had left? Bill shook his head. He didn't have any way of knowing since he was already paralytically drunk at Henry's place. Fergus was out – he'd gone home already. Alex had also left early and his return timings were logged in and out by the guards at the gate, so he was pretty unlikely. He, Bill, hadn't done it and neither had Henry, although there was only drunken recollection to go on, there. Those were the only four officers with grudges as far as he knew. So . . . who else, amongst the NCOs and soldiers, had had access to the mess that night? He didn't know but he would make it his business to find out, he thought sombrely.

It was just no good. This murder was hanging over everyone like a great dark pall. Morale was at an all-time low, and there had been accusations flying amongst the men, each accusing the other when their own alibi looked shaky. No, the whole fiasco had to be cleared up – no matter who had done it. He kicked the grass in exasperation.

Any day now, they would be drafting in a replacement for him and shipping him off to Bosnia. Christ, he'd really messed up his career this time! And loused things up for Laura too. Even if they did decide to get together after this six months was over – and the uneasy thought entered his head, not for the first time, that Laura had never enjoyed army life and never would – she would be uncomfortable returning to the battalion. So then what? Should he give up the one thing he really enjoyed doing and settle down in the country like his brother? Or perhaps move to London and spend his inheritance in double-quick time, if Laura had her way?

Either prospect did not thrill him. He didn't really mind the mine-clearing duty – as long as he made it home again in one piece. Bosnia at this point would be a fascinating place to be and this was part of the job he had been trained to do. So, all right, this was a punishment, but it really wasn't such a terrible one. At least, not to him. He grinned at his foolishness.

But, having to leave the battalion permanently, all his friends . . . for Laura's sake? The cold, snaking sensation in his belly made him feel sick. What sort of cad ruined a marriage and then refused to divvy up and marry the girl? Not his sort, anyway! But, he swallowed over the nausea rising in the back of his throat, could he make a marriage to Laura work? Could he make someone like that happy? Or would his marriage turn out to be a re-run of Hugh's?

He shook his head, furious at himself, at his stupidity. Christ, this was going to be the real punishment. Being ostracised from the life he loved, and married to a girl who, he suspected, was never going to be happy in England in the first place. And he, much as he might kick against the restraints of his upbringing, would never be happy anywhere else. He sighed and stared up at the cedar tree.

How long had that stood there? A hundred, a hundred and fifty years. Maybe longer? It made his own little problems seem insignificant. How many other men had stood beneath it, as he did now, mulling over their futures, regretting their pasts? The shadows the tree threw over the lawn suddenly made him glance at his watch and curse. He'd been standing about, mooning over his sorrows for nearly an hour and dinner had started at eight, ten minutes ago. Hastily he stepped out for the mess.

'Laura's what! Already?' Fergus was flabbergasted. He sat, staring into the distance for a moment while Emma shrugged her shoulders and took a deep breath.

'Well, you know Laura . . .' She had finished glazing the pie with egg yolk and bent down to slip it into the oven. When she stood up again, her face was flushed with heat. 'Evidently this "Neil Carlisle" bought the farm next to her parents in the time Laura's been over here. He's a widower and loaded, I suspect from what she wasn't saying but hinting at. Anyway, she met him almost immediately she returned home and, well, the long and the short of it is, the wedding's next month. Rather an indecently short interval since Hugh's death, I know, but then, she hadn't loved him for years . . .'

'Well, good for her!' Fergus exclaimed suddenly and generously. 'The lifestyle out there's much more her sort of thing and let's face it, the sooner she moves on and out of Bill's sphere, the better for both of them. But,' he hesitated, 'I really do think she should have told Bill first. Not asked you to do it. That really is stretching things a bit, I think.'

'Um, so do I!' Emma retorted. 'I tried to refuse but she said she simply couldn't do it, and then Bill would read about the wedding in the *Telegraph* instead, and think how awful that would be for him! Laura really is the limit, sometimes,' Emma bit her lip crossly.

'But you're fond of her anyway, aren't you?' Fergus smiled. 'Go on, admit it.'

Emma gave a rueful grimace. 'Oh, I suppose I am. She's such a madcap! But how am I supposed to tell Bill this?'

'I'll do it,' Fergus offered and Emma looked up at him gratefully.

'Oh, would you darling? You'll know so much better how to phrase it so he won't be humiliated—'

'I wouldn't worry so much, my sweet. I strongly suspect Bill has been coming to his senses in the last few weeks and realising just what a complete cock-up he's made of his life. I think this'll come as more of a relief than anything.'

'I do hope so! Then everything would be sorted out.'

Fergus gave her a strange, probing look. 'Except, of course, who killed Hugh.'

Emma eyed him sideways and tossed her head defiantly. 'Do you know?' she said in her clear, precise voice. 'I really don't give a damn who did it. As long as no one we know ever gets caught for it. And as long as the wrong man doesn't get put away. I must admit, I was worried about this local thug. It did seem all too pat, too convenient . . .' She glanced sideways at Fergus.

'Well, if he didn't do it, then the murderer's clearly willing to let an innocent man go down for it rather than confess. Better no one's ever caught than that,' Fergus added, hunting in the fridge for another beer.

'You didn't see anything when you popped back to the mess, did you?' Emma asked casually. But the tightness in the back of her throat made her voice thin and brittle. Fergus straightened up and looked at her carefully.

'Just your bag, lying where you said you'd left it. Hugh was nowhere in sight by then and most of the others were either comatose or snogging their girlfriends. All the boring old pads had gone home by then.' He smiled evenly and steadily at her, as though to reassure her. She nodded, a nervous smile on her face.

'So you're sure no one saw you?'

'No one. Or I'd have mentioned my return visit to the police. We've discussed all this before, Em.' He stroked her cheek. 'And we agreed it was better if no one knew. Otherwise I'm one of the few without an alibi and with a motive.'

'Alex was out and about at that time, too,' Emma added stubbornly.

'Yes, but he was logged in on the gate. I scooted out that hole in the fence at the bottom of the garden to avoid all the hassle of rousing the guard. No one knows I was out, no one needs to know. And I didn't do it, Emma. You do know that, don't you?' His eyes were deceptively mild, watching her, gauging. Emma smiled and nodded.

'If I don't, then no one does. And anyway, as long as the wrong man doesn't get caught, I frankly don't care.' She seemed to throw off her nervousness. 'I think Hugh deserved it!' She wiped her hands efficiently on the tea-towel and stood back to look at her husband. He raised his eyebrows.

'My, you're one tough little cookie, aren't you?'

'That's right.' She smiled sweetly. 'We army wives have to be. Now, how about some wine with dinner?

'Do you know, something's just occurred to me!' Bill, sitting opposite Alex at lunch in the mess the next day, leaned forward eagerly. 'You know how you might know someone if you see them in the same place every day, but not recognise them out in the street?'

'Like the greengrocer, you mean?' Alex smiled wearily.

He hadn't been sleeping well and was barely focusing on what Bill was saying. 'You'd know him in his green apron but wouldn't recognise him in a suit at church?'

'Exactly. Or one of us. People know us in uniform but not out of it. Well, I've suddenly realised that I did recognise the woman with Hugh that night, but I can't quite remember from where.'

'Is she army or not?'

'I don't know, can't think . . . I've never seen her in an army uniform, I know that much, but . . . I still think she wears something distinctive.' He paused as Sergeant Hoskins leaned over him to take his plate. 'Thanks . . . whoops, careful there.' Bill caught the knife as it tilted off the plate.

'Sorry, sir. Sorry.' Sergeant Hoskins seemed upset and Bill, glancing up at him, frowned.

'It's all right. No harm done. Don't worry about it.' The mess sergeant stepped back and hurried off to the kitchen. Bill looked after him in surprise.

'What's up with old Hoss? He seems a bit flustered, doesn't he?'

'Been looking a bit harassed of late. I'll have a word with him after lunch and just check everything's all right,' Alex murmured, wondering if Sergeant Hoskins was ill or had personal problems. But that only brought Alex's mind back to his own and he lapsed into a brooding silence.

'Anyway,' Bill continued, 'it occurs to me that this woman might be the key to it all. I mean, she might well be a complete outsider whom Hugh met while out shopping or something, mightn't she? And Hugh might have run foul of her husband. That would be a really plausible reason for murder, don't you think?'

There was a sudden crash from the far side of the room where Sergeant Hoskins had been attempting to carry out the newly refilled soup tureen to the sideboard. The remains of soup were splattered up the walls and over the furniture as well as over those lunchers who, unfortunately for them, had chosen to sit near the sideboard. Chairs were thrown back hastily, cries of pain and annoyance ringing out as hot soup, soaking through cotton battledress, sent men hopping up and down, and Sergeant Hoskins stared around him as though dazed and appalled. Alex walked quickly over to him and put a hand on his shoulder.

Sergeant Hoskins didn't react at first, then turned slowly and looked at Alex. 'The napkin slipped, I couldn't hold it, I, I . . . It was burning my hand, sir.'

'It's all right, Sergeant, it was an accident. Anyone could see that. Come on, let's go to see the doctor about that hand. You there,' Alex pointed to one of the mess waiters, 'Private Dutton, isn't it? Get some help cleaning this up, will you, and ask the cook if there's any more soup left. Right? Thank you.' He nodded as he drew Sergeant Hoskins down the table towards the door to the Sergeant's office. 'Tony,' he called, belatedly spying the doctor at the far end of the table, studiously ignoring the fracas. 'Come and have a look at this hand, will you?'

'Will it wait until I finish my meal?' Tony asked with exasperation and the sergeant hastily nodded. Alex, lips pursed in annoyance, gave the doctor a curt nod and led Sergeant Hoskins away.

'Let me see it,' Alex demanded, eyeing the smooth pink palm with misgiving. Already it looked shiny and taut, he thought, savagely angry with Tony. Sergeant Hoskins read Alex's grim mood and fell silent.

'We'll wrap it in a wet towel with some ice on it until the doctor finishes his meal, I think.' Alex sighed, caught another waiter scurrying past and relayed instructions for the towel and ice to be brought out. Then he gestured for the sergeant to sit in his own chair and Alex perched on his desk, his arms folded across his chest. He looked at Sergeant Hoskins steadily.

'Care to tell me about it, Hoss?

'About . . . spilling the soup, sir?'

'No.' Alex paused and gave the sergeant a slight smile. 'Not the soup. The reason you flinched when clearing Captain Ovington's plate, the reason the napkin slipped. Was it something to do with the conversation we were having, by any chance?'

Sergeant Hoskins tried unsuccessfully to look blank. 'I don't know what you mean, sir,' he replied stonily. Alex waited as the towel and ice appeared and was applied. When they were alone again, he stood up and went to look out of the window at the lawn and cedar tree in front of the mess.

'Your wife – Jenny, isn't it? Is she well?' he asked, speaking over his shoulder. He didn't turn around, knowing the sergeant would react differently if he knew he were being watched. Alex watched his reflection in the glass pane instead.

'Yes, she's all right, sir,' Sergeant Hoskins replied dully, but his face registered the pain and bewilderment he obviously felt. Alex bowed his head, understanding only too well the emotions the man was feeling.

'Was . . . was Jenny seeing Major Mallory, Hoss?' He turned around swiftly before the man could try to pretend, catching the look of despair flooding his eyes.

'I didn't do it, sir,' he blurted out, as though anxious to be rid of the deception, desperate to seek advice and share his burden. Alex sat down again, his mouth grimacing.

'Why didn't you say something earlier?'

'You know why, sir! Captain Ovington spelled it out pretty clearly over lunch, didn't he? I'm the one with the best motive for doing the bastard in, they'll say, and I'm not an officer so they won't think twice, just bang me up, won't they?' He sounded bitter. Alex nodded and gave a half shrug.

'You might have a point. Care to tell me about it?'

Sergeant Hoskins sighed as though from the bottom of his soul, raising his hands for a moment before letting them drop. He looked up again, wearily. 'He met her at the Naafi. Jenny works there. That's probably why Captain Ovington said he knew her in a uniform of some sort but couldn't think who she was.' He sighed again. 'Anyway, I don't know how long exactly it'd been going on. A month, six weeks, not much more. I've been doing a lot of extra duty here and the major always knew my schedule, it seemed. And the kids are away at school now, aren't they, so Jenny was alone a lot . . .'

Alex listened to the tale of a marriage's disintegration with a sick feeling of recognition. Hoss had let his career become all-important, working every spare moment and doing lots of overtime. Jenny had missed the children once they'd been sent off to school and had been lonely without Hoss. A smooth-talking, plausible man offering a better life had come along . . . and things had disastrously fallen into place.

'. . . Jenny got angry at me one night and boasted to me about it, said she was going to leave me. I begged her to think things over and she calmed down a bit and was, I think, pretty upset she'd said anything at all. I got the impression it was all a bit of a fantasy with her, like . . . but then he wound up dead and I was really glad . . . except I swear I didn't do the sod, I swear it!

'I was here all night, running ragged trying to clear the dinner, sort out the drinks, get breakfast up and ready in time for four-thirty. There just wasn't time for me to slide off, bash his brains in, and get back to work, sir, there just wasn't!' The sergeant sat back, rubbing his good hand over his face. Alex sat very still and then he nodded.

'No, I don't think there was unless you're a secret marathon runner.' Alex smiled. 'But, I am going to have to discuss this with the colonel. We'll decide then whether we need to inform the police or not.' He started to rise and then leaned forward and gripped Hoss's arm. 'I'm sorry about this, Hoss. I hope you and Jenny can make a go of it again. You know what Major Mallory was – there's no point in me saying further there. Just try not to let it sour you for the future.' He stood up and started to leave the room but the sergeant interrupted him.

'Do you believe me, sir?' he asked in a hoarse, strained voice. Alex turned and gave him a swift grin.

'One hundred per cent, Hoss, don't worry. And there are plenty of the rest of us with good motives too, so I wouldn't get too panicked! I'll send Tony in, pudding or no pudding!' And then he went out, pulling the door to behind him. Pity he couldn't tell Kate about all this, he thought coldly. Perhaps then she might see Richard for the shark he really was.

Over the next three days, Alex and Kate barely spoke to each other. Alex found that he was terribly busy catching up with all the work his new job as company commander generated and so spent long hours in his office, working late into the night. And Kate was working against a deadline of lunchtime on Friday to complete the brief for the redesign of the Chelsea Hotel in central Belfast. Neither saw each other for more than a few frostily polite moments a day and neither tried to apologise or repair the fracture in their marriage.

By Thursday 8th February events were turning nasty, according to the Intelligence briefs Alex had received and there were rumours of problems down in West Belfast. Alex wondered whether he ought to try to get himself on Fergus's reconnaissance flight as well. But he had an 'O' group ordered for 10:00am on Friday and didn't think he could change it. He'd talk it over with Fergus at lunch.

Katc, used tu tlie restrictions and quirks of life in Northern Ireland now, didn't notice the sudden step-up in security and was equally oblivious to the news. Yet more talk about the twin-track initiative to peace negotiations, yet more Trimble on about this, and Hume on about that . . . not to mention Gerry Adams warning yet again that the Peace process was in jeopardy if the Prime Minister didn't abandon his hard-line stance on the decommissioning of IRA arms before all-party talks.

Well, she, Kate was tired of it all. What she really wanted was to make a great success of this job and get lots more work because of it. Then Alex would stop taking her for granted as his wife and see just how much he ought to appreciate her. And Joanna could take her exhibition and stick it!

By eleven o'clock on Friday morning, Kate had dressed herself in a chic little pale pink suit. With Chanel-type pearls roping heavily over the ivory silk blouse, and her hair pulled back severely into a chignon at the nape of her neck, she was feeling excited and elated. She stared at her reflection in the mirror as she applied a lipstick in exactly the same shade as her woollen suit. Richard appreciated her looking the part of the successful design consultant and she had no intention of letting him down.

Emma would be back shortly, so Kate quickly collected up the boards in her zippered portfolio case and placed them in the back of her car. She looked up to see Emma approaching across the street, looking smart and fresh in a navy fitted dress to just above her knee, a gold chain around her neck, and large gold earrings. Her dark mink-coloured hair was pulled back with a tortoiseshell band and curled gently onto her shoulders. Very nice, Kate thought approvingly and waved Emma into the passenger seat.

'I know we'll be a bit early, but I thought we could have a drink first and settle our nerves,' Kate confided and Emma gave her a strained smile as they pulled out of the camp and waved their thanks to the guard holding up the toll-gate.

'Did you catch the news?' Emma asked, a shade too casually for Kate to notice. Instead she was concentrating on pulling into the fast-moving traffic on the A2 Bangor to Belfast expressway. After a couple of moments' silence, she glanced across at Emma.

'No? Why?'

'Um, well, it seems a bomb went off on Canary Wharf in the early hours this morning. Twenty-two injured, some seriously.' Emma swallowed carefully as Kate's head shot around to stare in horror at her.

'Watch your driving, for God's sake, Kate! You nearly side-swiped that van!'

'Has anyone claimed responsibility?' Kate demanded, refocusing on her driving. She pulled over into the slower lane and reduced her speed.

'A warning was evidently delivered in Dublin just an hour before, using an IRA codeword and saying the 17-month Peace was at an end.'

'Oh, dear God!' Kate's worst fears flooded her mind, jumbling one over the other until she could barely think straight. She couldn't imagine how Emma was sitting there so calmly. Did this mean Belfast would explode into violence again with soldiers deployed on the streets and in danger of their lives? Would bombs start going off all over the place? Was Alex at risk?

Obviously the same thought must have occurred to Emma because she commented reflectively, 'Lucky Alex didn't do his mercy run this week instead of last.'

Kate glanced at her, frowning. 'What do you mean, "mercy run"?'

'You know, with the baby,' Emma said. 'I have to say, I nearly broke down and wept when I heard how he'd saved that baby's life . . .' She paused as Kate's incomprehension became obvious. 'But surely Alex told you, didn't he?'

'Not a word,' Kate assured her grimly. 'But then, we've hardly been on the best of terms just lately.'

'Oh,' Emma replied hollowly, 'well, I'm sorry. I thought you knew.'

'Tell me, will you?' Kate changed lanes to bypass a bus belching out fumes as she passed the City Airport. Emma, cursing herself, reluctantly related the event to Kate whose face became more and more sombre. Finally, as they approached the hotel, Emma came to an end and

Kate swung into the hotel forecourt. She parked the car and turned to look at Emma.

'Quite the hero, then,' she said softly and Emma gave an awkward shrug. 'I wonder why he didn't tell me.'

'Well, I don't know, but you can ask him tonight, can't you? Make up with him, Kate, please! Now you see how fragile things are, how much at risk he and the other men are, surely you must feel he's more important than Richard.' There was silence while Kate sat there staring blankly out of the window. Emma gave it one more try.

'Talk to him,' she urged. 'Get him to tell you about the baby. And then he'll want to tell you all about the helicopter flight over Belfast, I imagine. Quite a useful recce, all things considered, and he'll find it easy to talk about. That'll break the ice and then, you know, things can go back to normal.' Emma smiled tentatively and Kate raised her eyebrows again.

'Was hc going up?'

'Oh, it wasn't confirmed.' Emma shrugged it off, appalled at how little Kate seemed to know about Alex's life at present. 'I know he mentioncd to Fergus that he'd like to go along with them but didn't know if he'd have enough time. Something about an 'O' group he couldn't change. Well.' Emma looked up at the hotel. 'I guess this is it. Let's go, shall we?'

'And what happens now that the Peace is at an end?' Kate looked around as she climbed out of her Golf and handed the keys to the valet with a faint imitation of a smile.

'I don't know,' Emma replied sadly. 'I really don't think anyone does. We'll just have to wait and see.'

Richard Christie finished his third cup of coffee and placed it down on the table. They had been over the plans again and again until he was familiar with every detail and had asked just about every imaginable question that he could think of. In turn, Kate and Emma had wanted to know how the Peace being at an end would affect the job. He had brushed the question aside as though of no importance and the girls had glanced at each other, surprised.

Now, as Richard shuffled through the boards again, he tapped his finger against the fringe Kate and Emma had selected for the curtains in the show bedroom. 'Very nice, but just how expensive is this stuff? Is it worth the extra?'

Kate shrugged nonchalantly. 'I know a warehouse where I can get it at about a third of the retail price but that's not really the point, is it, Richard? This is your show bedroom and you want to emulate the small, smart hotels that have sprung up in London. So, if you want to charge their prices, you have to give the finished effect. The Boxwood fabric is stunning – I've used it before like this – but it needs the final trim to look totally polished.'

'Well,' Richard rubbed his finger along his nose in contemplation, 'I just think that businessmen aren't going to notice trim—'

'If the sort of businessmen you're focusing on are willing to go for the big hotel look, then you've given us the wrong brief. You said small English country-look hotel. That calls for all the finish. Big hotel with the same decor in all the bedrooms doesn't. Which is it you want?' Kate asked firmly and Richard gave a deprecating grin.

'You know what I want, Kate,' his pale blue eyes twinkled with amusement, 'so don't go getting all tough with me. I'm just trying to keep costs down. This is the sort of question you'll have to field on Tuesday—'

'Ah,' Kate glanced away from Richard's attractive face and steeled herself to say it. 'I'm afraid there's rather a hitch about Tuesday . . . I can't be there.' She glanced up into Richard's face, seeing the quizzical frown, the grin slipping into puzzlement.

'What do you mean? It's the board meeting. You've known about it for a week or more.'

'I know and I'm dreadfully sorry, Richard.' She spread her hands wide, supplicating. 'If I could do anything about it, I would. Emma is quite willing to stand in—'

'With all due respect to Emma,' Richard gave a quick, offhand smile, 'I don't think—'

'I'm sorry, Richard.' Kate held up her hands now, forestalling the barrage she knew Richard would attempt to launch to make her change her mind. 'I know I've put you in a difficult position, but I truly can't do anything about it.' She glanced awkwardly at Emma who gave her a commiserating smile. 'But,' Kate continued, 'if you don't want to put the designs forward yourself, and you don't feel Emma can handle it alone, we can either reschedule or . . . you are quite within your rights to find another design firm.'

Richard stood up abruptly, his fingers combing through his short hair in irritation. 'You know there isn't time to get someone else and you know you're leaving me in an impossible situation, Kate. This really isn't good enough! What's got into you? Is it Alex?' His tone hardened, became dismissive.

But Kate looked at him coolly and impassively. 'I have another commitment that I cannot change, Richard. Let's just leave it at that, shall we?'

'No.' He swung around angrily. 'Let's not! The least you

could do is tell me just what this "other commitment" is that's so important to you that you'd jeopardise this job and my trust. No, more than my trust, my – friendship! My . . .,' He slapped his thigh as though at a loss suddenly for words, and then continued in a lower, quieter voice. '. . . but you know all that. There's no point in saying the obvious. I just thought you cared for me more than this.' There was a moment of deathly silence when Emma stared at her feet in acute embarrassment and Kate breathed in sharply.

'Oh, Richard,' Kate said finally, in a soft voice that held none of her earlier steel. 'I'm sorry . . . I'm truly very, very sorry. But I have to choose between something that means everything to my husband – and something that means everything to you. And I will always choose Alex. I'm sorry, Richard, but that's how it is.' She rose, gathered her bag and jacket, and gestured to Emma.

'Come on, Emma, I think we've shown Richard everything. Let's leave him to think matters over.' As she took Emma by the elbow and gently pushed her through the door, Kate glanced back once at Richard. He was standing rigidly with his back to her, staring out of the large paned window at the Belfast skyline. Nothing she could say would make any difference, she realised.

She closed the door softly behind her.

Chapter Sixteen

'Sorry Em,' Kate said finally, when they were in the car again and heading home. 'I've probably lost us the job and maybe any others we might have been offered on the strength of this one. I just didn't realise how much Richard was depending on me being there.'

'Don't worry about it. You did the right thing, Kate. I'm just relieved you've decided to back Alex up.'

'What else could I do? Besides, when Richard went and put it all on a personal level like that!'

'Um, well, maybe Alex wasn't all that far out when he said Richard was trying to woo you.' Emma grinned wryly at Kate.

'God, I hope not! We need to get the jobs because of our professional skills, not our figures!'

'We will,' Emma soothed, 'we will.' Idly she stretched forward and turned on the radio. 'You don't mind, do you? I thought we might try to catch the news?'

'No, no, go ahead. It's set on Cool FM but we'll probably

get better local news that way anyway. And let's face it, the Peace being over is kind of local, isn't it?' She gave an ironic smile to Emma who nodded and looked out the window. The news was just coming on and they both listened gravely to it, trying to imagine the devastation of a bomb like that going off around them. As it might well do now. Each shuddered with horror.

The day was cold and bleak, slanting rain and sullen clouds scudding low over the lough. How appropriate, Kate thought. A thoroughly miserable day for thoroughly miserable news. She glanced up through the windscreen and wondered if Alex was up there with Fergus, trying to see down through the intermittent cloud cover into Belfast's troubled west side. She'd make it up with him when he got home, she vowed.

If she apologised, he was bound to do the same, she realised. Neither of them wanted this dreadful coldness to continue between them and, besides, what did it say about the state of their marriage that he hadn't even told her about the dash with the baby? She shuddered again at the thought of him running alone and unprotected along the Falls Road and for a moment her eyes teared up, the images around her wavering into a blur that she blinked rapidly away.

She needed to tell him how much she loved him and how little Richard mattered to her. In her heart she knew he didn't care about Joanna, so why was she making such a big fuss about competing with her? It was crazy the way things had escalated between them into this state of cold hostility. Even more crazy now, when, with the Peace at an end, Alex was in danger all the time. How much was her pride worth when she balanced it against her love for him? Not very much, she admitted to herself, hollowly.

God, she just wanted him home so she could bury herself in his arms and tell him how much she loved him and how sorry she was—

'There's news just coming in,' the newsreader was continuing and Kate's thoughts broke off abruptly to focus on what was being announced on the radio, 'of an RAF helicopter crash just north of Belfast. From eyewitness accounts on the ground, the helicopter seemed to lose power in its tail rotor blade, sending it into a spin before it crashed into hills above Fort Whiterock. Emergency crews have yet to reach the site of the crash and there is no word yet on survivors. We'll bring you further news on the crash when we have it . . . And now, a word from our sponsor,' and the radio launched into a familiar jingle that jarred shrilly on Kate and Emma's ears. They glanced at each other just once, their eyes veering away almost immediately in terror.

There were scores of helicopters flying overhead every day, each reminded herself sharply. There was nothing to indicate that it was the flight Fergus and, perhaps, Alex had been on. Nothing except the sick dread in their stomachs or the coldness creeping along their limbs. Kate put her foot down and sped along the last of the expressway, turning up sharply for the barracks and barely pausing at the toll-gate as the guard inspected her identification.

'Come on, come on,' she muttered beneath her breath as the barrier lifted slowly, and then she lurched the car through and over the speed bumps with little regard to the suspension of the car. As she pulled into her driveway and climbed out, she noticed the padre returning to his car parked on the side of the road. He turned and looked at both of the girls, hesitated for a moment, and then began to walk towards them.

'No, oh God no, please, please God no,' Kate breathed over and over to herself, her heart suddenly racing and her lungs seeming to collapse within her. She stood rooted to the spot, unable to move, her legs feeling as though they were filled with sand. She tried to look at Emma but found she couldn't take her eyes off the padre's face as he approached. His kind grey eyes were filled with concern and compassion and Kate found she had to bite down on her hand to prevent herself screaming.

The colour had bleached from her face so that the skin was tinged with grey and drawn sharply over her cheekbones. Beside her, Emma simply closed her eyes as the world spun around her and she crumpled quietly onto the ground.

Kate immediately dropped down beside Emma, unable to catch her head before it contacted with the cement driveway. She looked up to see Father Ralph leaning down, his head blocking the filtering rays of sun through the clouds so that it seemed to be ringed with a halo. 'Who . . . ?' Kate began, but found her lips were frozen and refused to bend to speech. Father Ralph was kneeling down to scoop Emma up into his arms, and Kate staggered up beside him.

'The poor girl,' he said gently, looking down at Emma's white face, 'as if she didn't have enough sorrows.' He looked at Kate sadly. 'I was just coming across to see you, hoping you would come and help me break the news about Fergus, but I suppose you must have heard about the crash already?'

Kate stared at him, unable to think straight. And then she caught movement out of the corner of her eye and saw Alex running down the road towards them. Hating herself for the relief that burst through her, Kate wiped the tears from her eyes and forced herself to open the front door and let Father Ralph carry Emma in and place her on the sofa. Alex followed them, his face grim and pale.

'She knows?' he asked quickly, kneeling down beside Emma on the sofa, his great black army boots leaving tracks of mud across the carpet where he had run across the camp on hearing the news. Kate nodded, tears spilling down her cheeks to make the room waver and wash away. Gulping them back, she tried to speak.

'We heard about a crash on the radio and then when we saw the padre here . . .' Kate burst into fresh sobs, holding her hand over her face. 'Emma knew it had to be Fergus and I thought . . . oh God, I thought you were aboard too . . .'

Alex had been checking Emma's pupils in case she had cracked her skull when she fell, but now he stared aghast at Kate, realising what she meant.

'Oh, sweetheart, I'm so sorry. I should have told you I wasn't going up . . .' But Kate brushed his apology aside.

'It doesn't matter, as long as you're alive. Nothing matters. But, oh God, Fergus! Is he really dead?' When Alex nodded, she wept angrily and wretchedly for Emma. How was she supposed to live on without him and without the baby? How could life be so bitterly unfair for them?

Father Ralph laid a hand on her shoulder and turned her slightly away.

'Would you go to make some nice sweet tea for everyone, Kate? I think Emma'll need it when she comes around and she's beginning to stir now. I'd better go to call the doctor to look at her and maybe he could prescribe some sedatives to dull things for a while . . . take the edge off her grief until she's better able to cope with it.'

Alex, left alone with Emma, stroked the dark hair back

from her face, remembering how Fergus used to do it with such a tender touch, how both he and Emma had been so very in love. Shutting his eyes, Alex bowed his head, trying to block the flood of images surging through his mind.

Images of Fergus and he as platoon commanders together when they were just young lieutenants, callow and inexperienced but having such fun on exercise in Jamaica; how they had been mortared in Crossmaglen and Fergus had thought it was fireworks; how he had been Fergus's best man and nearly not made it to the wedding on time, with Fergus being so sick with nerves out the window of the car . . . Beside him on the sofa Emma stirred and groaned, her face pale against the dark of her hair.

'Shh, Emma, it's all right, shh,' he soothed her gently as her eyelashes fluttered open. But he knew, even as he said it, that he lied. It would never be all right again. Not for Emma and perhaps not for him.

'Alex? What . . . ?' But dimly the horror flooded back in to her confused mind and her eyes windened in terrified disbelief. Alex remembered that look in the eyes of the mother whose baby had stopped breathing. A desperation that things weren't really as bad as they seemed, that somehow, some miracle might be performed that would reverse it all, leaving them with a terrible scare but nothing more. But there was no hope in this case, Alex knew. Alex held the hand that gripped him with terrible force.

'Is he dead?' Emma was asking in a dazed, almost hushed tone. 'My Fergus, are you sure? It was his helicopter? Are you sure?' She gripped him again, her voice rising. Alex held her tightly against him.

'I'm sure, Emma. I'm so desperately sorry.' He felt his guts twisted tightly by the keening shriek of despair that broke from her. It was followed by sobs that shook her whole body, on and on and on, as though they would never stop and she would shake herself apart. Alex looked up over Emma's shoulder, his own face streaked with tears, to Kate. She ventured into the room awkwardly, holding the mugs of sweet tea on a small tray. Her face was still wet and blotched with red, swollen patches. With a rasping voice, she offered the tea. 'Do you think Emma wants some?'

But Alex shook his head once, sharply. 'Brandy. Get her a glass, will you?'

Kate went quickly over to the drinks tray and poured out a small amount into a whiskey tumbler, then held it out for Alex. Slowly, he forced Emma to sip a little. Father Ralph reappeared. 'The doctor's on his way, so not too much of that stuff. I don't know about sedatives and brandy mixing too well.'

Alex nodded. 'Just a sip. She needs it.' And the padre came over to sit beside Emma and take her hand. Both were Catholic and where Alex's sympathy and sorrow only seemed to pain Emma further, she was able to draw strength from Father Ralph's detached presence, his touch. She looked around dully and then took a deep, shuddering breath. 'He'll have gone without confessing his sins, Father,' she began in a tentative voice. 'He wasn't ready . . .'

Alex stood up. 'We'll be next door,' he murmured and withdrew with Kate, to leave the priest to comfort and reassure Emma in his own way.

Out in the kitchen, Kate leaned in against Alex and held him tightly to her, crying again, partly in grief for Fergus, partly in relief that Alex had not been with him. Alex simply held her, stroking her hair until the sobs slowly died away, leaving them both hollow and exhausted. They clung to each other instead, beyond apologising for the trivial arguments of the past. There was no point. This was what really mattered and Kate, leaning against Alex and feeling his deep, slow breathing, wondered if she would be able to cope in future with the fear every time Alex walked out of the front door. She closed her eyes, refusing to think about it.

'Do they, um,' Kate wiped her eyes awkwardly, 'know what happened? Something about the tail rotor?'

'It's too early to say.' Alex sighed deeply. 'They think something knocked out the tail rotor, but they've no idea what. The pilot reported that much over the radio, said they were going into a spin, and that was it. The wreckage is scattered over the hillside and there's not much left of anyone. That's how I know Fergus is dead.'

'How many were aboard?'

'Two RAF and two army. It was just one of the little gazelles. It couldn't fit any more than that. That's why I didn't go. Alex knew someone in the Royal Irish who wanted to go up too, and the place was already filled by the time I made up my mind.' He felt Emma cling even more tightly to him.

'That could be me in there,' she whispered, jerking her head to the sitting room where the padre and Emma were still withdrawn. 'And you could be dead on that hillside, in a thousand pieces, just like Fergus,' she whispered wretchedly. But Alex just shook his head at her, kissing her hair.

'But it's not. I'm not. And there's nothing we can do to change it one way or the other.' He glanced up as he saw the doctor approaching, and gently disentangled himself from Kate. 'Here's Tony. Are you up to making more tea?

And maybe a sandwich or two? I think Emma might need something soon.'

He went to let the doctor in.

The funeral was to be a full military affair at Winchester Cathedral. The colonel and Alex were representing the battalion since no more could be spared from Belfast in the state of unease following the breakdown of the Peace. Kate stood beside Alex, Joss and Suzy, one row back from Emma and her family. For a moment, she almost hadn't recognised Emma in her severe black dress and with her hair pulled back into a knot. Behind the dark veil there were lines of grief but also a look of acceptance, even serenity, that Kate found hard to understand. Only a week had passed since the crash. How could Emma accept Fergus's death already?

Kate had barely seen Emma since that terrible Friday. Her parents and Fergus's parents had arrived hours later and as soon as possible, she was whisked away home, looking frail and broken. Now, however, she stood firmly in the cathedral and there was a dignity, even strength there that surprised Kate. In time, yes, Kate had known Emma would steel herself to resume life. But so quickly? She shook her head in admiration.

Inside the cathedral, the regimental flags hung low over the congregation, and the bier in front of the nave was decked with flowers. The congregation were a mix of civilian and army, silently hushed and expectant.

Outside, the first of the drums began to beat in a slow, steady rhythm that sent instant shivers up Kate's back. She glanced quickly at Emma but there was no sign, no hesitation, as the coffin covered in the Union Jack was borne across the cloistered square towards the entry. As it arrived at the massive doors, the drummers inside the cathedral took up the beat, the sound reverberating hollowly around the great space and causing tears to slide unexpectedly down Kate's cheeks. She didn't turn to watch the approach, merely clenched her hands together tightly. In front of her, Emma stood rigidly erect almost as though to bend might be to collapse.

The pall-bearers were all members of Fergus's company and they carried the coffin to the bier and laid it carefully down, the weight of it sending one of them staggering for a moment before his balance was recovered. Then the flag was folded in triangles until it became a small packet. This was brought to Emma who stretched out her gloved hand and took it carefully.

The service was long, sombre and hushed, each hymn, each prayer seeming to wring the last drops of misery from the company gathered there. Then, finally, the coffin was lifted and the drums started beating again, and Emma followed it silently and painfully, her small figure still upright but her face now pale and tear-streaked behind the veil. Her father took her arm; Fergus's father needed to support his own wife down the long aisle. Slowly everyone trailed out after them.

By the time the coffin was again loaded in the hearse, for its journey to the small village in Dorset where Fergus and Emma had their house, Kate had managed to work her way through the throng to Emma's side. She touched her arm briefly and Emma turned and gave a weak smile.

'Kate! And Alex!' She threw her arms around each of them in turn. 'Oh, I'm so glad you're here. Fergus would have wanted that more than anything. Such a shame Bill wasn't allowed to come, but I can see he's probably still in disgrace . . .' She trailed off, looking around. 'I have a horror of military funerals. They seem so desperately gloomy and miserable, but I know Fergus would have wanted it. And, let's face it, it does seem to purge everything right out of you.' Kate and Alex nodded, unsure what to say, how to comfort. Emma smiled again, and gave them comfort instead.

'We weren't going to tell anyone, you know, until I was further along. But that last scan I went for . . . well, despite all their silly tests and shaking of heads, it seems I'm pregnant. Nine weeks today.' For a moment her smile wavered, almost broke down, but then she had herself in control again. 'I thought you'd like to know.'

'Oh, Emma! That's wonderful!' But Kate, having hugged Emma to her, was having to fight the tears and she turned away, blinking into the sunshine, leaving it for Alex to express their joy. So that explained the serenity, the hope she had seen on Emma's face. Oh, thank you, God, she murmured beneath her breath. At least there was something for Emma to look forward to, something of Fergus to keep with her forever. Perhaps it would be another boy, with merry eyes and curling hair? She hoped so.

'You'll come and see me, won't you?' Emma was asking, by the time Kate had recovered. 'Down in Dorset? I'm moving into the cottage. We always wanted to bring children up there, and I know Fergus would have . . .' But here her voice wavered and thickened, so that she simply smiled awkwardly and kissed them goodbye as they nodded and promised they'd be down very soon.

And then Emma disappeared into one of the waiting cars with her family, and the whole procession slowly edged away and out of the square. Kate hunted furiously for her handkerchief and finally accepted Alex's instead, clinging to him with her fair head bowed against his chest.

'Come on, my love,' he murmured, 'time to go home. Joss and Suzy are waiting.'

Chapter Seventeen

The coffee morning had been abandoned, the wives' club dinner still awaited, and Richard Christie had sent Kate a terse message that the backers for his project had decided not to proceed until the political situation was more stable. Kate crumpled the note in her hand and tossed it into the bin. Her business could wait. First, she had promised Emma she would help supervise the movers sent to shift all the Kennedy belongings home. Kate hoped Alex and Bill would be there to give a hand as they had promised.

Fergus's army clothing was collected up first and sent to the charity shop for sale. Emma had said she wanted nothing of his clothing except the more useful items like dinner jackets or tweed suits which might, one day, be of use to a son. Cuff-links, braces, studs and pins were all boxed up and put to one side as well. All photographs and mementoes were very carefully packed and then the movers were allowed in to deal with the rest.

Bill and Alex offered to clean out the garage and separate out useful items from general litter. Fergus, however, had been meticulous in his storage system, everything hung or stowed from the eaves and walls, or boxed and labelled. Even the hideous, mock Tudor lamps that each quarter's sitting room had until they were taken down by the newly entering pads, were neatly swinging from the rafters in the garage. Bill stood up on a box to lift them down and return them to the house and, as he pulled them, dislodged something else balanced on the central beam of the garage. A dark, heavy item clanged down on to the cement floor below. It was a poker.

Bill stared down at it, aghast. Then, slowly, he looked across at Alex. Alex was staring at the poker as well, deep creases appearing beside his mouth as he pressed his lips firmly together.

'Um, just toss that in with the golf clubs, why don't you, Alex?' Bill suggested, his tone as light as he could make it. But Alex had obviously done the same mental homework as Bill. He knew exactly what the poker meant. He gazed steadily at Bill until the latter flushed and looked away. There was a long period of silence while each of them grappled with the impossible.

'Finding this here,' Alex began at last, his voice slightly hoarse as he slowly walked forward and bent to pick the poker up in a rag, 'doesn't mean Fergus did it, Bill. He always kept the garage door unlocked, often open. If he were going to hide something this incriminating, he wouldn't be stupid enough to put it in here where anyone might dislodge it, just like you did.' Alex fell silent, staring at the long, slender piece of metal in his hand, imagining, without wanting to, the force with which it had been brought down upon Hugh's unprotected head. Involuntarily his hand clenched it more tightly.

'So . . . what? You're saying someone planted it? Someone who knew Fergus had a good motive for killing Hugh and wanted to shift the blame?' Bill sounded sceptical as he stepped down abruptly.

Alex shrugged. 'Think about it. How many people knew the reason why Emma lost the baby? I mean, they didn't tell anyone except Hugh, obviously, for all he denied it. And then, later, Kate. I knew, because Kate told me. Fergus said he mentioned it to you after Hugh's death, but asked you to keep it quiet. And . . . Laura knew, didn't she?'

Bill looked awkward. 'I don't know; she never talked about it to me.'

'Possibly not, but she did to Kate. And how did the police find out? Because they did. And I'll lay odds it was Laura who told them.'

'Not to be vindictive! If she did, which I'm not saying she did,' Bill paused crossly, 'it would only have been to give a fair picture of how many people detested Hugh and would, perhaps, have had reason to wish him dead. She would have been worried about me.'

'And about herself,' Alex added quietly. He raised the poker and examined it in the sunlight. 'It's been washed clean. There won't be any prints left on it, that's for sure, though I expect forensics could probably confirm it was the murder weapon. Whoever did leave it here had no intention of being caught. Even if someone else took the blame – a local thug, Fergus . . . it didn't much matter as long as it wasn't . . .' he shrugged awkwardly, 'her?'

'No! I don't believe it!' Bill snapped stubbornly. 'It could have been anyone who put it here well after the event. And

Laura never went out the gate again after she came back with Emma and Ferg—' He broke off as he realised the problem. If Fergus had done it, by the same premise, how had he passed the sentries without being seen?

Alex gave Bill a jaded smile. 'Come on, Bill! You know, as well as I do, that Emma's been complaining about that bloody hole in the perimeter fence for months. And as far as I know it still hasn't been repaired. Shall we go to look?'

With a troubled face Bill nodded. Alex laid down the poker on one of the packing boxes and led the way to the far corner of the garden, where the fence joined with the neighbour's. At some point, a few large cement blocks had been leaned against the fence and two had broken through it, leaving a gaping hole in the wire that, with a struggle, a man could certainly have climbed through. Or a woman.

'The main reason the police couldn't get anywhere with the murder enquiry, was the booking-in and-out system. All those people with grudges against Hugh were supposedly inside the wire when he was killed, or, like me, were logged out of the main gate and in again here at the side gate with no time to spare to deviate up the lane and smash a man's brains in. But we forgot this hole, didn't we? And the police never knew about it. Laura didn't tell them everything, clearly.'

'Laura, Laura! Why does it have to be her, especially, other than the fact that you never liked her much? Why couldn't it have been – you? Or me? Or Fergus . . . or anyone, for that matter?' Bill trailed off angrily. Alex turned and started walking slowly back towards the garage. Already the garden was looking neglected, the lawn covered in daisies and dandelions, the beds straggly with spring weeds choking the plants. Emma would have hated it.

'Why, especially, Laura?' Alex repeated uncertainly. Bill

caught up with him as he stood staring blankly at Laura's house. It backed onto the Kennedys' but there was no way Laura could have got out through the hole without either entering the Kennedys' garden, or their neighbour's. And that quarter was empty, wasn't it?

'Bill,' he sighed, and turned to face the troubled expression of a man who suspected, but refused to believe, the worst. 'Laura had motive – she hated Hugh, was trapped in a marriage she was desperate to be free of, and she was supposedly having an affair with you.' He ignored the flinch Bill gave.

'She had opportunity – she had come home earlier, very publicly after the fiasco on the bronco, with Fergus and Emma, and gone home to sleep alone. And she knew about the hole in the fence.'

'Maybe so, but what about means?' Bill broke in hotly. 'She couldn't have gone back to the mess to pick up the poker without having been seen, now, could she? And no one remembers her returning. She'd have stood out like a sore thumb in that shocking pink dress—'

'Ah, but what if the whole thing was premeditated?' Alex cut across Bill sharply. He had been thinking about it for a while, and something Kate had mentioned in passing suddenly fell into place. 'Laura turned up for the flower arranging on the morning of the ball and stayed for quite sometime in the mess. She even offered to carry out some of the boxes of flower clippings afterwards.' He paused, seeing the pallor on Bill's face. 'It would have been child's play to scoop up a poker in amongst the left-over leaves and branches and carry it out to the gardens in the back of the mess. Then she could have slipped the poker out and taken it home with her, wrapped in her jacket. Kate mentioned that Laura had suddenly disappeared, as oddly as she had appeared in the first place, but no one really thought much about it.' Alex gave a wry shrug. 'They just thought she'd had enough and left without saying goodbye.

'So now, Laura hides the poker at home, goes to the ball and stages a drama that was *bound* to have Hugh react angrily by hitting out at you, and you . . .' sighing, Alex gripped Bill's arm, as though to excuse the offence in advance, 'give exactly the performance she had been hoping for. You threatened Hugh with death.' He saw the horror deepen on Bill's face.

'I don't believe a word of this, Alex! And I won't listen to you any more!' Bill dragged his arm free and started for the gate, but Alex blocked his way.

'Hear me out, Bill. And refute it, if you can. I don't want to believe any of this either. But it makes sense. So just listen, will you? And then prove me wrong. I'll be glad to be wrong,' he urged.

Something in the darkly sombre blue eyes must have caught at Bill, reluctantly bringing him to a halt. He knew Alex, trusted him – with his life, as he'd proved in the past, so shouldn't he hear him out now? And how well did he really know Laura? Barely at all, a small voice echoed hollowly in his head.

'Go on then,' he snapped tersely.

Alex nodded and took a deep breath. 'Laura met this Neil Carlisle in Kenya after she returned from the funeral, according to what she told Emma. But what if she met him prior to that? What if she decided some months ago she wanted to be free of Hugh and marry rich Neil Carlisle? She knew Hugh wouldn't agree to divorce. In fact, he nearly strangled her when she mentioned it once in the past.

'Also, she's agreed to a Catholic wedding ceremony, according to Emma. So, obviously Carlisle is Catholic, since we know Laura isn't. And apparently he takes it seriously. No divorces for him, then.' He paused to see whether Bill was following him. From the look of sick dread on his friend's face, he knew he was. Remorselessly Alex continued.

'Laura needed to be free, but she was the most immediate and obvious suspect if Hugh were murdered . . . unless she set up someone else to take the blame. So she stages an affair with a brother officer. She's wildly indiscreet. She causes a scene in front of scores of witnesses that clearly underlines the jealous husband and vengeful suitor. And then she goes ahead and murders Hugh, leaving her dupe to take the fall . . . You.'

'But . . .' Bill scraped his fingers through his hair, massaging the pain in his temples that was building alarmingly. 'How would she know when Hugh was leaving the mess? How would she know what route home he would take? It's all very iffy, surely?'

'Not really. She came home, changed her clothes for something dark – perhaps a track suit, I don't know; and then slipped out the hole in the fence with the poker carefully hidden beside her trouser leg, just in case she was seen by someone. Then she simply waited in the park, maybe in some shrubs, near the front gate for Hugh to come through.

'We were all working on the premise that someone followed Hugh from the mess, weren't we? But Laura didn't need to. She already had the murder weapon handy – exactly the sort of weapon that a man, living in the mess, might have chosen – and she simply had to wait for Hugh to come out and to trail him down the lane, hidden behind the trees. At the right moment she stepped out behind him and clubbed him down. And don't tell me Laura isn't strong enough to have done it. Because we all saw her ride that bronco,' Alex added bitterly.

Bill swallowed and looked away, his eyes unconsciously fastening on Laura's house in the distance. 'She couldn't have known I'd have stayed with Henry and the other guys. That I'd have an alibi . . . Could she?' he asked quietly, finally turning to look into Alex's eyes. He read the answer there for himself. 'So,' he sighed with a slow, desperate sound, 'she meant me to be blamed. And when I wasn't, she planted the poker in Fergus's garage as a back-up.'

'Laura knew her house and garden would be searched. It was inevitable.' Alex grimaced wryly. 'She can't have known who else's house might have been searched. And Fergus always kept his garage unlocked. Perhaps she simply meant to hide the poker in the garage and retrieve it later, dispose of it. But she never had the opportunity.'

'There's no proof, Alex.' Bill shook his head, disgust in his tone, but not at Alex's scenario. No, it was directed at himself, at his stupidity, naïveté, vanity. Laura had duped them all. 'It's all very circumstantial. There's no way the police would even try to convict her on this sort of flimsy 'what if'-ing. But they might try to pin it on Fergus. He's dead, after all. That would solve it all very neatly, wouldn't it? And leave Emma without even Fergus's reputation intact.'

'Quite. I know.' Alex sighed. 'I've thought it through too and I realise there's nothing we can do – except this.' Then, much to Bill's surprise, Alex strode forward to the garage again, picked up the heavy metal rod, and slid it in with the golf-clubs. Then he carefully fastened the leather hood over the bag, holding everything securely in place. He turned to Bill and smiled tightly.

'I might borrow these for a game up at Clandeboye this afternoon, though I expect I'll lose most of the balls in the lake. Feel like a game?'

And Bill nodded, very sure suddenly that Fergus would have depended upon them to protect Emma. 'Why not? I expect those lakes are just full of balls – and all sorts of other things too, if they ever emptied them. It'll be nice to have one last game before I fly out tomorrow.' He smiled a lopsided grimace at Alex and swung the door of the garage down into place behind them. 'You won't go mentioning this to anyone, will you?'

Alex shook his head, pushing the hair back from his forehead, unaware that the scar stood out harshly in the sunlight. 'There's no reason to, is there? We'll just close ranks on this one, I think. Better to protect Fergus, than chance Laura being convicted.'

'Good.' Bill nodded firmly. 'Then that's settled.'

The following week, Alex received several tickets in the post to Joanna's viewing. He was on the verge of throwing them out when Kate, glancing across the kitchen table to him, raised her eyebrows.

'What're those?'

'Jo's thing at Ross's.' Alex shrugged dismissively. 'She's sent us some tickets to the private view. I was about to bin them.'

'Why?' Kate looked at Alex with a glinting smile. 'I think it might be fun to go to see it. She was good enough to come to our wedding. The least we can do is go to her exhibition.'

She carried on opening her own mail, not waiting to see Alex's expression.

Finally he spoke. 'You're sure?'

'Yes, of course.' She smiled at him again and he shook his head.

'I don't know what you have in mind.'

'Nothing. Not a thing, Alex. I'm just going to be polite to an old friend of yours, nothing more.' Her tone was light and amused. 'Oh, did I tell you that work's begun again on the Chelsea hotel? I tried to get in touch with Richard but he seems permanently unavailable. Funny, really, because I did happen to notice that the corian marble for the bathroom, that I specified in my layout, is being installed. I expect the curtains are already being made, too.' She made a moue of irritated exasperation. 'But that's Richard for you. I thought I might introduce Joanna to him. They seem well suited, all in all.'

'And you don't mind that this first venture has fallen apart? You can cope with Joanna's success?' Alex queried carefully. He watched his wife's eyes widen in astonishment.

'Her success? But . . . I'm married to you, aren't I?' And then she grinned, mischievously. 'That's all that counts with Joanna and I intend to let her know it. You've no idea how much fun it can be being an army wife, my love.'

'Oh, I'm sure I'm going to hear all about it. Just make sure Richard's there to hear it too,' Alex remarked pointedly. 'That seems only fair, after all.'

'I'll certainly do my best, darling. Besides, maybe I can wangle the money out of him that he owes Emma and me. I think she could do with it at the moment and if Richard tries to renege, well, Emma is a solicitor, after all.'

'Good,' Alex grunted, examining the telephone bill with misgiving. 'Then you can offset some of these expenses to tax. I really don't think I can afford you, Kate. You'll have to work, after all.'

'I intend to, my love.' Kate smiled soothingly. 'I intend to.'

Chapter Eighteen

On the night of the wives' club dinner, Kate sat next to Susan White, without recollecting having met Susan's husband in the past. But Susan remembered and smiled broadly.

'I hear my Whitey disgraced himself not so long ago.' She laughed with generosity and a certain rueful understanding. Looking at Kate, Susan was surprised more men hadn't disgraced themselves. Long, leggy blondes were always hard to resist. 'At the Open Day – he was trying to chat you up in the pub until Alex came and squashed him.'

Kate opened her mouth in dismayed astonishment. 'Oh, but that was just a bit of fun—'

'Don't think I don't know it. My Whitey's all bark and no bite. The other lads told me about it, poking fun at him, like. You needn't go looking all worried that I think you're trying to steal my husband!' And Susan went off into a peal of laughter that had Kate joining in, despite herself. The laughter was merry and infectious, and Susan obviously had no qualms about teasing Kate. Kate relaxed.

'Did you hear I was in disgrace for not doing the bake stall, as well?' she asked ruefully.

'Oh, yes, we all heard that and gave three cheers that you weren't another bloody,' but here Susan broke off and looked around furtively before continuing in a markedly lower voice, 'Amanda Toffee-Nose. We could all do without another like her, that's for sure.'

Kate glanced around, noting Amanda and her cronies seated at the head of the table some distance away. Most of the wives had just sat down willy-nilly in the large dining room, but Amanda had made sure of her position as usual. Suzy was much nearer, seated next to Sheila, the RSM's wife, with whom she was obviously on close and friendly terms. Kate breathed out slowly.

'Um, don't even start me on that one,' she muttered, aware of a certain disloyalty. But the grin on her face dispelled any serious gripe. 'So, I gather Whitey and Alex go back a long way together?'

'Right the way back to where Alex was just a sproglet right out of Sandhurst, trying to pretend he was a platoon commander, and my Whitey was one of his men, causing havoc left, right, and centre. Now Alex is a major and Whitey's . . . well, he's been up and down a bit, made it to colour sergeant, then down again for a bit,' Susan shrugged, 'and now he's going to be made up to sergeant again soon, if Alex has his way. Oh, yes, they've been in a lot of scrapes together but always come through, so I guess they're pretty good mates.'

'And you've known Alex a long time too, have you?' Kate was aware that she had seemed to have almost stepped into a family gathering, everyone knowing a side of her husband that she didn't, all of them knowing him for much longer than she had herself. It was disconcerting but fascinating.

'Oh, yes.' Susan rolled her eyes. 'I've known a lot of the young scamps who're suddenly all grown up and serious but Alex is still just the same to me, kisses me whenever I see him and asks about the children and teases me about Whitey. He's always been a good lad,' Susan grinned, 'unlike some of the others I could mention. Not exactly shy with the girls, just . . . I don't know, he stands back a bit thoughtful, like.'

'Reserved, mmm,' Kate agreed with a smile. 'And, of course, there was Joanna for a long, long time.'

'Ye-es, that's right.' Susan flashed a glance at Kate. 'You know Joanna then, do you?'

'Not terribly well. I've met her a few times, that's all. She's having a showing here in Belfast shortly of her sculptures, did you know?' Kate was aware of an avid interest in herself for more information on Joanna, and much as she might be ashamed of herself for it, she wasn't about to pass up the opportunity.

Susan grinned tightly. 'Is she now? Now that I hadn't heard. Well, if you see her, you ask her about Daniel's sculpture. See what she has to say about that! And you can tell her I'll be in to see her an'all!' For a moment, Kate had the distinct impression that Susan was angry about something but then she shrugged and gave a laugh. 'That'll flummox her, I won't doubt!'

'Daniel's sculpture?' Tentatively, Kate sought enlightenment but Susan just shook her head.

'My son. She'll know and I hope she'll have the grace to look embarrassed. But I doubt it, knowing her. Anyway,' abruptly she changed the subject, 'I don't suppose you play tennis, do you? We're one short to make up doubles on Tuesday evenings, and you look pretty sporty to me. And no children yet either.'

'Oh, well, yes, I do play but not seriously, not for years. I'm not very good,' Kate confessed.

'Neither are we. We're just in it for a bit of a laugh and a bit of exercise. You'll get to meet more people too, and see a bit of life outside of the officers' patch. Who knows, you might even enjoy it!' Susan was back to her teasing and Kate, laughing, agreed. This was just what she needed, she thought suddenly. To get to know everyone and not feel so cut off and nervous about the real army world. And, she added mentally, she'd get herself out and about more in the republic, go to see things, meet local people, not be so ivory-towered.

'What do you think's going to happen here?' Susan seemed to read her mind and Kate raised her eyebrows and shrugged.

'I think it's just about impossible to say. It could go either way. I'm sure you've heard all about the IRA just waiting for the word to start up all the violence again. They've certainly used the last few months to their advantage.'

'If I have to listen again to that two-faced Gerry Adams going on about how the others aren't serious about peace—' Susan cut in abruptly and Kate nodded.

'I know, I know, but we'll just have to wait for the elections to see which way it goes. I have to admit,' Kate shrugged again, 'I'm not hopeful.'

'Then all I can say is, the sooner we get moved to Germany, the better. I don't want my boys being blown to hell for someone else's bloody grievances.'

'Germany?' Kate was startled. 'Is that likely?'

'Oh, yes, that's our next posting.' Susan looked at her curiously. 'Didn't you know?'

'No, Alex hasn't said a word!'

'Oh, that'll be because they're all still waiting for the confirmation to come through, but it's ninety per cent certain. Or so we all hear, anyway. Some time early in the next year.' Susan smiled at Kate's astonishment.

'But how does everyone know?'

'The wives' grapevine, of course. Don't tell me you've been married for several months now and you haven't heard about it?' Susan gave her a sceptical look and Kate blew out her cheeks in exasperation.

'Not really. I certainly knew that Emma was always clued up on things long before I heard of them from Alex, but I just assumed Fergus was more forthcoming.'

'No, no, poor lass, she just knew a lot of other wives. How is she? Coping all right?' Suddenly reminded of the tragedy, Susan looked awkward and upset.

Kate gave a faint smile. 'Much better, I think. I talk to her a lot by telephone and we're going to go down and see her in a couple of weeks.'

'And still no word about what caused the crash?' Susan asked and Kate hesitated, then shook her head. She daren't say a word when it was so speculative anyway and Alex had told her in confidence. Obviously anything let slip here would be all over camp by breakfast the next day.

But she shivered slightly at the thought of a Russian sniper rifle able to shoot out a tail rotor at a distance of more than a mile. The theory was that they were trying it out quietly, on a target that would be difficult to prove had been knocked down by the rifle. A flak jacket would be child's play compared to that, Kate thought and then shook her head to clear it.

'Um, you know about the baby, do you, Susan?'

'Oh, yes.' Susan nodded with pleasure. 'About time that

poor lass had some luck her own way. You give her my love next time you talk to her, won't you? And tell her we've got lots of baby clothes and a cot and everything if she's interested.'

By this time the first course, a rather boring avocado and tasteless shrimp viniagrette, had come and gone and the main course of roast lamb had arrived. Kate eyed the plate without much hunger and nodded. 'Yes, I promise, I'll tell her. Um, any word about the, um, about Hugh's death?' If Susan was tuned into the grapevine, she probably knew far more than Kate would ever hear from Alex. Susan eyed her ironically.

'No, well, nothing new; she got away with it, didn't she?' Tucking into a large forkful of roast potato, Susan seemed indifferent to the gasp Kate gave. 'Not that I blame her entirely,' Susan added judiciously, after a pause. 'I mean, he was a complete plonker, wasn't he? But she shouldn't've got Bill involved, that's all I say. *Body Heat* all over again, wasn't it, and Bill being the schmuck!

'Hope he's all right over there in Bosnia. Shame about that young lad that got blown up, wasn't it? He was a PO with the battalion some years ago before he went to Sandhurst. Can't remember his name now . . . oh, well, a really nice boy. Such a shame. So Bill better be careful, hadn't he? Not that he isn't probably safer over there than when he was here with *her*!'

'Her? You don't mean Laura?' Kate was horrified that Susan seemed so sure, when there was absolutely no evidence.

'Of course. Everyone knows. She took *Body Heat* out from the video club five times in the last couple of months. I mean . . .' Susan sniffed sharply. 'Maybe she thought no one'd notice that, but my friend works there and she told me. Besides,' and here Susan looked uncomfortable but stubborn in her defence, 'she was seen that night, wasn't she? Outside the wire.' She raised her eyebrows significantly.

'By whom?' Kate asked in a hushed tone, aghast.

'One of the young girls, can't say who, because she wasn't supposed to be out herself but everyone on the officer's patch knew about that hole in the fence, didn't they? Anyway,' here Susan lowered her voice carefully, 'this young girl, whose Dad'd have her for breakfast if he knew about it, so she didn't dare tell the police, she saw Laura, didn't she? Wearing black jeans and a dark sweatshirt, climbing back through the hole. Just before three, this was. The girl was coming home from a nightclub but she knows Laura well, and she recognised her all right. And this girl, she's a good mate of my daughter's. So,' Susan shrugged again, 'now we all know, don't we? But there's no real proof.'

'But,' Kate protested, 'this girl should be made to go to the police. This is a murder, not just a bit of a skylark. Why hasn't someone given the police the information?'

'Because we'd be dropping this girl right in it. And there'd still not be enough proof to do Laura, would there? So, we all know, but we'll just close ranks on it because no good'll come of involving outsiders. Besides, Laura was never one of us. Never wanted to be. And Hugh . . . well, good riddance to bad rubbish.' She laughed at Kate's expression, suddenly light-hearted again.

'We look after our own, Kate. That's what matters. If there was any way Laura could be convicted, we'd do it. But there isn't, so just let it be.'

* * *

Which was what Kate was repeating to Alex that night in bed, while still protesting that the police should be informed. But Alex shook his head, equally adamant. 'No, there's no point. As Susan says, we all know – or strongly suspect, anyway. And the battalion's been through enough already and has to get its mind focused on the trouble ahead, not behind. So Susan's right. Just let it be, Kate, all right?'

Reluctantly, Kate had agreed, filing away the lesson for future reference. The battalion looked after its own, she repeated ruefully to herself, and closed ranks on outsiders, particularly those that lived in ivory towers. So she had better not be one, had she?

Climbing the wide, wooden stairs at Ross's, to the gallery above, Kate clung hard to Alex's arm. The high ceilinged hallway to their left, already filling with the light banter and laughter of a successful view, echoed like a void around her. With a deep breath, Kate drew herself up to face her old adversary.

There she was in the corner, surrounded by admirers, her fiery hair flung carelessly back as she puffed languidly on yet another cigarette. She didn't seem to have changed, Kate thought, but there was something in the angle with which she held her head, the way she laughed, that spoke of self-satisfaction and anticipation. Kate was only too aware of just why.

Alex, it seemed, had seen her too. Kate felt the very slightest stiffening of his body as her hand was tucked in more tightly against him. As yet, Joanna hadn't noticed them. They drifted, gently, to one side, out of her view as they examined the first of her sculptures. Entitled *The Divers*, the two birds entwined as they arrowed down towards an imaginary sea, the carving was smooth and uncluttered and yet exquisitely poised. Kate felt her heart thud down into her belly with disbelief. Alex pointed to the price, equally disbelieving.

'Good lord,' he murmured, his lips brushing against her hair, 'does anyone have that sort of money these day? Just for a nice sculpture?'

'It's more than nice, Alex!' Kate exclaimed, in spite of herself. 'It's stunning.'

'But how kind of you, Kate!' A smooth, satisfied voice announced behind them both. 'Stunning? Yes, well, I suppose it is, really. Certainly the birds themselves are.' Joanna's tight-lipped smile encompassed them both as they turned to face her.

'How are you, darling?' Joanna moved forward into Alex's arms, pressing herself against him despite his rigid bearing. He kissed her cheek lightly, smelling the heady scent she always wore that now cloyed and offended his nostrils. 'It's been simply ages, hasn't it? I shan't allow so long to pass without seeing you again, I promise you. Isn't this fun?' Joanna gestured around the large room where her sculptures were displayed to advantage against the plain white walls and wooden floor. 'Such a crush already, so early in the evening!' A complacent smile slid past Kate and latched itself onto Alex again.

'Yes, well, I'm so pleased that your work is finally being recognised,' Alex murmured coolly. 'Quite a different style from what you used to do, isn't it? Where did you find your inspiration?'

Joanna gave him an odd, probing glance before flicking the red hair back from her face. 'Oh, here and there,' she replied in an offhand tone.

'Did Daniel's work inspire you at all?' Kate asked sweetly, a suspicion of what Susan had been hinting at suddenly hardening into certainty in her mind. 'Susan asked me to tell you she'll be down to see you,' she added, noting the flare of alarm in Joanna's eyes for a brief moment before she had herself under control again. Joanna looked down at Kate and gave a dismissive laugh.

'Did she? I can't think why. Daniel's work is quite uninspired and I told her so at the time. God, what a bore when people keep thrusting their children's dismal efforts at you, expecting you to discover them for the world.' She puffed on her cigarette again, more assured as Kate did not contradict her. 'I'd advise you to tell Susan not to bother. She won't get anything from me.'

'Well.' Kate hesitated, shrugging, as she glanced up at Alex. 'If you say so. I promised I would mention it in passing and I'm sure she wouldn't miss it for the world, anyway. But we won't keep you, Joanna, when obviously other people will want to speak to you, and we really can't stay long anyway. We just popped in on the way out to dinner,' she added, gesturing towards the door. 'Our congratulations on your success at long last.' And with that parting shot Kate, smiling, strolled away on Alex's arm.

'Well done! Short and sweet. But no sign of Richard, is there?' Alex murmured, searching the crowd without success. 'Perhaps he decided discretion was the better part of valour?'

'Well, he has two weeks until we see Emma. If he hasn't replied to my letters or paid our invoice, I shall unleash Emma on him. We'll see how he likes that.' Kate shrugged, indifferent to Richard, the warm glow of her confrontation with Joanna still filling her with elation. 'Besides,' she angled her chin up so that she could see Alex's expression, 'I don't think the man knows the meaning of valour.' She squeezed his arm again. 'Let's go home, shall we? This isn't really my sort of thing.'

Chapter Nineteen

As they drove down the small, rutted farm lane at the end of the village of Lower Waterstone, the cottage came into sight. The woodland that it backed onto had been cut back at some time in the past to produce a sunny clearing, and the thatched, white-walled cobb cottage looked as though it had strayed from a fairy-tale. A low box hedge surrounded a tangle of flowers close to the house, with roses, not yet open, clambering up and over the windows and small porched entrance. Honeysuckle, clematis and jasmine trailed over the walled garden at the side, where a patch of smoothly striped lawn could be seen through the wrought-iron gate. The spaniels could be heard barking shrilly from somewhere out the back.

The sun shone down with the first warmth of that late spring and the bees droned, heavy and drugged with pollen, from flower to flower. Kate, standing by the arched gate, breathed in deeply the sweet smell of freshly cut grass and hay.

'Oh, this is so idyllic, Alex! And look, even the cowshed is thatched!'

'And, more importantly,' Alex murmured, coming to put an arm around Kate, 'the village is just a hundred yards away down the lane if Emma needs anything. Trust Fergus and Emma, they always do things so well. This really is a joy, isn't it? I wonder if there's another cottage somewhere around here with our name on it!'

But, at that moment, Emma opened the upstairs window and called down to them. 'Shan't be a mo'. I've just got to finish putting away the linen. Come on in, the door's not locked.'

The outer entrance hall was tiny but opened up into a surprisingly large inner hall that was flagstoned in pale, worn stone. The walls were a bright, sunny yellow and a huge blue and white porcelain footbath of wild spring flowers stood on a table at the foot of the stairs. A large antique brass lantern hung in the centre of the hall, and on either wall hung two oil paintings, flanked by candle sconces. One was a darkened family portrait of a long-dead ancestor, the other a stunning portrait of Fergus, obviously recently completed. They stood staring at it, at the smile twitching at his lips, the warm intelligence in his eyes, feeling as though Fergus had suddenly strayed into the room and was greeting them as always.

'Good, isn't it?' Emma asked with pride as she descended the stairs carefully, her belly suddenly much larger than they had remembered.

'Oh, it's wonderful, Em! When did you have it done?' Kate came forward with her arms open and embraced Emma tightly.

'My parents gave it to me as a surprise present. They'd had Fergus sit for it last time we were there, but it wasn't finished and the artist had to complete it from memory and photographs. But it's good, isn't it? It's really caught him as he was.'

She spoke calmly and warmly of Fergus, not yet over his death, still missing him terribly, but beyond that dreadful wasteland of pain that had engulfed her at first. Alex smiled and kissed her.

'I nearly shook his hand,' he teased. 'No, it's brilliant. And so is this.' He gently patted her stomach and Emma blushed rosily.

'Can you believe how big I've got! I thought it might be twins at first but they say it's just one whopper!' She laughed and gestured for them to follow her into the sitting room. 'Come and see how much I've done. I've been dying to show it off to you both and get Kate's input.' The initial awkward meeting when memories of Fergus were bound to intrude painfully passed away smoothly as they looked around the house and admired it all.

To the left of the entrance hall was a generous sized room with a huge fireplace of old stone. Half of the low beamed ceiling was cut back to provide a soaring cathedral roof and gallery overhead. French doors led out onto the side-walled garden and the room was flooded by light from oriole windows high overhead.

The floors were covered in seagrass and oriental rugs and the antique mahogany chest on chest, pembroke tables and faded floral chintz sofas from the quarter looked much more at home against the mellow age of the cottage. Kate gasped in appreciation.

'My God! You'd never guess from outside that this existed. It's stunning, Emma. Did you have an architect do it for you?'

'Yes, well, most of the ceiling had fallen down anyway so we had the option of opening it up like this. Of course, it meant we lost one bedroom but it was worth it to get this light in here. You really should have seen what a mess this place was when we first bought it. But it's been five years and a lot of hard work and whatever money we had to get it like this. The dining room's on the other side and the kitchen's been made out of some farm buildings at the back. Come and see.'

The dining room was in the same yellow as the hall but trimmed in sky blue and the simple padded chairs were in a rough linen damask of the same shade of blue. The oak table gleamed in the sunshine and the windows were framed by the pink buds of clematis just opening. An ornate gilt mirror hung over the fireplace and fine willow pattern plates adorned the walls, but otherwise the room was done simply, in keeping with the cottage's style.

The kitchen, a series of small larders, washrooms and pig-pens had been knocked together into one large low-ceilinged room with a refectory table at the far end that overlooked the garden. Light and bright, with old pine beams against stark white plaster and a stone floor, the kitchen had very few built-in pieces apart from an Aga in what had been the inglenook and a butler's sink cleverly disguised in a white painted dresser. The room looked as though it had evolved over the years and was comfortably expecting to evolve over many more to come.

And through the far french doors leading out onto a small terrace and lawn, a stream could be seen meandering past the end of the garden with a simple stone belvedere overlooking it and a shallow flight of steps down to the water. On the far side, willows draped their branches languidly in the water, and the first flush of spring green underplanted by a carpet of bluebells was lit in the clear sunshine.

Upstairs, the master bedroom and tiny en suite bathroom were done in a faded pink Zoffany toile and Colefax roses chintz, the spare bedroom in a green and pale blue lilac pattern against white half-panelling, and the nursery, as yet unfinished, in white with pale yellow checked lining to the curtains. Kate stared at the waiting crib with a small smile playing on her lips.

'I confess I'm envious beyond belief. This is exactly what I've always wanted, Em. It's totally gorgeous! Isn't it, Alex?'

'I'd buy it tomorrow if I thought we could afford it. It's truly stunning, Emma, and I can't think of a better place to bring up a child.'

Emma beamed with pleasure. 'Good, I was hoping you'd say that. Because I've got something to show you both.'

And she led them downstairs again and out the back of the house, through another arched wrought-iron gate and along a dirt track that led, several hundred yards away, to a jumble of barn buildings forming a courtyard in the distance. She gestured towards the buildings.

'The local farmer's thinking of putting these up for sale. Now, I know they'll need a lot of work, and I know—' but she broke off before she could list the pitfalls, seeing instead the instant excitement in Kate.

'Oh, darling, it could be wonderful! And we'd be right next to Emma and she can tell us who all the best local workmen are and her architect too . . . not to mention getting Milly to help as well and sweetheart, just think, our children could grow up together and oh, let's go to see it, please!'

And Alex was laughing, knowing he was lost even before he started. 'Can we afford it, Em? How much is he asking?'

'The price is a bit steep at the moment, considering the amount of work that needs to be done and there no planning permission granted yet, either, but there's nearly two acres with it and it opens up onto farmland and this wood with the stream going through it, and you could make a really fabulous house out of it—'

'How much?' Alex raised his eyebrows and Emma broke off, laughing.

'Oh well, he's asking one-fifty, I gather, but I think you can knock him down quite a bit on that,' she said tentatively and Alex groaned.

'Even with the best will in the world, Emma, no bank'll give us a mortgage that size with all the work that needs to be done.'

'So we'll have to sell my London flat, won't we?' Kate said suddenly, looking at both of them.

Alex frowned. 'I thought you wanted to hang onto that?'

'Yes, when I thought we might be returning to live in London from time to time. But, as Emma so rightly points out, you can't bring up children in London – at least, not as happily as here. And if we're going to be shifted around from pillar to post with the army, this would act as our roots. Our little ones would be able to picture their own bedroom, even if they can only visit on long weekends and holidays, and they'll know where they're from. And I won't feel as frustrated having to dismantle a quarter all the time if I know I have a beautiful house waiting for me here. Oh, please, Alex . . . at least consider it!'

But Alex didn't really need convincing. It was what he had always wanted too, not the London flat that Kate had always been so keen on. And he wanted to be around for Emma and her baby, not just for their sake, but because he felt they were family. He grinned. 'Come on then, let's go to have a look at it, shall we? And have you told Em the good news yet?'

Emma looked puzzled, but she had sensed a difference in Kate ever since she had arrived. And she knew what Kate was going to say, could read it in the glowing eyes and happy, carefree laugh.

'I'm expecting too! Bit of a mistake, actually, but wonderful now we're used to the idea. There'll be about five months between them, I think, so they can grow up best friends.'

'More like they'll hate each other! Friends' children never get on,' Alex retorted, but Emma just laughed and embraced them both.

'Congratulations. I did wonder, I must admit. Well, then, it's settled. You must buy the place. It's made for children. Now, I'm going to make the tea and put my feet up. You go to explore. And then, later, we can go to visit Fergus.'

She said it so naturally, as though it were part of her daily routine, that the other two merely nodded and smiled. Visit Fergus . . . Kate looked around at the glowing countryside and thought nothing could be more normal, more . . . right. Fergus was still there with them, just a bit removed, over there in the churchyard, that was all.

She wondered, briefly and idly, if Laura ever thought of Hugh but then realised, instantly, what a foolish thought that was. Hugh was truly gone, neither mourned nor, if most people had their way, remembered. She shuddered at the thought.

'Em? Before you go, um, did you hear any more from Laura at all? About the wedding – or anything?'

Emma laughed, a shade bitterly. 'Not a thing. But that's Laura for you. Out of sight, out of mind. She didn't even call or write when Fergus was killed. I suppose she's too caught up in her new life and you know what they say about red hair and volatility, don't you?' She sighed slightly.

'Um, well, I just wondered.' Kate shrugged. 'I don't expect we'll be seeing her back to visit for a long time, if ever, then?'

'Not if she's wise, no,' Emma retorted and Alex raised his eyebrows.

'Meaning . . . ?'

'Meaning, red hair will out,' Emma said slowly, and then flashed a rueful smile at them both. 'Such an old wives' tale, but, in this case, I think we've all slowly come to the same conclusion, haven't we?'

'And even if we haven't, it saves the battalion ripping itself apart searching for the truth,' Alex agreed sombrely.

'Enough,' Kate announced, refusing to ruin the day with bad memories. 'It's over, it's done. And maybe we'll never know for sure. Now, let's go to see this house, shall we?'

'All right, all right!' Alex threw up his hands in self-defence. 'Come on, let's go to take a look, shall we? But I warn you, Kate, we'll still be pushed to get all the renovations done.'

'Not if I work too,' she contradicted, as they ambled arm in arm towards the buildings.

'You think you can manage that and a baby too?' He kissed her hair, looking around at the glory of the late afternoon sunlight gilding the trees and fields beyond.

'I'm an army wife, my love,' she smiled. 'And you know very well, we can handle anything.'